Praise for Douglas Woolf

"Woolf's great qualities . . . independence of approach. . . . . of style. . . . If you want to re-e . . . . it might have been seen by a Smollett, a Sterne, a Fielding or in places a Cervantes don't miss *Wall to Wall*."

—Robert R. Kirsch, *Los Angeles Times*—

"Satire and hilariously clever situation comedy bloom from the out-of-phase dialogue and action of *Fade Out*. Displaying a completely fresh virtuosity of prose, the author leaves one with a haunting sense of the tenuous and fortuitous nature of life."

—*Library Journal*—

"Douglas Woolf writes authentically about the milieus in which his characters move. . . . Small things become almost matters of life and death. Tragedy lurks in a spilled cup of Orange Crush."

—*Best Sellers*—

"Woolf's work is single-minded in impulse—like Swift, a more obviously enraged but related ironist, he sets out to depict commonly ignored or denied priciples of order."

—Larry Kart, *Chicago Tribune*—

Other Books by

Douglas Woolf

Ya! and John-Juan

two novels by
Douglas Woolf
introduction by
Robert Creeley

Ya! and John-Juan

DALKEY ARCHIVE PRESS

Portions of *Ya!* first appeared in *Delta* magazine.
Portions of *John-Juan* first appeared in *Origin* magazine.

Library of Congress Cataloging-in-Publication Data

Woolf, Douglas, 1922-1992.
    Ya! ; & John-Juan : two novels / by Douglas Woolf ; introduction by Robert Creeley.
        p. cm.
    ISBN 1-56478-281-6 (pbk. : alk. paper)
        1. Psychological fiction, American. I. Title: Ya! ; and John-Juan. II. Title: Ya!. III. Woolf,
    Douglas, 1922-1992 John-Juan. IV. Title: John-Juan. V. Title.

    PS3573.O646 Y3 2002
    813'.54—dc21

                                                                        2002073504

Partially funded by grants from the Lannan Foundation and the Illinois Arts Council, a state
agency.

Dalkey Archive Press books are published by the Center for Book Culture, a nonprofit organization with offices in Chicago and Normal, Illinois.

www.centerforbookculture.org

Printed on permanent/durable acid-free paper and bound in the United States of America.

Various World: Notes for Douglas Woolf

Douglas Woolf was an uncannily reflective person—as though he chose to take his color and shape from the surrounding world rather than to force upon it his own determinations and judgement. However, what he did exercise, unremittingly, was an acute perception, *his* witness, *his* recognition, *his* fact in being there, wherever there was or might be. In the seeming chaos of his incessant shifts of place and employment, he was persistently and minutely practical, however unlocated he may have seemed to others in more usual lives. Choosing to be a writer or, more to the point, finding that he was a writer and had to be one, he practiced an almost religious avoidance of other, overreaching patterns such as professions or familiar vocations must argue. The doctor or the carpenter is real, long before anyone is actually there as a specific person. Just so the teacher, the nurse, the soldier or anyone society has thus made a name for. There is no name simply for Douglas Woolf. Even that name itself seems often curiously unreal.

If I am to be responsible to this extraordinary person's life, I must briefly rehearse its details, such as I know them, a scatter of particular memories of our all too few meetings, letters, mutual friends such as his exceptional Grove Press editor, Donald M. Allen, others such as the writers

Edward Dorn, Bobbie Louise Hawkins, the people who were his family. In some ways Douglas Woolf was as elusive as the proverbial woodland creature, known to be there but rarely if ever seen. I know he was son of a successful New York businessman, that his mother had difficult bouts of mental illness, being occasionally hospitalized at McLean's near Boston, that he had driven an ambulance for the American Field Service in North Africa during the Second World War and had also been in the Army Air Force, that he had gone to Harvard, dropping out before graduation. But having said that, the trail grows cold or rather grows increasingly singular—Good Humor man in Tucson, sweeper of a municipal racetrack in Spokane, householder in an abandoned miner's cabin in Wallace, Idaho. I was in touch with him in all these situations but it was very hard to join the symbolic dots so as to make some defining picture.

Our first contact was entirely by chance. Living with my family in Mallorca in the early fifties, together with my wife, Ann, I had begun the Divers Press, which published collections of poetry and translation by Paul Blackburn, Charles Olson, Irving Layton, Robert Duncan and myself among others. I thought of the press as a chance to publish that work of contemporaries which had all too little hope of being published. But other than the first edition of my stories, *The Gold Diggers*, we had found no prose. Then, altogether unexpectedly, a manuscript arrived in the mail, a novel no less, *The Hypocritic Days* by Douglas Woolf.

In some ways it was an obvious "first novel" insofar as the construction had a wandering impulse at times. There was no tight, determining hand seeing to all details if that's ever the imagined necessity. But the people in the story were almost heart-breakingly present, the ex-jockey father,

Chick, with the large son, Charles, the tenderness and confusion between them, the nudges of affection and pain—"Chick moved silently around him with sideways face to remove his dish. 'Sit down, there, Big Fella,' he said, 'we still have our dessert.' " It was so gentle, so particular to ways people live together, and if it was otherwise the complex passage from teenager to adult in the proposedly garish world at Hollywood's edge, it was in the intimate focus, the unobtrusive detailing of gesture, conversation, place, that Douglas Woolf's genius was clear. One gets some sense of this, thinking of what he's said of his need to write: "If there were only one reader left in the world, I would write to that one as lovingly as I do now." "Lovingly" is the apt word. There is always a story to tell in his writing, always the people to be found there as I did "Chick" and "Charles." So we published the book in January, 1955, in several hundred copies, a compact format with a cover by the Japanese poet Katue Kitasono, the font our standby Mercedes with Futura heads. It was hardly a best seller. I remember being delighted that someone in Connecticut ordered twenty copies. It turned out it was his mother. The novel itself is dedicated to his wife Yvonne.

Perhaps the reason for his unsuccessful sales is that it has never been easy, and may, in fact, be impossible, to make a simple characterization for this writer. At times he is compared to Jonathan Swift but that seems to me displacing of both. Woolf is not angry, or certainly not in the same way as Swift. His intent is not, as I read him, satire in the first place anymore than it was Richard Brautigan's, who shares with Douglas Woolf both the insistent gentleness of manner and also his "loner" life. If one were to make them persons of a group, to include Mark Twain, Nathaniel West, Stephen Crane and Malcolm Lowry for starters, then perhaps one gets a little closer. However "comic" these writers may at times seem, they are not laughing. They all seem finally to be just where they have placed their diverse characters, in a world without appeal, without relief or response.

In like sense, I never felt that Douglas Woolf was making anything up, certainly not as some fantasized or invented "reality." Given the order of things, "worlds" such as those to be found in either *Ya!* or *John-Juan* will happen as facts of thought itself. What was it Descartes said? "I think, therefore I am." That credo can become with equal simplicity, "I think, therefore it is." The poet William Carlos Williams put it most succinctly in saying, "A new world is only a new mind." Our "world," or "worlds," are what we think they are, neither more nor less, and so we go about our daily businesses, determined in our purpose, convinced in our rightness. That's what thought's for—to make a world possible.

So if one finds oneself in a world with no memory of how one came to be there, wearing solely pajamas, then one continues as thought and one's experience and the case provides. Left here, right there. Toothbrush for teeth and good health. What's different then in Douglas Woolf's relation to these curious matters, how, in this case, does "John/Juan" serve him as a writer? How does this truncated but vivid character take place in the reader's own world? I think suddenly of Nathaniel West's "Miss Lonelyhearts" becoming entangled with his own sad respondents, of Stephen Crane's young soldier in a thicket of trees, hearing the large cannon ball coming toward him, and of Malcolm Lowry's drunkenly poignant "Consul," collapsed in a corner of some garden, urinating, as he tries to explain his situation to the person who has discovered him. What matter discretion, call it, in any world where all *is*, even tossed out bottles and cans stuffed with shit and wadded Kleenex? The padding, swooping "runners," who would collect all such, burying it for subsequent salvage, are heralds of present environmental concerns no doubt. But it is rather Douglas Woolf's construction of this curiously ambivalent cluster of survivors, of their apparent "queen," of their intensive ordering of all significant details of human life, their equal abstractness, absence of relations among themselves, even "good" and "bad" a vague appellation they cannot themselves control except by doing what they are told to do.

It is John-Juan's own particulars which most define the world then realized: the absence of a usual history caused by amnesia, the physical way he is persuaded or pulled to move in a kaleidoscopically changing company of others, the incessant distortion of any locating habit of language, his prized watch disappearing into the vagina of a teasing young woman just met, and his dress, one battered set of pajamas. What can he do? Go with the flow, as one says, and consider. No doubt this curious stage would make a useful ground for any imagination of satire writ as large as one might hope to manage. However, there seems to be no satire, no necessary condemnation, even of the malevolent border authorities who end the chaotic and surreal story by pounding him thoroughly, breaking his bones. It's as though the author had taken the various bits and pieces of an all too real life and thought then of how they might conjoin in some place that only the mind could propose, some border—familiar enough from Douglas Woolf's passing in and out of Mexico—where a redefinition of who and what one thought one was is always in order, in fact, required. The echo of name sounds familiar—*Robert* or *Bob*, *Bill* or

Willy. Is the person *changed?* Heavens no—or it would not be the case for said person, just for all else surrounding? "A rose by any other name would smell as sweet. . . ." They would think of something to call it.

In *Ya!* the autobiographical grounding seems to come forward markedly. For example, the extraordinary sequences having to do with the protagonist Al's meager job "at Portal 8" in "the Coliseum" selling "Pipsi" (he first calls it "Pepsi") must come from Douglas Woolf's own transient employment in like circumstances. There is a painfully meticulous tracking of money, most particularly of coins, all through the novel, endlessly reiterated budgeting, balancing of one coin's expenditure against a small cache of others saved for "hockey" in some hazy future. The pacing, the calculations of what's in hand, the purchases made so poignantly are, as one reads of them, heartbreaking. " 'I'll take one of those,' Al said, whipping out twelve cents." Yet it would be utterly beside any point apparent to say that that effect only is either this book's intent—so to move the reader to some compassionate response—or the general disposition of the writer, to bring us into some box of apposite guilt and displacement. Paradoxically there is no advice to be found, which says, for instance, the reader should practice Al's terrifying virtues, be humble, find pleasure in the absolute minims of survival, go on foot even through such drifts of mid-winter snow as have caused the highway to close and trucks and buses to stop moving. Our hero walks on, or rather contrives to slide as follows:

> This was a lazy mode of travel, once one got the swing of it. Eyes closed, knees raised, slide downward on a wave, partway up to its next gentle undulation. Now

crawl to the nearest treetop, hang there a moment. Shove off again, gliding each time a little farther. The proud sun stood at his back, to guide and not to blind him. The highway lay to his left, not far away. The undulating telephone wires were visible! He swung onward, paralleling. Ahead, treetops stood out against purest blue, beckoning him to the summit. If he could slide uphill this well, imagine sailing down the other side. Thus he did not much mind slithering on his belly the last steep half mile.

This beckoning world seems a veiled paradise of unexpected kind. I know I am not out there myself, hands chapped and raw, worn pants stiff with frozen snow, shoes, if any, caked blocks in which, somewhere, I presume are my still surviving feet. And my tenderly secured packages! Christmas, after all, is just around the corner and I am on my way to see my only beloved daughter. Who would not feel all possible?

Again the father "Al" approaches his destination with such a deliberation of means. Careful not to arouse curiosity, as one says, he contrives to complete both his shopping and the last miles to where his daughter lives with the aggressively successful relatives. This is to be Al's shamed entrance into the world of all that he cannot manage or provide. But his angel, the daughter he has come to see, not only receives him with recognition and securing love but then chooses to escape the drear company with him. When they are at last free, as it were, he is hit by hunger, realizing he had not thought of food for them both. But she has brought unexpected sandwiches taken from the relatives' hoard, so that their hunger is amply fed. "Not bad for your first night, 88! Maybe tomorrow would be better. You never lose hope. . . ." It is just about with these words that the novel ends—happily. That old hotel with its battered sign, reading at night *YA* because the *LE* had blacked out, was trying to tell us something after all. *YA!*

One never does quite lose hope—despite all the horrors and despairs surrounding. If I am persuaded that Douglas Woolf is neither a satirist nor an ironist primarily, it is because the worlds his various characters find themselves in are, each one, places which do not apply to any other world so simply. They are there where they are and he has found means to live in them because he believes, as I do, that they are not merely reflections of some anterior "real" world. If one were, for example, even for a minute asked to think of our present world as anything other than a malignant joke, a satire upon the very principles it claims as its authority, what would he or she manage to offer in response? Is it to be finally, as e. e. cummings wrote, "listen: there's a hell of a good universe next door; let's go"? It is Douglas Woolf's immense and consistent acceptance of what he's been given, his fascination with what can be made of it, so that the salt left in a small bag of peanuts has use, the peels of an apple, and this is just where his story begins, always. It is not Robinson Crusoe's. The hero is not headed back at last to civilization and wealth. It is like Cervantes or rather his ageless friend, Don Quixote, who even when defeated still hears the echoes of his transforming dreams. I know there are good guys and bad guys in Douglas Woolf's books, and he makes sure we know which is which. But his pleasure, and therefore mine, is in making the world, any world, a place still of one's own.

ROBERT CREELEY
2002

YA!

For Gail and Lorraine

Note: I began *Ya!* in Mexico in the fall of 1965. After a brief interval as a civil servant in New Mexico, I continued the book during a second stay in Old Mexico in the winter of 1967, and finished it (after some sightseeing on my way back north) that same spring, in New.

D. W.

Out in the early morning, a gentle snow brushed his face, the blacktop was white. Everywhere the old folk sat behind their windshield wipers waiting for the parking lot to clear so that they could get home to bed. Here and there a red-eyed flashlight waved at them. Beneath these lights the attendants huddled in their parkas like red-nosed Eskimos. Al stepped among them carefully. If ever those drivers decided it was time to move out, a pedestrian would not want to be caught too near a beckoning light. He called to one: "Traffic a little slow just now?"

"Ninety cents a hour, they can sit all night."

"Hell yes." With help like that he reached the street before the rush. Down by the corner, on a bench, a life-size snowman sat. Nearby hung a weak street lamp, which seemed to be spewing snow on that white man alone and on his bench. Upon his shoulders and arms and the back of the bench snow was piled to the depth of an inch. A few leftover flakes swirled at his feet. One knew he was alive by his sputtering pipe, and he spoke.

"Don't these big-assed buses ever stop?"

"You'd think they would."

"This here's a big-assed bus stop, isn't it?"

"It sure looks like one."

"I been sitting here since eleven o'clock. Every damn one is either barrel-assing for the garage or all filled up."

Al shook his head. "Did I see you working the show tonight?"

"Me? Yeah, you did."

"How'd you make out with the drinks?"

"Oh, big-assed," he said. Even his frowning eyebrows were turning white.

"It looked like you were running circles around the kids."

The snowman sucked snow through his big pipe. "Shit. I thought he said his drinks was a dime apiece. By the time anyone told me they was fifteen cents I was in the big-assed hole five ninety-eight."

"Ow. You have to pay up?"

"Me? You can't suck honey from a welfare check. I gave him seventy-five cents."

"That still hurts."

"Hell, I kept my bus fare out."

"You coming back for the Auto Show?"

"Pepsi on the Auto Show. I'm going to stay right home and wait my check. If I'd known how these buses was going to run I could have walked and been home by now."

"Hell yes, you could." Here came one now, sliding out of the parking lot, half filled with the last remnants of the ambulatory audience. Sucking his pipe, the snowman eyed it disgustedly. Al raised a hand. The astonished bus driver hit his brakes, skidded to a big-assed stop half a block beyond. Al turned back to the bench. "Man, there's your bus."

The snowman pocketed his pipe, heaved to his feet, and shook himself. Cold, or the weight of remaining snow, seemed to impede his progress as he stamped after the bus, but soon his arms began to swing and he gained a little momentum by the time he got to it. Al could hear him stamp each step as he climbed in. He could see him stamp down the aisle, past his watchful audience without glancing to right or left, drop heavily onto the wide back seat as the bus blasted off. Stepping around the broken pile of snow before the bench, Al followed south.

Now he had the sidewalks to himself, and quietly. No one had ever walked on them before, they were being made fresh tonight. They were being made of a perfect material that required a perfect temperature to set. Rubber soles pressed their marks on it reverently. Each step was its own discovery waiting to be lost. If conditions continued perfect for one hour more, the world would be all new again.

Not tonight. Up on the bridge ahead a red light blinked emergency, two big men were out and running toward a little one. He was leaning against the rail and vomiting. "Hey! Hold it there! Hold it there!" They grabbed hold of him. "What do you think you're doing out here?"

"Me? I–I–I . . ."

"Don't you know you could fall off of there?"

"I . . ."

"Christ, you can't even talk. What are you, froze or stoned or what?"

"Ah–ah–ah! I didn't recognize you officers at first. That your car there?"

"Where? Yeah, that's our car."

"Ah–ah–ah! You're officers from the Patrol!"

"Yeah, we're from—"

"Good! Good! I thought you was some of them city boys —you got to be careful with them!"

"That right?"

"I know you officers from the Patrol. I like your work!"

"That ri—"

"Get 'em! Get 'em! Get 'em! Get 'em!"

"O.K., now—"

"Get 'em! Get 'em! Get 'em!'"

"Look, dad, you don't belong up here at night, you know that. You better get in this nice warm car and we'll take a little ride down south." They began dragging him toward the car.

"Get 'em! Get 'em! Get 'em!'"

Al stepped carefully around the scene, eyeing it with only the politest curiosity. Behind him he could hear doors open, slam. A laconic voice spoke on radio. The motor started up. "Get 'em! Get 'em!'" the old man croaked, and then he seemed to be vomiting. The car slunk quietly by. Twenty feet farther on, its chains suddenly bit ice, the car leaped south. Just before the crest of the bridge it hit a post. It bounced off, spun slowly north, and then slid cockeyed to a stop. Al was half blinded by its one light. He slowed a little as he passed, but the officers did not seem to wish to notice him. They were on radio. Their motor still turned, their heater worked, as did their blinking light. The old man himself seemed to be having a lovely time. "*Get 'em! Get 'em!*" he encouraged them from the back, drooling happily on their red necks. Suddenly sirens were everywhere, and heading here. Al quickened pace, anxious to be off that bridge before they met. He made it, as cars raced by him from the south. They wailed and blinked. Inside each car, the cops peered straight ahead. They weren't interested in him tonight, they had a rendezvous to keep!

Four dollars and thirty-eight cents. What time was it? He had earned himself a little drink. Pretty good show, first night, Old Gus had said. Al was passing now various establishments despite their allures—Blatz!—he was intent on a certain one, last night's. There a man need not have been born within the city limits to join the bar; the owner himself was from out of town. What had first attracted Al was the place's name, The Refugee. It was something about that second *e*, right here in Washington. It told a stranger he was not the first to pass this way, and reminded him of other times when things had been worse. In such a place there were no close examinations to be passed; any man over twenty-one was at liberty to state his case or not. In such a friendly place he could line up his after-hours drinks like sympathetic jurors in advance, if only he could get there by one o'clock.

The joint was off the path, of course, under another bridge, but with all the cops meeting out of town Al felt free to run. The snow was partly melting here, what with the hot lines and sewers running underneath the streets, but his rubber soles could take a hold on anything save ice. They had long ago established that. In Texas the aisles ran beer by ten o'clock, which was quite all right, while in Colorado at any hour you had to watch for frozen spit. In fact he liked this slushy track, and soon sighted shelter up ahead. Not to look conspicuous, he walked the last ten steps. The door seemed to open without his help.

"Bienvenido! Adiós! You made it just in time!"

"Good! Gracias! I did?"

"How many you want tonight?"

"Make it two and two, I guess."

The Refugee was already pouring them. Had Al already had a few, he probably would have ordered three and three, but coming in out of the cold that would have seemed too much like greed to him. Now looking at the other juries lined up all along the bar, he wondered if he had perhaps shown too much restraint instead. No, that was all right. Tomorrow he would try to make it faster, right after the Auto Show. To-morrow, after an abstemious night, he would be able to afford four and four. It paid a man to look ahead like that. Dropping a dollar on the bar for The Refugee, who had gone to latch the door, he downed a shot of sherry first.

That was a drawback here, not of the joint specifically but of the town—to get a real shot a man had to find a tie and visit a cocktail lounge. The tavern was set aside for the working man and bum. His boilermakers came a little slow, but cheap. But then, after one or two of those, all discriminations were well forgot. For example, the big working man in the very center of the bar was, by this time, Chief. "Hey, buddy, who won the fight tonight?" he roared.

Al put down his drink, and showed surprise. "Didn't you watch it here?"

"The blinking TV went out the middle of round five—"

"Round six—"

"I said round five!"

"O.K., O.K."

Rolling a cigarette, Al shook his head. "Me, I was at the travelogue. . . ."

"The . . . ?" The big man stared wide-eyed at him, as though he had uncovered some sort of intellectual or culture nut in their midst. Al was preparing to explain, but the man turned to his other side. "*Hey, buddy*, who won the fight?"

The man addressed was at the farther end. When he turned his head he revealed a swollen, purple eye. He looked at the big man with the other one. "Who wants to know?" he asked.

"Arriba, señores!" cried The Refugee, but they were all too intent. The big man was on his feet. He walked toward the other man, who was big himself. When the approaching target was in range, the seated man slammed him in the eye. The Refugee was too late to deflect the blow, but he was there in time to catch the stricken man before he fell flat on his back, save him that additional embarrassment. He led him staggering to his stool, flashed a smile up and down the bar. "Arriba, señores! We don't got time to fight tonight. We got to close this joint!"

He stood behind his gladiator, patting his broad back, encouraging him to drink, get back his strength. The big man drank, for strength, but otherwise ignored The Refugee. He still was unsure who had won the fight. Both fighters had to crane their necks in order to glare at one another with an open eye. It didn't end until the other, right-eyed one had finished all his drinks, growled good night to The Refugee, and banged out of there.

"Arriba, señores!" cried The Refugee, behind his bar again and mopping up. Now everyone began talking and drinking fast, with an overflowing friendliness. Even the big bruised one, when they slapped his back, cracked little grins of acknowledgment. He hadn't shown up so badly after all. Blind aggression wasn't everything in this life—there was restraint. He had not wanted to break up the place, and everyone must have noticed that no man had cared to try him a second time, one-eyed or not.

"Two and two?" The Refugee had finally reached Al's dollar bill.

"Sí, keep the change," Al said. "Nice show tonight."

"Ah, sí, that was a clásico."

"You refereed it well."

Broadly smiling, nodding, The Refugee remopped Al's bar space with a graceful hand that held not only his cloth but Al's folded bill.

"Where did you come from, señor?" Al asked.

"Señor? Madrid y Habana. I was trying to go to México. I got to New York all right, but then they had a mixed-up bus —you had to get off at Kansas City to go to México! By the time I found out this it was two days too late, so they let me out here. I owed them five hundred miles, they said, but I didn't know where to look for it. I stayed right here. . . . Arriba, señores! Bottoms up!"

It was time. They drained their drinks, slapped their empties to the bar with finality. Zipping their coats on the way to the door, they called good night to The Refugee. Gathering empties six in each hand, he waved them on. "Adiós! Come back again!"

"Adiós! Adiós!" they called from the door. Going out, they grinned obliquely at one another, for they had spoken in a foreign tongue.

Now there were people in the streets at last, but each man seemed to own a different part of town. Within a block Al was by himself again, on untrodden slush. The city center was preparing to look a mess again, so that when the commuters arrived a few hours hence they would have something to complain about. The two or three streets they knew by night, where the movie theaters, lodges, and cocktail lounges stood, they had already left in filth. A tremendous machine was following after them, sucking grey slush with a perverted appetite. It called to mind another machine, an ancient steam roller it had seemed, on which Al and a friend had hitched a ride one night in Capetown years ago. Their friendly driver had been delighted to accept a few slugs of brandy as their fare and to point out some remarkable life to them, for his part of town lived at night. Later they had left their bottle in the good care of a generous lady friend of his. Nighttime in Washington did not jig-jig. It had been much warmer then, of course. He too perhaps. In any case he stepped wide of this unnatural machine lest it might think to slurp him up, and did not even wave at the white, goggled driver huddled in his cage above. Clearly the man had his mind on slush. The snow itself had stopped. So had most of the blandishments, excepting for some probable reason the blue and purple ones. There in his cab sat a driver half asleep, waiting for a minor miracle or a gun to bring him awake. Al looked away from him. Across the street a narrow shop was partly lighted up, and he crossed incredulously to it. Was that a reading man he saw inside, or a newspaper hung up to shield the light? Could it be business someone intended to attract, so early in the morning and in such a gloom? Al expected to find the door bolted inside or out, but it was not. That was indeed a man in there, and he seemed ready to faint or call the cops.

"Good morning!" Al called hearteningly, closing the door against the cold.

This man was not to be taken in thus easily.

"Are you open for business still, or yet?"

That did it: "Sure am."

Now Al approached a step. "Are those Washington apples there?"

"Them's Wenatchee Reds."

"Aha, Wenatchee Reds!" Moving slowly, he chose four of the reddest ones. "Do you have milk?"

His man was getting in the spirit of the thing; he went to the cooler himself and brought a carton back. "Sure do," he said.

"How much are those donuts there?"

"These here?"

"Yes."

"Them's thirty-five."

"How much are those other ones?"

"Same price."

"I guess I'll take the sugared ones."

"The sugared ones." The man slid them along the counter, where they came to rest nicely beside Al's milk. "Something else?"

"Guess I'll need a little tobacco too." Being closest to the tobacco rack, Al chose a tin, though his man was quite ready to do all the work. "That should do it now."

"Cigarette papers?"

"I have plenty, thanks."

"Gum?"

"No, thanks."

His man wanted to make sure they had everything before he began adding up. He looked around his store a bit. Al did too, then smiled and shook his head. It was time to settle their account. There was a machine to do the work, but a man had to punch the keys just right. He had to heft each article before he punched. Some he had to study carefully first. The apples were the trickiest, for they had no labels and were Wenatchee Reds. Here went another dollar bill, Al knew, plus how much change, the question was. The machine had a secret tape; its feeder himself could hardly make it out. "Let's see now." He counted each item against his numerals. "Oh-oh, I almost forgot the dang-blang tax!" Ruefully he punched. "There now. That's it! One twenty-eight." Wenatchee Reds were a little high tonight, but so was the price of confidence. This man was already sacking Al's groceries before Al had his change all counted out. Even then he didn't pick it up at once, but wiped his hands on his apron first. "Yes, sir, just right! Watch that sack! I put your donuts on the top."

"Thanks."

"There you go! Little cold out there tonight?"

"Oh, not too bad."

"Well, come back again."

"O.K., you bet."

"Good night!"

"Good night!"

"Good night!"

"Good night!" Al made sure the door was closed. With a bag of groceries in his arms, he felt himself acquire a new solidity, a sense of belonging to this day; either one, the old one or the new. It was scarcely two o'clock. No matter how one looked at it, he was well ahead. He could have breakfast twice—as soon as he reached his room, again before he went to work. There might even be something left over for tonight. The old day had not begun that full. For breakfast he had eaten bread, with a kind of banana he had bought two days before, somewhere in Idaho—it might have been grown there too. For lunch he had had to dig into his Colorado hockey funds, half a dollar's worth; hockey simply could not support many days like that. The cows of Texas had already done all they could to help him out of state, and out of Colorado too. Thank Washington therefore for Old Gus, if not for a travelogue. At dinnertime there had been cold corn, purchased from a Goodwill refugee with dripping eyes and shaking hands. Tonight he would treat himself to a ice cream bar, like Santa Claus. Later, four and four, for sure. It seemed he had spoken too soon to his friend at the grocery store. The night indeed was cold. Two and two were clearly not enough for any man, not when his place of work was forty-some blocks from home, his favorite stop less than halfway between.

Yet to a man so lately from Colorado nothing of this kind could prove really difficult, once he understood it was too late for remedy. For it was not all that cold, even if on this side of town he was beginning to encounter snow again. Yes, that was snow all right, and there ahead, with a set of giant footprints leading straight to the door, loomed home. Somehow copying those steps, he arrived there fast.

Just above the beaten door a sign said HOTEL YA in mauve; its LE was dark. The door itself said *yee,* and said it again louder as it scraped closed. In the hall the light was more like burnt umber, a mixture of the reddish glow that marked the third-floor fire escape and whatever yellow lights were still left on, including the one in the can on the second floor. No one was behind the desk, but his key was on its allotted hook. He stepped apologetically on every second stair, taking care not to slip in the big puddles of melting snow on every third or fourth, or was it fifth? In the can he paused long enough to feel relieved that it was only two and two tonight. Now he took the stairs by threes himself, missing all but one last pile of slush. From there three far-flung tracks led to a narrowly open door, beyond which the great pioneering feet themselves could be seen hanging over the end of the bed to dry.

"Hey, I thought I might find you up."

"How you say?"

"I followed your footprints partway home."

"Oh ya." Henry sucked his teeth and rolled his eyes aside. "I had to go to the bus station for a candy bar."

"Ah." Ten blocks each way, and Henry had waited to eat when he got home. The crumpled wrapper lay on the floor near his shoes and socks, a five-cent Pay Day bar. Al found himself rolling his eyes aside. Since he was standing there, he rested his sack on the dresser, next to a crumpled one.

"Sit down and stay awhile."

Henry had glanced at the chair standing nearby for him, and Al sat down on it. "Thanks."

"How you make out tonight?"

"Ow-wow," Al said, but Henry was watching him. "I cleared a few bucks."

Henry rolled his eyes, and Al leaned forward to open the donuts up. Taking one, he placed the package on the edge of the dresser, where Henry might see it. "You have any luck yourself?"

"Shit," Henry said, and his stomach growled.

Al held the donuts out to him. "Take two," he said, and Henry did. "You went over there?"

"Shit yes, I went."

"Shit," Al said, taking two himself. "I didn't suggest, I only mentioned it."

Henry waved a donut soothingly. "Man, I know that."

They ate awhile.

"Well, you didn't miss much."

"I guess. They said they might be able to use me later for sweeping up, but I don't think I could stand the draft they got."

"I noticed that. They seem to like to have all their color in their travelogues. There's milk to wash those donuts down."

"Ah." Henry drank. "You going to try to make this town?"

"I guess. I have some family out on the Coast. I'd like to make a little stake before I head over there."

"You'll do all right."

"Let's hope," Al said, drinking milk.

"Me, I haven't got anyone this side of Los Angeles. I'm leaving fast."

"When's that?"

"First thing in the morning, while I still have my strength."

Their milk was gone. "Have an apple," Al offered, tossing Henry one. He did not bother to mention it was a Wenatchee Red. "You try those other places you had in mind?"

"Hell yes, I ran my ass everywhere. I was even over at the post office, but they already hired their Christmas help."

"That's tough luck."

"Ya."

They yawned.

"Well, it feels like it's getting late." Al stood up. "There's an extra apple you may want."

"That's all right."

"You don't smoke?"

"Not me," Henry said. "Somebody might want me to play basketball."

Al collected his garbage, and Henry rose from the bed to go to the door with him. They shook hands there. "Good luck to you, Henry."

"Thanks, hey." Henry held his door open until Al had found and unlocked his own. Then they both closed at once.

Inside, Al placed his own apple on the dresser, crumpled his sack. The tobacco he tossed on the bed. He hung his jacket on the chair, sat on the bed to take off his shoes and socks. He stood up again to count his take, his working change, and his savings account. Now he could lie down at last and stretch his feet to dry. Rolling a cigarette, he rolled his eyes. He had forgotten to turn off the dirty light. He stood up and kicked it off, first try, cold foot. Back on the bed again and all fired up, he flicked his match, watched it sputter out in the puddle beside his shoes. His pants felt almost dry to him. He thought to sleep in his clothes tonight, in case he woke up late, was in a hurry to get to work. Maybe the Auto Show would turn out to be a big-assed success, he could get moving out of here himself. You never know. . . .

"Oh ya, indeed," he said.

2

It was early. He could tell, because he had been down there yesterday in just such a light, in case anybody wanted him for anything. You never know. . . . He had not had to leave his clothes on after all, but it was all right he had, for his chamber lady was an unhappy one. She was waiting at the door for him: "You leaving now?"

"Good morning! I'll be right back."

She had already stripped down Henry's room. His sheets were heaped in front of the fire escape, and in her big wire basket lay apple cores. The stairs were not yet swept, but dry. Down in the can he brushed his teeth and shaved as best he could in the dirty light. The water itself was yellow and cold, probably reclaimed slush. A farsighted man, he had carried a little sample bar of Cashier Bouquet all the way from, he believed, New Mexico. He was never never without some kind of razor blade; his traveling kit had a built-in strop to it, from California. Luckily he had showered in Colorado before he left; he only had to put a little bouquet on his underarms. After a glance at the toilet he decided to wait for the Auto Show.

"You be here again tonight?"

"We'll see," he advised, and closed the door on her red-lighted face. For an instant he thought his Wenatchee Red was gone, but then remembered he had put it behind his sack before he left. In Denver the other night he had lost a ten-cent Whiz Bar in less time than it had taken to get no answer on the telephone, three flights down, of course. That was all right by now; his lady had been a smiling one, and thin. He sat on the chair to eat, and then made himself look forward, to a ice cream bar.

There was not much else. His traveling kit was zipped. In the hall the lady had finally given up on him, begun to sweep, or brush. He had to wait for her to stir things around a bit before he could safely reach the steps; her broom looked to have a sharp point on the end of it. Below, the Hotel Ya was way ahead: two with suitcases and big Texas hats and boots were signing up, and the smiling clerk was giving Henry's room to them. Al did not stop to leave his key; he had a back pocket quite big enough. Yee, the day was a dirty one. Grey slush lay on everything. Passing cars and trucks spat black. Somewhere during the night the machine had lost its appetite. A befouled clock said not yet eight, as he had guessed. Had it been later he might have splurged on a big-assed bus, but as things stood he chose to mush to work by an unfamiliar route, in search of restaurants. Not that he would be patronizing one today, of course, but you never knew when such a day might come. It paid a man to look ahead. Yesterday's had been a flytrap dreaming of businessmen.

He still hadn't chosen by the time he reached the bridge, the dangerous one. Now he redirected his attention to that misplaced pole, in quest of traces of patrol car white. There they were, and a little dent, and at the foot of the pole a few turds of mud. He could not say for certain which poles the others had hit, so he had to guess. Here came one of the survivors cruising slowly now, eyeing everything suspiciously. Al took care not to walk too close to the railings, as of course the poles. Everything went just fine. That one for the moment seemed satisfied.

There loomed the Coliseum up ahead, and already the gleaming beasts were being driven with greatest care through the slippery streets. They entered the parking lot in single file, where an attendant waved them toward the wide-open doors. Here and there in that long line snorted the transportation of the tardy parking boys. At ninety cents an hour, they were in a hurry to get their parkas on. Their colleague waved them toward the back of the lot, where they raced together in a squealing pack. The gleaming beasts moved stately on, for they were the chosen ones. Each paused briefly before the doors, but then moved calmly through without a sound.

Al followed in, though by a narrower door, marked COM-MISSARY. It seemed they weren't ready yet for him. The room was dark, but soon he could see the floor was wet, with water, and everything waited neatly in its allotted place. No people were in sight. Not to be standing there in his tracks, Al stepped lightly to the can, here called MEN. This room too was freshly watered down, though the nearest sink showed blood—perhaps only where some early gladiator had shaved himself. In here the stall doors swung free. Yesterday, upstairs, Al had almost cost himself a dime, by stumbling into GENTLE-MEN. With all this sudden cleanliness, a man could consent to sit awhile, wait for his Wenatchee Red to begin to work. It was between nine and nine-fifteen, he guessed; Old Gus wouldn't be needing him just yet. Al rolled himself a cigarette, put on his cap. It was then he noticed there was no paper in the box. With all this sudden cleanliness, he had not thought to check. Up, redressed, he tried stall two: this box had one sheet at least, but oh, how well he had warmed that other seat!

And what a way for man to waste his time, he thought; for

all he knew that sheet in there was the only one. It paid a man
to look ahead like that. Hadn't Old Gus been good enough
to trust him with his paper cap? Didn't it say Orange Crush?
He would try his luck another time, after lunch perhaps.

The commissary floor was drier now; one could see where
Al had walked on it. A man stood just outside a doorway
looking in. "Good morning!" Al called to him.

"Oh, it's you," Gus said.

Not needed now, Al tiptoed out. All the beasts were in, but
here came Santa Claus on foot. He was so red-nosed today it
hurt. All that profit had not reached the bank, it looked, but
had been deposited somewhere handy at an early hour. Six
and six? Al waited for Santa to say good morning first.

"You're early, Eighty-eight."

"Ya, a bit."

Santa Claus peered past Al into the commissary, and advised, "We best wait for that floor to dry."

"We best."

So they watched the parking boys. Not needed yet, these
stood together in a group waving its arms against the cold.
One drove in late, and they laughed at him. Hey hey, they
said. Then suddenly appeared a customer. Park here, they
called, all moving and motioning, showing where. That car
didn't know *what* to do, being first, but finally it stalled or
parked. Each boy had some good word to give, and the out-
numbered customer mumbled something back. Santa Claus
and Al went in.

"Hello there, boys!" *Gus.*

"Hello, hello!" they said.

Santa Claus knew just what to do, but somehow Al could
not quite pick it up, no matter how carefully he watched. Go
to your ice cream box, flip back its lid, go to the freezer and
look in that, move to the sink, wet a cloth, go to your box,

close it up, carefully and firmly check both taps for drips, disappear somewhere in back. . . . Al went to a neutral wall, leaned waiting there to see what next. It seemed he had instinctively chosen his allotted place; soon some of the other boys arrived and stood next to him, watching Santa Claus go about his work. In fact it began to appear that no one was allowed to stand anywhere else except Santa Claus, and Gus himself.

"Old Nick sure has a lot to do today."

"I think he's looking for a dime he dropped."

"No, he's looking for Gus's ass to lick."

"Whenever he thinks he's found the mark his nose gets in the way of it."

"Hey hey . . ."

At eleven o'clock they went to put their jackets on; they had only been waiting for last night's sweat to dry. Now it was time to form a line before Gus's window, behind Santa's back. Gus hadn't quite finished his paper work, but he interrupted that to get Santa's bars. Santa paid cash for his. All others charged. They had to wait a little longer for their loads, but soon they were staggering one by one away in debt. Some made matters worse by stopping to borrow a roll of change at the cashier's cage.

"You're on Pepsi, Eighty-eight. I'm giving you Main Floor Northeast, Portal Eight. Charley there will show you where to put your box."

"Great!"

"What's that?"

"O.K.!"

Accepting his yellow chit, Al wrapped his arms around his Pepsi jug. Charley where, what box? Never mind; he staggered smiling off in search of Portal 8. It was good he knew northeast. His jug was an awkward one, and greased. At nine dollars, Old Gus must have put pure olive oil in it. Oh yes, it leaked.

"Eighty-eight! You forgot your cups!"

This was Pete, upon the run. Using a downward thrust, he rammed one long carton between Al's chest and jug. Circling, he drove home the other one.

"Thanks!"

Now with two horns or tentacles waving above his head, Al had little difficulty finding Portal 8. If people were in the way they watched out for him. His only worry was the beasts, each standing so quietly in its allotted place. Al let himself be guided partly by his sense of smell, relying on his feelers to distinguish bulk. Glancing sidewise, he saw the other boys already setting up their shops. Al eased his goods onto the floor, while his Pepsi sloshed and his cups slid out.

"Over here, Eighty-eight!" Charley at last, waving, pointing to Al's box behind a Cadillac. "Over here!" Charley couldn't wait for him to pick up his cups.

"Ah, here?"

"Go get your jug and put it on your box."

That box didn't look like it would support his cups, but Al went for his jug. Charley was all gone by the time he got back. Al eased his jug toward his box, not very far. Now he lowered it sloshing to the floor again, and moved his box over against the wall, in spite of everything Charley had said. When he had his box tilted well he balanced his jug, which was growing lighter now, on top, and leaned his cups against it diagonally from the southeast and the southwest, to help hold it up and warn the public off.

The public just now was the vendor of that Cadillac, in great need of drink. He held out coins with a trembling hand; Al's trembled too as he approached his jug, plucked a cup, opened the spout, or spit-tit. What came out was a yellowish froth. Somebody had fed his Pepsi jug some Orange Crush, and the jug was gagging on it. Suddenly it coughed, spat red. Nothing else happened for a little while. Then it was gagging again, drooling a greenish bile.

The man with the money had turned green himself. "You've got your jug placed all wrong! You got to have your spout tipping toward the floor!" cried that desperate man, taking hold of the jug.

"Don't touch it!" Al warned, and grasped his jug in both his arms. Hugging tight, he glared at the man. Did he try to tell him how to drive his Cadillacs? Meanwhile the jug was piddling on the floor. "Take the cup!"

The shaken man took the cup, found the spout while Al held up the jug. The cup quickly filled, the stuff was spilling over onto the man's shaking hand. "Turn off the spout!"

"Which way does this fugger turn off?"

"To the left!"

There was a gargling noise as the stream tapered gradually down to a drip. The man waited for every last drop to fall into his cup, spill over the brim, trickle onto his hand, down his wrist to his watch. Then he stood up. He stood with his back to the jug, drinking his drink. He did not go near his Cadillac until he had finished, wiped himself with his handkerchief, left his coins piled on the floor by his cup.

Now Al dared release his jug. He carefully balanced everything again, reset his cups. He stirred the mess on the floor with his foot. Then he wiped his hands on his cap, picked up his coins, and leaned back to rest. The Cadillac vendor was resting in his front seat, drying himself. No one else was in sight. All things considered, not such a bad start: *one out of one.*

Here came number two, all dressed in black suit and black tie, like a doctor or president. Even the Cadillac vendor's coat and pants didn't match. This one had a red eye, but no thirst. He sized up Al's shop like some kind of visiting specialist from the East. He seemed to be counting Al's cups, weighing his jug. Surely he wasn't thinking of taking over the joint, or knocking it off? No no. He glanced at Al's cap and Al found himself standing almost erect. His smile, however, came a little too late, at the man's stiff back. One out of two.

"I'll take a shot of that, Eighty-eight." Santa Claus's hands shook his money belt. "Make it quick."

"Coming up." Al flipped his spout.

"That's all right, Eighty-eight," Santa called, shouldering his pack. "I see Charley has a fast jug."

What to call that? One out of a little too much. Al could see why Santa was always on ass cream bars. Santa's hands shook too much, unless he was pocketing a dime—far too much for the corn and the nuts, not to mention these drinks. Spinning his lid, Al ladled himself an early lunch, drank deep. Now came a boy on the run; passing, he hit Al full in the face with a cloth. "Stay a minute, boy. . . ."

"Mr. Costello wants you should wipe your mess."

"Oh, he does?" Al wiped his mess with his foot on the cloth, kicked it into his box. His shop swayed but did not collapse. Through Portal 8 he could see Charley's fast jug, its spout giving Orange Crush like a horse. Charley had his cups invitingly displayed in neat little stacks that encircled his jug; at a customer's approach he whipped a cup from one of his stacks, held forth a nice drink while his customer fumbled for coins. When business was slow he sat down and leaned back to rest, on his extra box. He gave Al a little wave from down there.

The noon whistle blew, and they opened the doors. That first customer walked in, still mumbling to himself. His first stop was at Charley's well-liked shop. One out of four, or the third in a row, he drank deep as he wandered by. Al decided to speak.

"How's it go, Charley?"

"Not too bad," Charley said, leaning back.

"What's the cut on these drinks?"

"Fifteen percent."

Two cents plus. "Sixty cups?"

"That's right." Charley was counting his stacks. "I've already dumped six," he said, and leaned back to rest.

"Not bad," six to one. "Where can a man trade a crate for a box, Charley?"

"What's that?"

"Where can—"

"Hey, you got a bite," Charley said.

A man stood eyeing Al's stand from some distance off, whether as shopper or engineer it was hard to make out. Al hastened. "Good afternoon! Care for a drink?"

The man eyed Al in his semiprofessional way. "You in business?" he asked.

"Sure am," Al said, gently whipping out a cup.

His fast draw caught the man by surprise. He went for his wallet instead of his change. "Got change for a dollar?"

"Sure have," Al said with a fast draw and a laugh.

The man was less ready to give up his dollar than Al was his drink, but they did at last make the exchange. Al watched while his customer raised the cup to his nose, took a sniff. Now he rotated the cup. Finding nothing to read there, he read Al's jug and his cap. Once more he sniffed. "What is this stuff?"

"That's Pipsi."

The man tried to look Al in the eye, but could not quite bring himself to it. Without further word he walked off, not gulping, but sipping, his Pipsi. He eyed the Cadillac and its vendor on his way by. Those two eyed him back. That vendor was less aggressive than most, especially the Fordmen. He did not run and hop all around, showing off. He stood in silence beside his big beast, as if waiting for it to speak for itself. Each beast did have a label glued to its brow, giving some facts. To him, that was apparently enough. As it happened, his beast too was green.

Now a few carloads of customers drifted in; it was snowing again. They had all had their lunch, had had plenty to drink. They only glanced at Al's jug. Most of them gathered around the Fordmen, who were growing excited. In the still, exhausted air of the Coliseum, one could hear them slapping their fenders and slamming their doors: those beasts were not dead, only hibernating. Customers stood a long time observing, nodding their heads. When they moved on from the beasts to the birds, they seemed all nodded out. A few winced at the Cadillac's label on their way by. One man circled the beast with plain longing a number of times, didn't leave until its vendor gave him a green little smile.

At two Al had sold three, when the lights went out. All the beasts hooted. The Fordmen stopped beating their flanks. Now a team of some kind could be felt trotting past. They could be heard on some steps. All at once a blast of musical noise stunned even the beasts. It came from a high place to the south, where that team had arrived. The Fordmen had lent them their keys. Each member leaped forward to take his turn at the mike, while those left behind took no turns drowning him out. They were Negro, but someone upstairs had taken care to bathe them in a blue-purple light. A tremendous blast from the brass turned it green. Blast! It turned red. Blast! Blue-purple again. Blast! Blast! Blast! Blast! Everything went black—they had shattered that light. Through a gate to the west staggered a shining white beast, pursued by a nervous halo of gold. A golden-haired lady braced herself in the front, beside the grim driver in black. The haughty beast moved coughing past the other beasts, jerked to a stop at the foot of the stage.

"In-tro-du-cing Miss Betsy Smith and the power steering power braking fully automatic *loaded* new—"

To a crashing of cymbals a doorman in uniform opened Miss Betsy Smith's door, and the nervous spotlight followed her out. Now a smaller spot, calmer, pure white, accompanied her to the ladder, or stairs, while the other eyed the glum beast waiting for her to return, the glaring driver hunched over his wheel. Well-stacked if not *loaded*, very high-heeled, Betsy Smith lifted the edge of her skirt with one dainty hand, gripped the stairs with the other. Under the pitiless light, one could see her trembling toes testing those rungs. Her left foot was the scout, followed doglike by her right. When at last her left hand reached the stage, the master of ceremonies grabbed her wrist, hauled her up. She stood straight, her chin high, her smile bravely answering the treble salute of trombones. In the sudden quiet that followed, she continued to smile. She seemed willing to stay there, smiling, all night, but the master of ceremonies led her back to the steps. He had things to say at the mike.

"Thank you, Miss Betsy Smith and the makers of—"

Betsy Smith tripped. Gasps, and scattered remnants of applause, accompanied her bumpy descent. This time the doorman, or master at arms, hauled her up. With his aid she hobbled back to the beast, that unbreakable smile held only a little less high. He aided her in, slammed her door tight. Betsy Smith waved and the beast leaped away to applause. Its halo, caught daydreaming, ran to catch up, finally spotted the beast's tail flicking out Portal 8.

Bowing to applause, the halo was dreaming again, for a

beast could be heard staggering in from the west. Meanwhile the halo basked in a new wave of applause. Would it never wake up? Ah! Starting suddenly, it darted left and right a few times, then took off, to the south! In panic it flew from portal to portal down there, until a roar from the beast brought it up short. Turning pink, pretending to ignore the applause, it crept to the foot of the stage, where black beast and driver sat waiting. Quickly the doorman opened the door, the master of ceremonies announced, but smiling Miss Virginia Martin made no move to climb to his side. She waved at the hand he held out. "Thank *you*, Miss Virginia Martin . . ." and a treble salute. Unaided she made her way back to the beast, which sprang off at the slam of her door. This time the halo was ready, in fact a half jump in advance. It went straight to Portal 8, and from there watched the beast duck out Portal 7.

"Give me that mother pricker!"

A sure hand guided the halo due west, in time to spot a little red beast dashing in. There was applause, but it was rather halfhearted. Some of the joy had gone out of the show. Now by comparison the halo seemed too damned efficient, the beasts were warmed up and almost obedient, and the ever-smiling misses had altogether stopped taking risks. Only when it came time for the grand finale did the heavy atmosphere liven a little. Then the combined roar of the parading beasts and the Lampbreakers finally shattered the master of ceremonies, and with so many beasts at one time the distracted halo had difficulty choosing.

The lights finally went on, revealing a parade not of beasts but of stumbling people. They wandered about blinking their eyes at tame beasts and wild Fordmen, whose merciless beatings seemed anticlimactic. They blinked in the same dazed way at the hot dogs, popcorn, and Pipsi. They were not hungry, nor thirsty, nor happy, but they had paid a dollar to get

into this salesroom, and outside it was snowing. So they hung
on, earning back some of their money. Uniformed men and
boys patrolled them in silence.

One man was drinking. He had already patronized Charley's
stand, and now Al's too attracted his attention. Stocky in a
sturdy wool jacket, he had a straightforward way of walking,
and talking. Unblinking, he looked a man very straight in the
eye. "Here, I'll take one."

"Coming up," Al said, his spout already spitting.

"How much you get?"

"Fifteen."

"No, how much *you* get?"

"Fifteen, percent."

"Fifteen! In San Diego they get twenty. That's three cents
a cup, figure it out for yourself. We've got the management
by the nuts. Some boys clear twenty dollars per night after
dues. With a take like that a man doesn't half mind paying his
dues, right?" It wasn't really a question, and the foamy cup
was now ready, presenting a problem for even such a man as
this one. Taking the cup, he looked Al straight and hard in
the eye. "Here you go, buddy. I like to see a man get his fair
share." He winked and nodded. "The bastards owe it to you,
right?"

Glancing at the coins in his hand, the dime, the nickel, the
shiny new penny, Al blinked, and nodded. "Well, thank
you!"

"O.K., buddy." The man nodded once more before he
strode off, swilling his Pepsi.

Al slipped the nickel and dime into his money belt, the
penny into his savings pocket. Vigilant Charley, reclining on
his throne, was grinning. Al gave him a nod. Smirking,
Charley flipped his bright penny high in the air and caught
it. Al waved, but Charley was up on his feet now, slipping

his penny into his pocket with one hand and fussing his cups with the other.

"How's it going, Eighty-eight?" It was the red-eyed president speaking.

"Just fine!" Al said, adjusting his cap in lieu of his cups.

"If you need more rags, let us know."

"Thank you!"

The president nodded his head, acting nice. He had only stopped by for a chat. "How's it going, Twenty-three?"

"Like a gun, Mr. Costello! I've already dropped forty-one."

"If you need more cups, let us know."

"Sure will, Mr. Costello!"

Beaming Charley watched the friendly president depart, then nodded sidewise at Al. *In.*

A wet rag smacked Al in the face. *"Boy?"* But the boy was far gone, delivering Charley his cups. Waving, Al kicked the rag behind his box. Now he felt a draft at his back and some people blew in; it was family hour, mostly freeloading Ford-wives with kids. The wives were immune, but each kid had a dime he was all eager to spend.

"Those drinks a dime, mister?"

No, he had to admit they were not. No, neither could he make up the deficit; their mothers would have to do that. Not a chance, they assured. He suggested they share. Looking at one another, they wrinkled their noses. He looked too, for many were the times he had sold a single ice cream bar to cooperative gangs of seven or eight. He believed he could still find them running on certain streets. He let these boys go, but soon they were back.

"How much for a half cup?"

"Same price."

"How come?"

"I have to pay the boss by the cup."

"We only want *half* a cup."
"I pay for the *cup*, not the drink."
They were gone longer this time.
"O.K., we'll take one, mister."
"Just one?"
"One."
Under their steady gaze Al drew a slow one, without too much head. He handed it carefully to the boy with the dimes, and the empty-handed boy took the change.
"Hey, he gave me a full one at least," the one said, walking away.
"Yeah, he did," said his friend.
Al dropped dimes in his money belt, while Charley fussed with his cups. Now Al took advantage of this breather to size up the crowd. The big boys had no dimes, they were spending their dollars on a machine that analyzed their handwriting electronically with the help of some holes punched by a fat pitchman in business suit. Whatever the machine wrote made them proud. Tucking their cards into hip pockets, they strolled in solemn troops among the beasts. At their approach Fordmen ceased slamming doors, for these boys were concerned with more serious matters. Generally speaking they spoke only to themselves, but when they did have a question it was well to be ready. As for girls, there were few.
"How much for a refill, mister?"
"Boy?"
"How much for a refill?" The boy with the nickel was back, with a cup.
"Refills are five."
"I'll take one."
They had washed out their cup. Under the boy's steady gaze, Al filled with the same care as before. The boy seemed well satisfied as he walked slowly back to his friend waiting

just beyond Portal 8. His friend nodded approval, and Al slipped five cents into his savings account. Thank God, he would not soon be in the market for cars.

"Charley, how about keeping an eye on my stand for a minute?"

From his throne Charley nodded, and Al wandered off among the beasts. To a man no longer buying it was like viewing a herd, a vegetarian tour of the stockyards, though at close range he did note a few distinctions. One had eight eyes in place of the usual four, another had rabbit ears. For the most part, however, he could not even distinguish the beasts from the birds. In fact none of them looked like the real thing, more like aficionados lined up to view Le Grand Prix, wearing goggles. Closing his nose against the fartful air, Al eyed soft drink stands, en passant. These vendors did not look as happy as Charley, though one growing boy flashed a shiny cigarette lighter: "It's a Cadillac!" Bien fait, mon petit. Even the garbage man wasn't unloading much today. His banners, balloons, and plastic dolls did not seem to relate to anything meaningful. Miss Betsy Smith smiled and said, "Hello!" Al smiled after her, but she was heading for a telephone. A slack-jawed security guard stood before it. Al followed some of the boys up to the balcony.

The action was up here. Up here no beast looked like any other. One had silver intestines, another gold, one, a rejuvenated nag, had leopard skin grafted onto her seat. One thing they all had in common was manifold goiters, and their mechanical heart pumps had all been lately repainted. In front of each beast stood a large, legible placard giving far more exhaustive information than any downstairs—the horsepower, the ring size, the valve size, the bore. Each placard sported a ribbon, red, white, or blue, and always nearby at least one boy stood on guard. These were older boys in their twenties or thirty. The younger boys stood before them in troops, asking reverent questions. Al approached an old one left momentarily deserted, hunched in a striped leather jacket that matched his beast's seat.

"How long it take you to build that machine?"

"Two years."

"Drive it very much?"

"Not yet. Going to drive it to the L.A. show next spring, if it's ready by then."

"They give you prizes at these shows?"

The old one scowled. "Prizes?"

"Money or gas or anything?"

The old one turned his striped back. "Can't you see that *ribbon?*" he mumbled.

Le Grand Prix, it was blue. Al wandered away, not needed here. It was time he got back down to business. His stand was still standing, but poor old Charley was tiring. "Where you been, hey?"

"How many drinks have you dropped, Charley?"

"Fifty."

Al nodded, leaned close. "I've been checking around. You're the odds-on favorite to win the Prize."

"Huh?"

"You're *in.*"

Al went to his cups under Charley's proud, perplexed stare. From the balcony, Al's old boy and a few others stared down. Mr. Costello stared from the floor. Al himself could scarcely believe, at an intense moment like this, when three lovely people approached with true thirst. By the time they were all served and sent away sniffing, his audience had lost interest. Providentially too, the lights went out before it had time to reassemble. Not wanting to overtax Charley, who more than likely could not stare so well in the dark, Al took his cups with him this trip. Thanks to their guidance alone, since the roar of the beasts was quite deafening, he somehow side-stepped the incoming beasts, made his way to COMMISSARY.

"More cups, Eighty-eight?"

"No, just leaving these here for a minute while I go to the can."

Old Gustus thoughtfully watched how he did that.

"Hey, cups don't go there, Eighty-eight, that's for bars!" Santa was right on the job.

"Ah. Sorry!" Al hastened to correct his bad blunder. He took his cups with him, Old Gustus and Santa watching with interest. See there: that's how he opens the door. Ah, that's how he closes it.

Inside was not pretty. Not only the usual blood and whis-kers, but from the door to stall one dripped an orangish vomit like an abandoned experiment in pip art drying slowly. Some-one had tried to efface it with that last piece of paper. For that and some other reasons stall two had lost its attraction. Stall three was its own kind of disgrace, but nearest the win-dow. MEN can't be choosers, and Al was in a hurry.

As consolation he almost treated himself to a soft paper cup, but thought better. Twelve and a half cents. GENTLEMEN themselves didn't pay that. Instead Al improvised, doing quite well by himself. GENTLEMEN didn't wear paper hats. Thanks, Old Gustus. As for the washing of hands, Al had a generous supply of wet rags back at the stand. Thus there was no fur-ther reason to tarry.

He had his apology ready—an Orange Crush hat made bad public relations for a man trying to dump Pipsi—but Old Gus took no notice. He was bent over his books and chewing his pencil. It seemed he might not even have spoken had he not found himself suddenly in darkness.

"Hit that damn switch!"

"What switch is that, Gus?"

"That freaking line breaker!"

Al's cautious feelers did find a wall somewhere but no line breakers of any kind. In the distance sounded a fierce crashing, or gnashing, as of two beasts locking bumpers in mortal contest. Now came a few seconds of silence, followed by scattered sounds of restlessness, which in turn became a crescendo of bellows. The beasts were stampeding. Nearby, Gus was hitting that line breaker. "Dead as shit!" he announced.

"Same out there." Al had found the commissary door, and in a flickering beam of light could be seen beasts without halos, paralyzed. Now, four by four, their eyes began to light up in the dark, revealing the problem. They were trying to escape through Portal 8, but found their way blocked by those two locked in terrible contest. The defective security guards were running in all directions, their side holsters swinging dangerously. In the confusion one could imagine the boys dumping drinks by the dozens. Here came some of them now.

"Get back to your stands!" Gus roared.

"Man, it's murder out there—"

"Mr. Costello said—"

"It's all over—"

"Hell yes—"

"What is it, a blackout?"

"No, just the storm. You can see lights in the city."

"Them are headlights."

"On top of the Federal Building?"

"The Federal Building has its own power."

"Yeah? What about the Church of Christ? Does it have its own power?"

"Well . . ."

"Man your stands!" Gus was up on the counter waving a parking lot flashlight.

"Everyone quiet!" Mr. Costello filled the doorway, his right hand raised like a president's. "Check these men in, Gus. Make sure nobody's missing."

"O.K., line up, you guys!" Gus commanded. "Nick, go get everyone in here!"

"I told him it was all over—"

"Hell yes."

"How you do, Forty-seven?"

"*Cool*, man." His jacket was deep orange.

Al ducked through the door in quest of his stand. The beasts were quieter now, were in fact almost docile as men shoved them about, jumped up and down on their bumpers. Only the bright glare of their eyes in the darkness warned what they might be thinking. In their midst loomed the Cadillac, thundering, like a great green brontosaurus reawakened in the Age of the Poodle. Lesser beasts and people steered wide. Up in the balcony, the old guard stood ready to meet any challenge. Al's jug, on the other hand, lay rocking on its stomach, face down in the sticky pool of its own making. People were skidding and cursing.

"That your jug there?"

"Yes, it is."

"You better look to her."

Closing his eyes, Al waited a decent time for that man to move on before he looked to her. Then, leaning his cups against his crate, he tipped her straight, slapped her lid on, spread damp cloths over her little accident. Oh, wasn't she a sweet armful. When he felt he had some kind of hold on her, he stooped for his feelers.

"You can leave your box there, Eighty-eight."

"You know I will, Charley," Al assured, staggering cheek to cheek toward COMMISSARY. The sluggish beasts jostled him.

"Eighty-eight, *Gus* wants you."

Saluting Santa Claus with his feelers, Al plunged onward.

"Here comes Eighty-eight!"

"Here he is, Gus."

"Has he got his jug?"

"Yeah, he's got her."

"Grab his cups."

Somebody clipped Al's feelers, and he rested jug-first against the wall for a moment before dropping her.

"You find Fifty-five, Nick?"

"No, he must have skipped. Eighty-eight's coming though."

"Eighty-eight's here!"

"He just come in, Nick."

"Jugs don't go there, Eighty-eight!"

Al bent to correct his little mistake.

"Here's your chit, Eighty-eight."

Al hastened to Gustus, who tended his books beneath twin halos provided by two boys aiming parking lot flashlights. "Little bad luck today, but we'll hit 'em tomorrow!" Gus promised.

"Thanks." Lucky eighty-eight cents, and that included six cents treasury money.

"You can pay at the cashier's cage."

Four sixty-five for the lady, and that included Social Security.

"That's tomorrow at ten, Eighty-eight."

"Ten?"

"Don't forget to turn in your coat and your money belt."

"Right."

"You can keep your hat."

"Thanks!"

Out at last, Al breathed deep. He would be wearing a snow cap again tonight. Each beast wore one, and to see them all charging the red-nosed parking boys was a dramatic sight.

In contrast to yesterday, the mood tonight was headlong escape. This led, of course, to little accidents. Any beast not yet moving was hit. Owners could still be seen tumbling through the flickering doorways of the Coliseum, like mice deserting a burning wastebasket. No, these were fleas. They scurried everywhere in quest of certain beasts. Fastidious.

Breathing deep, Al zigzagged across the unparking lot, for he had a date with The Refugee. Four and four was not eighty-eight, but on a night like this a man could in all conscience dip into his savings account. Thanks to the storm he was early enough, and quiet. While the cops were kept busy helping the parka boys, the Phantom of Portal 8 lay tracks to the south. The snow was his light. Jingling merrily if not so loudly as Santa Claus, he glided over the bridge.

Old whoever it was appeared to be right: whatever the facts about the Federal Building and the Church, the south side of town did have power. It glowed in the distance like the dawn of the twentieth century. Meanwhile the nineties were not so gay as Al might have expected. Without their bright blandishments the pubs appeared to be sleeping, but Al did not stop to awaken them. He was faithful, and progressive. Thus, turning onto the street of The Refugee, his surprise and sorrow at finding few tracks there. Not one led to or from that dark door! Al stood before it a few minutes, silently cursing the backward fathers and his own backward memory, then mushed on into a dark blue Sunday in Washington.

Up ahead, that gluttonous machine was getting all that it wanted, Sunday or no. In fact Sunday was better than ever: yesterday stale beer, today vintage champagne. Playfully it blew him some spray, which he spat back. The begoggled driver wagged him a mitten. Al nodded. Keep your mind on the gutter, sport. Further on, Al's apple magnate was at least tending to business. He was reading his newspaper by candle-light tonight, probably checking the latest quotations from Wenatchee. At the thought Al's stomach did stir a little. It was true he hadn't really eaten since morning. Stamping snow from his shoes, he saw his friend look up smiling. Al pushed in without further invitation. "Good evening!"

"Good evening! You're early!"

Al blew on his hands, nodding agreement. "Sunday."

"Still snowing out there?"

"Faster than the machine can swill it."

"Well, I saved a quart of milk for you!"

"Thanks!" Some Wenatchee Reds too, even bigger than last night's. But Al's eye was caught by another allurement.

"Apples tonight?"

"How much is that apple wine there?"

The man looked at a big, ticking clock behind him. Eleven-thirty. "I never expected to see you this early!"

"No, me either. . . . How much is that apple wine?"

The man studied his windows. "That snow sure keeps the cops busy out there, don't it?"

"Man, you know it."

The man studied his shelves now. "That apple there?" he said finally. "That's ninety-nine a pint. It's made from Wenatchees."

"O.K., I'll take one."

"Donuts tonight?" his merchant asked, sacking.

"No, I think I'll try peanuts tonight."

"One of these big bags?"

"Better make it two small ones."

"There you go. Tobacco?"

"No, but matches. Not that many. A couple of books will do fine. . . . All right, four."

"Papers?"

"No, I have those."

"Gum?"

"I think I will have a Wenatchee," Al said, selecting one of the biggest and reddest. That sufficed. His neighborhood merchant brought his adding machine into working position, looked around him just once more before beginning his reckoning.

"Let's see, that apple was ninety-nine a pint, wasn't it?"

"Yes, that's what you said."

That settled, the other prices came easier. Clearly the man's attention to the financial page was paying off handsomely. The dang-blang tax caught him momentarily unready, but he was getting the hang of it. "There we go! Dollar sixty."

"Dollar sixty." No man to argue on Sunday in Washington, Al counted out quickly from both pockets.

"Just right! Watch that sack now, don't forget that bottle!"

"I won't!"

"Handle that door all right?"

"Yes. Thanks!"

"Good night!"

"Good night!"

"See you tomorrow!"

"Good luck to you!" Al called, and waved from the sidewalk. Now with a sack in his arms he was off sailing like Santa Claus again, though jingling less loudly than ever. Here came competition. He did not wave to the machine and its palsy driver, but inhaled spray with what he felt to be a jolly expression. Down, Prancer! Otherwise, not a creature was stirring. The sleeping city had, however, left on its lights here to show him his way. All that he lacked were great footsteps to follow. If he lacked Henry's guidance in that way, at least he didn't permit himself to eat dinner before he reached home.

Home tonight presented almost a cheerful winter scene, thick new welcome mat on the step before the door, mauve glow of HOTEL YA amid swirling flakes, ever faithful glimmer of second-floor can above. Al stepped carefully over the mat, and the door said *keeey* to the nodding clerk. Flashing his key, Al waved him back to sleep. Mounting the stairs, he left the ladies a gift on every third step. He had nothing for the can just now. On the third floor the cowboys were snoring peacefully in Henry's bed, visions of sugar plums caught in their throats. Al tiptoed quietly by. Zeeee, in his own room it was no better; here it was not just the noise, it was the vibration.

What he did first was to open his sack. Later would be soon enough to settle accounts, eighty-eight cents was easy in relation to a dollar sixty. His pockets felt about right. He did of course remember to take off his shoes, and not to forget to check his traveling kit. The first bag of peanuts he placed on the floor by his bed, along with his tobacco and matches. He did not crumple his sack tonight, but folded it carefully and weighted it down with Big Red. Breakfast would be ready when he woke up at eight. He felt a sudden longing for meat. Meanwhile, he noted, his wine was a full twenty percent; a man could be sure there were plenty of calories and vitamins in that. Think of all that vitamin A! His chamber lady had rinsed out his apple jelly glass, or had herself a drink from his carafe. He dried well with his sheet. Now it was time to enjoy a short apéritif before he sat down to eat. No, he had his first course standing up, sat down to his second with a glass of good table wine, yellow.

Reclining, drinking deep, he grinned at the mirror. The sons of bitching Fordmen never had it this good, even with meat. The unconscious cowboys would never make out. He alone was awake, watching his day settle into place. He had not done too badly, given the difficult odds, not to mention that jug. You better look to her! Here you go, buddy! As for that refill, it still bothered him somewhat. So careful so young. He thought of those three lovely people instead, how beautifully they had turned away the cool stares. A man could almost feel pity for the poor old balcony boys, however dangerous they might be when they ran out of parts. Pity poor old starry-eyed Mrs. Costello too; her poor old son would never be a real President. Man your stands, men! You can keep your hat, Eighty-eight! Thanks, dear old Gus. I'll make out, I'll make out! No man can be Charley every day, that's what makes life interesting. Poor old Fordmen don't know that. They too have their problems.

He was starving, so he counted his money instead. That didn't last long. Thanks to a greedy idea dreamed up by the greedy Fordmen, he was seventy-two cents worse off than last night and two times as hungry. If he hadn't been taken in by those salesmen, he might now be barreling through the night like Henry instead of caught here famished listening to a duet of plump cowboys relishing their visions of strange fruit. Ever so loudly, he got up to pour himself more vitamin A. It was getting cold in here; he took his bottle to bed with him. Under the cover now, thinking less strenuously, he felt those calories begin to take hold. Tomorrow lunch surely, but meanwhile no big hurry. With only three hundred miles to go, he could even lie abed in the morning if he cared to. Probably not. It would be wonderful to see her again. Christmas was—what now?—two days away. He had no gift, not that he could be sure what she would like, no real shopping funds either. The mother thumping Fordmen had taken care of that.

He decided to save some vitamin A for tomorrow; he might

need it. It pays. He got up to kick out the light, warm foot, second try. He did not even visit the can, conserving energy. Good night, Big Red. Until tomorrow. À bientôt, hasta mañana, goodwill toward MEN—and GENTLEMEN. . . .

3

It was a little late. He lay abed only long enough for one cigarette and thought. Today was here, and he was shaking. One might almost have imagined this was his day to unload garbage at the Policemen's Ballet. Perhaps his trouble was simple hunger, together with an excess of vitamin A, he tried to console himself. Right now Big Red did not look good to him. He was overdue at headquarters, of course. Quickly up and shod, he headed there determinedly, with kit.

"You going to be here again tonight?"

"We'll see!"

Down there he made full use of all facilities, shaved, sat, and showered before he checked out. In the cowboys' room, the lady was sweeping sugar plums under the bed. Almost he wished she had done the same with Big Red, but it was time he thought of health. Salt from his peanut bags helped. Then, not to drown the sodden cockroach caught in his glass, he drank deep from his carafe. Big Core he placed on his peanut bags, next to his glass, giving the cockroach something to live for: the roach did seem to perk up. It was time to pack now.

His vitamin A bottle took up exactly the spare room in his kit, his sack fit his kit like a sheath. He was off.

"You leaving now?"

Zipping and buttoning his coat, leaping her sheets: "Going out to play in the snow!" Her stairs were not cleanly but dry; difficult to say whether she had accepted her gifts. The lady on floor two was more in the spirit: she was humming "Jingle Bells" to the tune of "White Christmas," and mopping. Al felt sure she would have smiled at the slosh of his belly had she been quiet enough to hear. He waved her goodbye. In the dark lobby the nodding clerk had not looked lately at the fading calendar behind him. He hung up Al's key without looking.

"Checking out?"

"Yeah, time to pay up for last night," out of both pockets.

"Heading west?"

"May be. Merry Christmas!"

"'Christmas."

They had brought the welcome mat in, in dirty pieces. The door complained, but outside a fresh one was even now being laid gently. Al stepped over. It was a day of atonement for having rendered the earth in the parking lot's image. Bowing one's head, one could almost imagine that one walked on unprofaned ground. Yet at this moment fanatical men on all sides were scraping with shovels; the city had sent out all available machines, with emergency crews running ahead of them; the churches were trusting in young boys on vacation. Al turned west onto a quieter street, whose citizens were apparently behind in their taxes and tithes.

On the other hand, it could simply have been that last night's gay machine had run out on the party just here. Clearly it had had more than a little too much. It lay in the gutter drooling a grey vomit from the corners of its mouth.

Al averted his eyes. (Someone had already loosened its collar.) He trod lightly, for a wall-to-wall train of pure white
was being spread over the machine's obscene tracks. The
occasional pedestrians seemed not to care; they scuffed and
tore in their hurry. One little girl danced on her toes: step on
that veil and you bruise your mother's face.

More than once he almost gave in to the pale allurements
of neighborhood grocers waiting for him, the narrow steamy
cafés, but he did not allow himself. Today he wanted to
choose in a bright light from high colorful stacks lining wide
aisles, and somewhere out there someone surely had thought
of that. Meanwhile only the very curious could guess that he
was leaving their town. Few could know that his sack held a
kit. He carried it in the crook of his arm, like two pounds of
graham crackers. Four pounds of canned beef, make that. He
quickened his pace. All things considered, he was moving
quite well. Behind him the quickening snow covered his
tracks.

He was passing through a semisolid neighborhood, of big
square houses set somewhat apart, smaller ones often crowding between, like a nineteenth-century graveyard that was
still being used. Without reading the inscriptions one could
determine occupants by comparing sizes and shapes: There
was the old man, there was his son. In some cases grand-
children had been crammed into the back. But most of these
lay up ahead in the new memorial park, neatly aligned in
small, freshly sodded plots; even with the big new inscriptions
one could not tell them apart. Here they had begun cramming
dogs into the back. Al skirted around, in search of the mourn-
ing-supply shop.

There it was, the familiar glass-and-stone front, the digni-
fied LAST STOPPE AND SHOPPE engraved on the frieze. Early
mourners were nudging one another into the patrolled park-

ing lot, where the grey snow was being shaped into heathen monuments. Al nodded to an open-faced plowman, who was most generous in welcoming him. It was not only suspicious, but risky, to be arriving on foot. In stepping aside for the ladies, one did not look at handbags, asses, or eyes. One did not stand aside too long either, but ducked in just as soon as seemed possible without being run down. Then again stepped aside. Having already a grocery sack was particularly awkward. After a moment's consideration, Al joined the cart race, propped his sack in the baby seat. A baby, seated nearby, frowned. Nodding, Al shoved on.

His was one of the new four-wheel-brake jobs. It liked to inch sidewise, crab into the ladies. Leaning hard on his handlebar, he was able to lift his front end clear of the track, which helped a little. More than once he was caught spinning his wheels by hard-driving ladies playing chicken. They veered off at the very last instant, sideswiping. He dared not park, leave his kit unattended. It seemed inadvisable to abandon his cart at this juncture. So he kept to the less dangerous stretches, the canned carnes and beans, avoiding the frozen desserts, facial tissues, and dog foods. They did have true beef, amid the stacks of sham meats. Sixty-nine cents, imported. For twenty cents more he could have had a whole canned chicken. The real bargains were in chicken of the sea, and flocks of ladies were fishing. Al settled on beef.

A quart of milk caught his eye. Maneuvering over, he plucked it out of the grasp of a formidable lady. His cart was beginning to look tenanted, but he had already far exceeded his budget. What man will do for appearance' sake! However, at canned fruits he chose applesauce, not even hiding the label. He counted on rounding things out with cigarette papers, if they had heard of them. The home stretch was the challenge. Carts were lined up ten deep at the tape,

each bearing enough provisions to last for eternity. Hanging
on to each handlebar was the larger part of a family. Al stood
close behind one smiling mother, in hopes she might note a
discrepancy. Instead, two more cut in front of him. He tried
a grandmother next. After one shrewd glance, she pressed
forward. He caught the eye of a teen-age housewife, but she
seemed ready to exchange glances forever.

He quit. Abandoning his cart in midtrack, he returned with
particular care each item to its own stack or bin. It surprised
him to find milk the hardest to give up. (Vitamin A was forty-
nine cents a pint, he noted.) Now it was a question of sidling
past ladies all intent on the tape; there was no escaping except
through those slots. Circling first, he chose a silver-haired
judge with a benign expression and a Manager badge. He
could read if anyone here could.

"Want to check that sack, *sir?*"

A squad of carry-out boys turned to watch and to listen.
Smiling, partway unsheathing, exposing his kit, Al bowed to
the jury.

"Check, *sir.*" The judge waved him on. Yet two carry-out
boys lounged shoulder to shoulder in front of the Out door.
Nodding, Al sidled between. Now *everyone* knew. Walking
straight past a patrolman, he raised his face to the newcome
snow. His plowman nodded farewell.

He steered west without further delay. He should definitely
have done business with a neighborhood merchant long long
ago, but it was too late and crowded to think of going back.
Perhaps somewhere out here was a store still selling food by
the armsful. Meanwhile regret contained no vitamin A. Time
was better spent welcoming the snow, which soon was melting
less quickly on his forehead and cheeks. Although he was not
quite ready to laugh, he said, "Ha!" And there was the new
highway right where he had known it would be, slicing

through farmyard and dell. Keep Washington Green! Nearby languished the old, a weed patch now. One stunted building clung to its edge, with two doddering pumps waiting in front as though they still looked for some old-timer to stop by. Above the door, "Feed and Grocery" had been painted in ancient grey. Al walked in.

"Good morning! . . . Hello!"

"Say?"

"How are you today?"

"Say?"

"Do you have milk? Milk by the quart? Fresh *milk?*"

"No milk. Just that bread there."

"I'll take it."

"Say?"

"How *much?*"

"Thirty-five!"

"Here!"

The grocery merchant peered before accepting Al's coins. It was a good thing Al had the right change; they might have had to wait a few days for the breadman to pass through. Somehow the cash register had not forgotten its figures, but with the slam of its drawer came a most frightening noise. What, did he have that prodigy wired up with a burglar alarm? No no, the alarm had been sent in by the pumps. They stood rather stiffly, eyeing a stranger. The merchant and his customer eyed too from inside. Who would have thought little folk could make such a noise? Finally the service station attendant shuffled muttering to the door, and Al followed out with his grocery. He lingered just long enough to make sure the attendant, stooping to the wagon, had everything well in hand. "Say? Say?"

This bread had not been touched by man. Machines had sanipacked, sealing the freshness in. Only the crust was stale.

Within was tenderized flour dough, fortified with vitamin A. This kept it moist. Air holes had been added as a preservative. Plus a bit of salt to whet the thirst. Eight ounces dissolved in the mouth almost as quickly as the newcome snow. The thin film of scum which clung to the gums was mother of bread. Throwing back his head, Al drank deep.

"Heading west?"

That little red wagon again.

"Say?" His inclination was to walk off his lunch, but this man was a pushing one. His little door slapped Al in the shins. "Hop in!"

"Well, thanks!" Al said, sinking in. At this range little more could be seen than back there at the pumps. The man wore a thin smile on his lips, and somewhere behind those green shades were his eyes. They studied Al closing the door. Al clapped his heels, dumping snow. "Keep Washington Green!"

He won a little cackle with that.

"Care for bread?"

"No, thanks." The man wrinkled his nose. He was adjusting his shades, if Al cared to think so. Al withdrew his offering, and now at last the man did tend to his driving, gripping his little gears with soft hands. "There's a seat belt beside you."

"Ah," Al thanked, studying it. This was more like a Gemini harness. It would take at least two or three orbits to figure it out; by that time they would probably have landed. "Thanks, I'll count on a snowbank."

That was worth a half cackle. "It's really very simple. You put that deal there over your head."

The man sought to show him. "That's all right," Al said, ducking the halter. "You'll probably want somebody out front to wipe off your windshield."

The displeased pilot consoled himself by smiling or leering

more fully. He turned up his radio and adjusted his goggles. Could he see snow through them? one wondered. Aloud, "Hey, that snow sure falls, doesn't it," Al suggested.

"The paper predicted four inches in Seattle."

Meanwhile there was twice that much outside, and the radio was predicting two feet in the mountains. "It's sure coming down out there," Al said.

"I don't believe I got your name?"

"Al."

"Will Watson. Heading for L.A., Al?"

"Not right away," Al said, giving Will Watson's tenderized hand back to the steering wheel. "Hey, if this snow doesn't let up we'll be lucky to make Seattle."

Cackling, Will Watson turned down his radio and his heater. "What's your line, Al?"

"Ah, whatever I can find. Sometimes I do groundskeeping, route driving, peddling, whatever is handy."

"Jack of all trades, huh?"

"Not all. Hey, that snow sure piles, doesn't it?"

"What? My my, they ought to plow this highway."

"They're plowing it. Look out ahead!"

Z-i-i-i-i-p, the little wagon slithered and swayed. That snowplow wanted half of the road! Sliding past, Will Watson peeped his horn. "Go to driving school!"

"Ya!" Al called, waving.

The shaken pilot tightened his harness, pressed on. "Will, what's your line?"

"I'm in visual education."

"Ah, you're in Hollywood?"

"No, I'm not in that end yet. I'm in distribution, out of San Francisco. I have my plans though," Will Watson said, flashing his teeth and his gums, his face too taking on color. He paused, sharing, and Al half cackled. "It's the new medium, and I plan to be in at the top. The people don't read anymore, Al, you know that."

"Ah," Al said, reading Will Watson's newspaper. NEW PEACE SLAYING.

"Oh, they still read the papers. That's de rigueur, so to speak. I'm talking about *reading*. Nobody does anymore, not in America. Know why, Al? There are no more writers in America."

Refolding the newspaper, Al returned it to Will Watson's side. "You say you live in San Francisco, Will?"

"If you're heading that way, Al, I'll be glad to take you."

"That's very good of you. Thanks very—"

Z-i-i-i-i-p, the pilot leaned on his steering wheel, slithered around monumental snowbanks to a cleared stretch of runway that led straight to a monument of glass. His little wheels chewed ice at the door. OASIS 90 COAST TO COAST. "Lunch time," he announced, deftly unstrapping.

"Thanks, I've eaten," Al said, climbing out.

"They have good hamburgers. . . ."

"Couldn't possibly." Al waved his bread.

"Have a cup of coffee on me, Al. . . ."

"I've got to be moving. Thanks very much for the lift!" Al called, waving.

The pilot stared after Al over his fuselage. One could almost feel pity for him standing there so stiffly beside his little machine, adjusting his goggles, here on earth. When he turned himself toward OASIS 90, his feet covered ground most cautiously, for they were unused. In truth Al wasn't moving so well himself; it had been something worse than stuffy in that wagon. But he gulped newcome snow and hurried onward. There was a hopeful-looking station up ahead, on a narrowing mountain road. Soon they would straighten and widen, but just now their stakes were disappearing beneath the snow.

That station was safe for at least one more day. Meanwhile trucks were invited. A hopeful man was out making room for them with a shovel. He had been waiting for Al to come by, the occasion to straighten his aching back. "What do you say?"

"Hello!" Al said, waving. "Have a little snow!"

"Heading west?"

"Ya. Need some help here?"

"No, I can handle her. Got me a little plow in back if I need her. Heading from Spokane?"

"No, Denver."

"Pass through here often?"

"No, not very often."

"For a minute there I thought you was Bert Hayes."

"No, I don't know him!" Al called, waving. "You're pumping too hard, attendant," he muttered, "and I don't even have me a car." Thank God again, he would not soon be in the market for that salesmanship, which last night he had *helped* to sharpen. How much for a refill, mister? That nickel seemed to hang heavy in his pocket as he continued uphill. A couple of years ago, this much newcome snow would have earned him an honest dollar. Throwing back his head, he gulped deeply.

No one claimed him, not surprisingly. These drivers were doing all their pushing and pumping on pedals; the snow was doing its best to bring them to a standstill without their asking. Chains themselves were almost quiet. Was he doomed to hike to the top of this mountain? If so, it was time he headed cross country: that little red wagon was due, and Will Watson would stop, certainly. Then it would be Al's turn to do the pushing. At the thought, he was already ten steps from the highway. What brought him back was a great blowing of air brakes, a great swirling of snow up ahead. When the atmosphere cleared partly, the biggest beast in captivity could be seen waiting docilely. What heart! What tractability! Al ran forward to praise.

The door wheezed open, wheezed closed, controlled by the driver. "Many thanks!"

Taciturn, the driver nodded and studied his mirrors. Al leaned back out of the way. The driver eased into gear, accelerated the motor. Studying his mirrors, he released the clutch very gradually. The beast was moving. It edged forward ever so slowly, the driver studying its great tracks in his mirrors. Two hundred yards later, now fully on the highway, the driver eased into second. The beast crept on for two hundred yards more. The driver eased into third. Now the beast seemed to creep a little faster. They covered the next two hundred yards perhaps a little less slowly. The driver eased into fourth.

"How many gears does this job have?"

"Seven."

The driver was eyeing his mirrors, and Al drew back out of the way. From somewhere below came a faint peeping. When it passed in front of them, the driver gave it one blast with his horn. The little red wagon skittered away like a balloon in an updraft. Al leaned back grinning.

Gear five was a long time in coming. The driver was trying for it, but the steep grade prevented. Once he had to shift back into third for two hundred yards, coax her a little. When he eased her into fourth again, she held steady. The driver leaned back, reached up on his shelf for a package of chewing gum. Steering one-handed, watching his mirrors, he shook a stick out for Al. "Chew?"

"Thanks," Al said, accepting.

The driver shook out two for himself, unwrapped them without taking his hands from the wheel. Lowering his window, he spat out his old. He chucked the fresh gum into his mouth and threw out the wrappers. Al, about to use the ashtray, thought better. There he hung for a moment leaning forward. Then he rolled down his window. Rolling it up again, he dropped his wrapper into a coat pocket. The driver glanced over.

"Hitchhiking ain't what it used to be," he said, chewing.

"Man, you're not kidding."

"I've been on the bum myself. It's a rough go anyhow you look at it."

"Boy, you can say that again."

"People don't care anymore. They'll leave a man standing by the side of the road like he was no bettern a stone. They'll leave him standing there like he was no bettern a fucking stone."

"You know it."

"I betcha a year ago this minute I was standing flat-assed on the side of the road myself, without a shit to call my own. I betcha I stood there three or four hours without a dime in my jeans, not even knowing where my next meal was coming from, wondering how I was going to con somebody out of a few bucks so I could buy me a couple bottles of bad booze, get me a dose of claps from some floozy. Man, didn't I cuss those drivers whizzing by leaving me standing there like a goddam one-armed beggar!"

"Ya."

"No more of that jazz for me anymore," the driver assured. His tongue had a way of wallowing in his mouth when he talked, all mixed up with his gum, so that little splashes of saliva dampened the soft yellow hairs above his pink lips, and his thin yellow sideburns fluttered in the wind. "No more of that lowlife for this man," he went on. "I got me a job now and I aim to hold onto it. My pappy give me this rig, and I aim to make him proud. 'Joe Day, take care of this little rig,' my pappy said. 'Take real good care of her, Joe Day.' The last time he give me a rig I piled her into a fire station the very day. No more of that jazz. When I'm driving to Seattle, I'm driving to *Seattle*, know what I mean? When I'm driving to Portland, I'm driving to *Portland*. When I'm driving to Frisco, I'm driving to *Frisco*. When I'm driving to Diego, I'm driving to *Diego*. When I'm driving to L.A., I'm driving to *L.A.* When I'm driving to Denver, I'm driving to *Denver*. When I'm driving to Dallas, I'm driving to *Dallas*. When I'm driving to Salt Lake, I'm driving to Salt *Lake*. When I'm driving to Pocatello, I'm driving to *Pocatello*—know what I mean?"

"Ya!"

"When I get home, I'm going to polish my rig. I'm going to polish her good. I'm going to polish her hood. I'm going to polish her cab. I'm going to polish her mirrors. I'm going to polish her amber reflectors. I'm going to polish her red re-flectors. I'm going to polish her taillights. I'm going to polish her bumpers. I'm going to polish her nuts. I'm going to polish her . . . gas cap. . . . 'You're doing good, Joe Day,' my pappy's going to say, 'you're doing real good.' " The driver paused to shift into third gear. "After ten, twelve trips like that," he went on, coaxing her, "it's going to be 'Good-bye old pappy, good-bye old mammy!' I'm going to buy me a little house. I've already got her picked out. Ninety-nine dollars down and ninety-nine dollars a month. I'm going to buy me a colored telyvision, twenty-nine dollars down and twenty-nine dollars a month. I already have me four radios. I'm going to buy me a hi-fi and stereous console with FM. I'm going to buy me a family-room suite. I'm going to buy me a bedyroom suite. I'm going to buy me a kitchen suite. I'm going to buy me dishes and silverware with my monygrammy on them: J.D. Then I'm going to marry me the sweetest little girl in the

world. I've already got her picked out. I've already bought
the engagement ring, four ninety-nine down and four ninety-
nine a month. When I marry that girl I'm going to swear to
be true. No more chasing slash for this man. My wife is going
to know she married a true man when she marries Joe Day.
When I go to Seattle, I'm going to *Seattle,* know what I
mean?"

"Ya! Ya!"

"When I get home the little wife is going to have my dinner
waiting for me. After we eat, she'll bring me my slippers and
my telyvision schedule. If I have a blisterous on my hand,
she'll rub a little Corn Huskers on it. Then maybe I'll have
me a cold beer. Then we'll watch telyvision awhile. Then
we'll go into the bedyroom and knock off a piece. We're
going to have ten, twelve kids. I'm going to keep that little
girl so full of babies she won't have *time* to chase. None of
this birth patrol jazz for this man. Know who's behind this
birth patrol jazz? It's the Catholics and Jews! The Catholics
and Jews want to crowd us white men out. They want us to
birth patrol while they crowd us white men out with their
ten, twelve babies apiece. . . ."

Joe Day paused to shift into second. Studying his mirrors,
he braked gently for two hundred yards. He eased into first.
He braked her for two hundred yards more. The beast was
coming to a stop. Studying her great tracks in his mirrors, he
edged her very slowly off the road, crept to a standstill. The
beast was not moving. Studying the dials, he accelerated the
motor for a moment, then switched it off. The doors wheezed
open, under his control. OASIS 91! "Coffee?" he said.

"No, thanks!" Al called, waving his bread.

Joe Day took no notice, for he was busy kicking his tires.

"Whataya say?" asked an old one manning the pumps.

"Good afternoon!" Al said.

He was in a mood to run all day and all night, but he eased into low going around the next bend. When he felt sure he was no longer in view, he lifted his face to the newcome snow. Breathing deep, he headed cross country. What called him back was the honk of a Model A horn. A skinny, humpbacked machine stood shivering on the road, its makeshift truckbed wrapped in a canvas shawl. There weren't any doors. Al went in. "Thanks!"

The driver shifted into gear and the machine lurched forward. Gripping the shaking steering wheel with his canvas gloves, he spat out the doorway. "This ain't no night to be hiking!"

"You're not kidding."

"I can only take you a piece."

"Every little piece helps."

"Got to get these apples to shelter."

"Ah," Al said, leaning back, breathing snow. They were chugging along at a fairly steady rate now, sputtering and spitting, canvas shawl flapping, palsied steering wheel mostly in hand. The driver held her to the center of the road. He could see straight ahead, for he had a windshield wiper. His eyes he kept clear by constantly blinking. Yet snow was beginning to pile up on his lashes. His white whiskers glistened with snow and spittle. "Looks like we're in for a blizzard," Al said, breaking the silence.

"She's beginning to pile up," the driver admitted. "I remember back in forty-eight, snow piled up so high this pass was closed for a month."

"That was nineteen forty-eight?"

"Nineteen forty-eight. They had to bring in plows to hunt out the plows. The telephone linemen had to come to work with shovels."

Al laughed. "I can picture it."

"See that pine there, that big one yonder, how she leans to the easterly, all cramped over at the middle? She was buried for a month and a half in that storm. In forty-eight she was just a youngster, about twenty or twenty-five feet. See that cedar next beyond? Only her tippy top was showing, she was about thirty then. Her little baby next by wasn't born then—he came along maybe a year or two later. His daddy stood just yonder—he fell about ten years ago. You could see him lying there if the snow warn't piled quite so high." The driver switched on his lights, if he had any. They made no impression on the snow or the darkening air, but he left them so. "Up yonder is where Betsy and I had to stop that time. She was up to her waist by now, and she tried hard, but she couldn't quite do her. She was still a youngster then, of course, twenty-two. I managed to steer her into a little cove of hemlocks just yonder, for company (they was her size then). She took to hibernating just as natural as a chipmunk. She still had her doors. When I led the plows to her four weeks later, they wanted to tow her home, but I said no. I dried her points and her plugs, gave her a crank, and before you could say Henry Ford she was zipping up the hill just as smart as we are now. She was a pretty little thing in those days, a real eye-catcher. Her windows never did roll real well after that though, and a couple of years later I took off her doors and stored them in the shed. I still oil them from time to time, just in case. . . . You never know," he said, blinking.

"That's right," Al said, blinking too.

"Looks like we'll make her all the way to the barn tonight though," the driver said, spitting lustily. He gave her a little more gas, just in case. "My turnoff is just around that next bend. We'll be hitting her fast, so brace yourself. Once we hit the turnoff a few yards, we'll be going real slow. You'll be able to jump out easy then."

"Right."

Spitting one last whopper, the driver crouched over his wheel, bracing himself as he poured on the gas. Al braced too, and they chugged around the next bend. "Here we go!" yelled the driver, spinning his wheel suddenly, hitting a snowbank head on. Somehow they churned through. The other side was less deep, but they were moving much slower now. One might have thought they were at a standstill, spinning their wheels, were it not for the cedars and pines gliding majestically by. "You'll have no trouble catching a ride here!" the driver called. "Think I hear a big one groaning up the hill right now."

"So do I."

Taking a hand from the wheel, the driver reached under the seat. "Have an apple, son."

"Ah, thanks very much!"

"Good luck to you, son!"

"Good luck to you too!" Al called, jumping out. He landed knee deep in snow, not even teetering. Betsy crept by. She was not quite up to her waist, but her knees or her hips. He watched just long enough to be sure that she was going to make it all right, then headed cross country himself. By now the groan of that beast on the highway was filling the woods. From a little grove of hemlocks of his own size, Al watched it grind by in first gear.

Pocketing his apple and half of his hand, he paralleled those great tracks toward the west. He was alone now, except for the trees. The snow itself by now had become as common as air, perhaps even more plentiful. The trees had a variety that he could distinguish. That crooked pine yonder was about sixty, her gnarled husband closer to seventy. Their lovely daughter had been born in '49 or '50. She had three younger brothers. No, that one just next by was probably her husband; these days the youngsters just couldn't wait. Yet her daddy did look proud, despite himself. Probably close by her side were her babies, already under the cover. Did she know that down the road a piece she had a fine cousin?

It was time he watched a little more closely where he was going. Snow and darkness were falling together and the highway was tricky, not yet having been straightened and widened. It began to look less like a wound than a scar, and sometimes he lost sight of it. Too, the snow up here was considerably deeper, almost up to his waist in some places. Once he slid fifty yards into a steep canyon that took him quite some time to climb out of; only when he reached the far rim and looked back did he realize he had been trapped by a gravel pit. There were other hazards, most of them natural. Old bodies lay everywhere waiting to catch him at shin level, topple him over. Often nearby were the gaping holes their roots had torn open. Al spent five minutes finding his kit after being trapped by one playful grandfather, only to lose his bread in the old man's root hole. Luckily, that bread floated. If there were any bear traps around he was above them, so far, and up ahead now were headlights.

There were dozens. They all pointed in the same direction, west, peering hard at a snowbank bigger than they were. The little red wagon up front was in fact peering inside it. A great beast brought up the rear, sidewise, snow wall to snow wall. Inside its cab, the driver studied his mirrors. Al hastened by at a distance. Over the next crest he slowed to breathe and consider. No more trucks, big or little, no more wagons, until he reached the top, perhaps a mile or two beyond it. Those on that side would be pointing east, mostly. Meanwhile not even the scar of a road to serve him as guideline. He could see no horizon ahead, but the terrain underfoot seemed to be rising ever more steeply. The air too seemed to grow colder, the swarming snow was no longer refreshing. It stung his face and his mouth, which he held open for gasping. What was it one did on such an occasion—make oneself a snug bed under the snow, next to one of those bodies? He had reached a decision: *Keep on walking.*

He switched his bread and kit to his other hand, which involved switching his apple pocket. Now he could thaw out half of his left hand, while he froze the unfrozen half of his right. His head served as best it could to fend off branches. These were becoming more plentiful, for the piling snow was bearing him up to the trees, when he didn't sink down to his shoulders. He thought of seeking the highway, which he would have to himself now, but he recalled the height of that snowslide, plus the depth of that gravel pit. He might trip on a snowplow. What would happen if one tripped on a telephone line? Surely snow was a poor conductor; one would be far from grounded. He wedged onward.

Somewhere ahead or beside howled dogs or coyotes, their howls rather garbled. They sounded angry, probably with hunger. Snow was little more than an appetizer, which buried the dinner. "Yowwww, for a quick lunch!" he muttered, slowing. Wolves these days were not likely, were they? He veered left, hoping to keep somewhere between the highway and Canada. As for bears, they were hibernating. Bears like honey. Do mountain lions? Ah, no matter, cats don't like to get their feet wet. They like birds, and there were none around that he knew of. They were probably all snuggled up in their nests, watching him wade through their branches.

He was not so much wading this time as hanging. Two

stout boughs had caught him under the armpits, another fanned out beneath him. By lifting his legs out of the snow he could sit on it. He leaned back and rested, crossing his ankles. With his half-frozen left hand he dug into his shirt pocket for his tobacco. Using mostly that hand, he rolled himself a crooked, very wet cigarette. He often scratched a match one-handed, by bending it over with his thumb to the striking surface; tonight he finally managed half-handed. Inhaling deep, he leaned back in the cheerful cigarette light. Washington was green in here. Reaching out, he brushed a bit of snow from one of his branches. It floated down to his floor. He patted the floor, packing and smoothing, filled in a few hollows. Not to disturb the snow on his roof, he drew from the edges. The snow seemed several feet deeper out there than inside, constituting his walls.

He placed his kit and bread on the shelf beside him. His sack had long ago dissolved. His bread would have also, had it not been saniplastipacked. Looking about him, he decided he had everything now but the fire. He scooped and packed a little hollow by his side, fashioned in it a tiny tent of brown needles from his branches, around a timely sheet of toilet paper. You never know. . . . Now came the trick of scratching match half-handed, made more difficult this time by the striking surface being wetter. Keep calm, keep calm, don't mess up that surface altogether. Ea-sy does it. The match flared up, and with shaking hand he held it to the toilet paper. Pffft. His armpit boughs prevented him from leaning sideways, but he craned his neck and blew on the glowing embers. One by one he blew them out. Leaning back, inhaling, he rested his head a moment before he put away his matches.

Never mind, in such a house a fire was luxury, frivolity. It was already quite warm in here. He had his cigarette for light. A larger fire might attract whatever animals, or burn the very roof above his head while he sat hanging helplessly. He rolled himself another cigarette, a straighter one, and lit it with the butt before that pfffted out. *That* was thinking. He scattered the brown needles upon his floor, but tucked the charred paper back inside his kit. You never . . . Now he had an ashtray, and he snuffed out the butt in it. Time for a little apéritif. Taking the vitamin A bottle from his kit, he examined it against the glowing light. He could have saved more, of course, but he was thankful to have been this much provident. Ah, vitamin A tasted far better here tonight, straight out of the refrigerator. His boughs were just right for tilting backward. Temporarily satisfied, and appetized, he propped the bottle on the floor, not the bench. Taking his pocket knife from his kit, he halved his Wenatchee evenly. The paler half he set face down in the floor to keep, the red red half he sliced. He aligned the slices on the shelf. Now it was time to think of bread. Peeling the topmost layer off, he wrapped it around two apple slices, the two farthest from him first, and leaned back to sup.

Apple sandwiches were not bad at all, when cold and moist, even without peanut salt. Smiling to himself, he rolled another. His day was turning out quite all right, for all the cabs and wagons. One thought of those drivers huddled behind their wheels, chewing gum and LSD, listening to their radios and heaters. Whatever they heard would not be pleasant. Leer on. Enjoy your mirrors. Read your paper. One could feel pity. At least Joe Day had himself a little bedyroom back there, Will Watson had his harness. They could roll their windows against the snow and wolves and piny air. What *was* this house, hemlock? Certainly it was well constructed. The roof told that. Whatever snowflakes drifted in came through the window curtains. This house had no doors, as such. It did have several stories, narrowing, like a pagoda. One simply found one's proper level, as he had, in case of flood or blizzard. Even now his floor was rising slowly. He could tell by the level of his bottle, which was disappearing faster than he was drinking. Well, if this turned out to be another '48, he would at least have started halfway to the surface.

One inch, three apple dumplings later, he still was hungry. What was it one did in such an occasion—hunt for berries? Not in here. There was always bark, he seemed to remember. This bark looked scaly. Needles? He chose a youngish one and nibbled: bitter green. Aha; two stories above his head he spied small balls of brown among all the green and white, a fine crop of pine cones. Pine nuts! Grasping his boughs, lifting himself stiff-armed on the parallel bars, he swung his legs several times before he sprang. Now he was standing in his second story, reaching up and through his third. He made a hasty harvest, eased himself downstairs again amid a little snow flurry. Seated, comfortably adjusted in his armpit boughs, he set to shelling. A good year; these cones were loaded. Shaking three or four unsalted nuts onto his sweating palm, he licked, chewed, and spat almost simultaneously. This house was hemlock.

Ah well, dessert was waiting in the refrigerator. He made another cigarette and lit it, giving the apple ice a few minutes more to set. That should do it. Tilting back, he let dessert slide onto his tongue in little slivers, which he chewed slowly. He drained to the last melting drop, then rinsed his bottle and drank that cold water. All in all, quite refreshing. If he found himself hungry later, he could always sniff his gum wrapper. He washed and dried his silverware, placed it in his kit for morning, but what to do about his dishes? After a moment's hesitation, he dug a cupboard. Ordinarily he did not like to do this, but this bottle was not the kind one carried everywhere and always. Perhaps no one would ever find it.

No, someone would most surely, but it did have at least a local label, and in any case its label would have long since dissolved by the time it worked its way to earth through all those stories. Perhaps in time the bottle itself would disintegrate, replenish the earth's supply of silicate, depleted by all that mining. He closed the cupboard tightly. His other dish he did not put in there, but shook out and folded it for travel. Plastic will not disintegrate. Nature has no need of it.

He lay back. After what they called the shortest day of the year, he found himself a little weary. Fresh air will do that. Tomorrow, he supposed, would be longer, certainly deeper. He would need his strength. He hoped to wake up and early. Tomorrow for sure, let's hope, Joan Marie. . . .

4

It was hard to say. Someone had closed the shutters during the night, and lowered the roof. There was light up there, the question was how much. Al lay abed a little longer before going up to see. Meanwhile he rolled and lit a cigarette two-handed. Something, he detected, had been chewing on his Wenatchee. Something small-toothed. With his flaming match Al set to tracking. Ah, there the culprit lay, curled up beside his travel kit, tail in paws, full white stomach heaving. "Good morning," Al called quietly. The pack rat opened his eyes, blinked once, and stared. "Will you be staying again tonight?" His guest left through the wall. Al did not follow, but used the stairs, went through the ceiling. Well that he had thought to take his shower yesterday; these today were as cold as ice. You never know. What he expected to find outside he did not know either. Opening his eyes, he blinked and tried to stare: it was sunlight, reflected by a dazzling expanse of white which he and a nearby treetop looked upon at astounded eye level. That tree still wore a soft, floppy nightcap, as did all the others. Great waves of white swelled from tree to tree most beautifully and blindingly. After one last squint, Al climbed back inside, giving it a little more time to set.

Downstairs, Big Red and Brown did not look good to him, but he made himself eat the inmost parts. The cuttings he left for his little friend, who had left something behind for him—pine nuts. Or *were* those nuts? In the bathroom, he brushed his teeth, relieved himself of vitamin A. Later would be soon enough to shave and sit. A good thing he had thought to launder in Colorado before he left. This shirt didn't look quite good, but he buttoned high his coat. He was ready to go, he guessed. His home looked different in the light of day, more like a tree buried in who could say how many feet of snow. Was that crust done yet? He stuck his kit inside his coat, handle looped to belt, in case. Then he climbed up and out. White! Through narrowed lashes he surveyed the scene in little shimmering glimpses. The crust had already sunk several inches. Not quite a '48, it came only knee high to grandfathers, who loomed grandly in their night robes. Night-caps were beginning to shed their tassels; little puffs of them lay here and there upon the glistening crust. Al made his own test seat-first. It bore him up, for all the groaning. Above, grandfathers bent to listen. Say? Say? Al waved reassurance. He tried one foot, conditionally, and quickly lost it. Never mind, his pants he had bought almost new in Texass.

This was a lazy mode of travel, once one got the swing of

it. Eyes closed, knees raised, slide downward on a wave, partway up its next gentle undulation. Now crawl to the nearest
treetop, hang there a moment. Shove off again, gliding each
time a little farther. The proud sun stood at his back, to guide
and not to blind him. The highway lay to his left, not far
away. The undulating telephone wires were visible! He
swung onward, paralleling. Ahead, treetops stood out against
purest blue, beckoning him to the summit. If he could slide
uphill this well, imagine sailing down the other side. Thus he
did not much mind slithering on his belly the last steep half
mile.

The summit, when and if he had reached it, looked westward to another, higher summit, and then perhaps another.
After a little sail, he slithered on. His kit was chafing. Un-
fastening his coat and belt, he strapped it to his back instead.
How man is governed by appearances: humpbacked, he felt
less jolly. Never mind, once he reached that farthest summit
he would sail like Santa. Meanwhile the telephone wires were
no longer undulating, but climbing sharply. For his part, he
was finding it harder and harder to maintain the ground that
he had slithered. More than once he felt himself inching backward, raw-nosed, hunchbacked, spread-eagle. Man your stands,
men! Saluting, he chewed on up the second summit. From
there at last he could see the eastbound traffic, lined up watching plows clamber on the snowbanks. A little red wagon
crouched in the lead, cold-nosed. For a moment Al feared
that in his slithering he had somehow wound back to where
he had started, but no, this wagon was a mate. The interesting
question was, how many miles of wordless books were those
two holding up between them. The people don't read anymore, they knew that well.

He saw a way to avoid another summit. By sailing south
and east a mile or so, he could hit the highway where it cut

through a man-chewed notch, remindful of today's Wenatchee. Had his little friend seen *that* yet? Best of all, it lay
well beyond the traffic. Unstrapping and rearranging, Al set
sail most cheerfully. This crust up here was even faster. He
covered a quarter mile in less time than it took a plow to
budge a faceful. When it came to climbing, no need to slither;
this crust could bear him upright. Thus he returned to civilization like a true explorer, aiming for that notch with measured steps, somehow missing gravel pits. One plow had not,
he noted professionally. A wrecking car was hauling it out,
all crooked-shoveled. That's right, haul her there, haul her.
Ea-sy does it. Hold her there. Back to the shop for that job,
beyond a doubt. The engineers, for all their problems, noted
Al's approach.

"Whataya say?"

"Good morning! Heading for the shop with her?"

"Yeah, we are."

"Hitch a ride?"

"Nah, we aren't insured for that."

"Ah." Civilization! Technicalities! He paid his Social Security. Yet he did not stop to argue, for a glance from that
flaming eye had bespoken something nonassurable. He strode
on, down a highway freshly scraped and his alone.

Not for long it wasn't. Halfway through that notch, here
came the hell-bent wrecking car, snowplow swinging from its
shoulder like a lethal pack of schoolbooks. Drawing abreast,
it swung at Al. They were insured for that. He slithered up
the snowbank just in time, to see the plow leap into another
gravel pit, carrying the wrecking car slung on its back. After
a very quiet moment, the engineers climbed down. They stood
studying together in a little group. No matter how they
looked at it, they were in need of another plow. Al walked
around.

Now he did have the highway to himself, freshly scraped and guarded by a wrecking car. The going was almost all downhill, and steep. If he got tired of walking, he could sail awhile. One way or another, he would get to town before the sun went down. The time, now that he could look back at the sun through trees, was morning still. As things seemed back there, he would be off the highway long before the west-bound cars got through. Peer on. He could smile, for he would not be in the market soon, only for pants or shoes. Yet around the next bend a little surprise awaited him. A kind of grocery store it was, with a delivery truck parked in front, pointing west. The driver had come as far as he could today. He was discussing with the merchant, who stood before his door. Now the driver ran inside his truck, ran out again. Two loaves! Al ran to congratulate. He met the driver running too. "Good morning!"

"Good morning!"

"Going back to town?"

The driver looked quickly east and west. "You can duck in back."

"Thanks!" Al said, running in behind him.

Closing his door, the driver waved to the merchant for both of them. "Keep down low," he warned, and Al lay back— just in time, for this road was a slithering one. At least it was soft in here, and in such concentration the smell was good. He thought to say something about apple sandwiches, as a kind of testimonial, but on second thought decided not. The driver might think he was begging lunch. Some of his pastries did look quite eatable, particularly the nut-and-chocolate-frosted ones which Al rocked against whenever the truck swung left. In fact he might have had a few inadvertent bites by now, had they not been saniplastipacked. The bread itself looked all too much. The driver seemed to think so too, for he made

many anxious stops. What, was he trying to sell those mer-
chants for the second time today? Most often he came trotting back without a bite. Once, after a great deal of talk, he
came on the run. Nodding to Al, he ran off with a pastry tray,
the nut-and-chocolate-frosted one. But it looked almost the
same when he came trotting back.

"I'll take one of those," Al said, whipping out twelve cents.

Nodding, pocketing the change, the driver marked up his
sale. Now they were off and sailing down the hill, sweet and
soft. The driver made no more stops. Passing the milkman, he
gaily honked. He carried a well-liked product in his truck,
good to the last sticky lick. He had a rather kind head himself,
smooth and round, brown on top. When he opened his door at
the edge of town, he nodded to Al almost apologetically. "You
better hop out here," he said.

"Right. Many thanks!"

"Good luck."

"Good luck to you. . . ."

A passing bread truck had screeched to a stop; its driver
was out and running across the street. He shot a look at Al
en courant. "What d'you say?"

"Hello!" Al said, on the walk. The snow down here was
thin and turning black. Plows and shovels had scraped it into
little piles, which boys were breaking up. For some reason
they did not throw at Al; perhaps they noticed an intimacy in
his step which they did not feel themselves. For another thing,
of course, he wore no hat. Nonetheless he decided against
stopping at a nearby telephone booth: they would know they
had him trapped, once he put his money in. Besides, he was
not ready yet. Those last few miles had sailed by all too fast
for him. He hoped the boys did not notice that he faltered a
little bit.

He did stop at the second booth, alone on a parking lot.

The door said *saaay?* Say, what if he had spent his last dime on pastry? No, he still had three. He was shaking. Putting his coin on the little shelf, he leaned back to roll and light a spilling cigarette. Inhaling tobacco deep, he found his letter and shook it out. Where was that number, anyway? Right there in front of him. He found the hole, dropped the coin. Stooping for it, he dropped it in the hole this time. He began to dial. Three or four numbers along, he paused. Had he dialed one number twice? The mind and the finger will play tricks like that. He hung up, in case. His coin came back, so he dropped it in the hole and dialed all the way.

The phone took a long time to buzz, and when the buzz came it was a lethargic one. It seemed to know that no one was at home, why get all worked up over an empty house? Al was in sympathy. That's all right, we tried, we tried, this coin returner is an efficient one, later will be— "Mr. Warner's residence. . . ."

"Is Joan there?"

"No, she's out shopping."

"Ah."

"Is this Mr. James?"

"Yes, it is."

"Mrs. Warner said to ask if you will be coming to dinner tonight."

"What time is that?"

"I don't know. Seven or eight o'clock."

"Aha. Well, I have some business to attend to first. I'll call back later."

"What time?"

"What time is it now?"

"I don't know. Around one o'clock."

"I'll call around five."

"I'll tell Mrs. Warner that."

"Many thanks. Good b—" The lady looked for no acknowledgment; her only wish was to be of service to him. Al hung up too. Most of his cigarette had shaken out. Opening the door for fresh air, *saaay*, he rolled and lit a firmer one. Now he had some time again, and much to do with it. He headed north. A patrol car swung around a corner, slowed. This place was a policemen's ball, he remembered that. Sauntering, he let them go. Thanks, I'll call you if I have need of you, I know you're busy, boys. Ahead, two more were cruising the other way. Al sauntered after them. At this rate, he wasn't getting anywhere. There was one other possibility. He strode.

It was a day of little accidents. These drivers were not enough acquainted with that slippery substance undertire. They paid their taxes, their streets were scraped, but too much of their money had been spent on new lampposts which had sprung up overnight. Too, those extra patrol cars were in the way. They should have kept on going, instead of stopping right there to investigate. Thus it turned out a good day after all for a striding visitor. Within less than half an hour, he was in sight of Century 21. He quickened pace, for he had lots to do in there.

Nothing had changed very much. The buildings were of course a little older, faded if not cracked, the tower leaned perhaps a little more noticeably toward the monorail, but this remained an impressive memorial. After all this time, one had to look around for MEN. Not for paper though—stall one! Seated, Al could congratulate himself on having thought to wait. Shaving was easy too. They had warm water here, and soap. Had they remembered showers, he might have taken another one. An opportunist, he combed his hair in the clean looking glass instead. Now he was ready for COMMISSARY. Left, then right? No, that was San Antonio. In Century 21, it was *up*, then right. The door hung open to him, and for a second he thought the man inside was Gus. Whoever it was remembered him in the same mixed-up way, probably as 86. "How's it going there?"

"O.K.!"

"That snow let up yet?"

"Ya, finally. How are things going these days?"

"Not bad."

"Got anything good coming up?"

"Not right now. Not till Friday. Mr. Worthington has the Christmas Party this afternoon; he could probably use another man. His office is at Portal Six."

"Portal Six. Many thanks!" Waving, Al went at once, to Portal 1. San Antonio again. That was all right, no one saw, and the door at Portal 6 still hung wide for him.

The businessman inside, a Mr. Worthington, took one quick look at Al and waved him in.

"Come on in!"

"Thanks!" Al said, joining a group of sheepish Santa Clauses, all bearded up like pregnant goats. He felt conspicuous. Mr. Worthington himself was tall and thin, but he stood well apart. When he addressed his men, he included Al as best he could.

"All right, you have the pitch now, men. You ask each kid what he wants from Santa Claus. Make sure he's sitting so that he faces your radio. Be sure it's on. We'll be getting straight Christmas music on XXI from three to six. That's fourteen ninety, isn't it, Glenn?" he called over his shoulder to an athletic young man who was combing beards.

"Fourteen ninety, Worth."

"Fourteen ninety, men. Turn your volume up. When you're sure a kid's had a good look at your radio, give him

a lollipop. Then let him go. That's all you have to do. Our
salesmen will catch the parents as they file through the doors.
Let's check those radios out before we hit the floor."

Each man attended to his own radio, pinned to his red coat
where ordinarily his number was, above the heart. Those
radios were in the form of comic bugs, gay and colorful. Their
shiny eyes were dials.

"What did he say that station was?"

"XXI, square!"

"Where's that?"

"Fourteen—"

A wildman's voice drowned them out, raving louder and
louder with each successful Santa Claus. Mr. Worthington
checked his watch. "That's it, men!" he yelled. "Good work!
Is everybody on the beam?" He went from Santa to Santa,
bending low to put his ear to each raving beast. He had to
tune in one red-faced Santa Claus himself. Another he dialed
and dialed, at last unpinned. "Glenn, bring this man another
radio!" Glenn came on the run. Trading radios with him, Mr.
Worthington held the new one to his ear, above the din. As
he spun dials, his eyes lit up. Now he pinned, and clapped
that Santa on the back. "Fine, men! Turn off! Turn off!" He
covered his ears as volume leaped, but uncovered as Santas
began to get their touch. One red-faced, shaking Santa still
could not, and wincing Mr. Worthington turned him off. In
the quiet, he turned to Al and briefly studied him. "Glenn!"

"Coming, Worth," with beard and coat.

"We'll want to set that stomach straight."

"Ah, my kit!" From the door Al waved, and called: "I'll
take care of it!"

He headed fast for Portal 1, for he had business to attend.
He would have to make do with what funds on hand. To buy
the want ads at this latish hour would be like buying the

obituary page at sight of death, and the library was probably closed today. Everyone was deep in town, like New Year's Eve. Their mood of course was far less gay, for they still had a long week to go, and they were burdened with packages. Yet they wanted more and more. Look at me, aren't I going to have a big one though! They eyed askance those few who had chosen with loving care. When they came to Al they seemed to say: What sect are you—Confusionist? Sidling into an alley, he unstrapped and brought forth his kit, not to disarm the shoppers but to forestall the clerks. Now he sailed on again, set his tiller for Big Marché.

Canal one went by without his catching more than a spinning glimpse of it. Canal two looked like a two-way cul-de-sac: those fighting in could make no headway against those fighting out. He chose canal three, for a strong side current swept many shoppers to another big market across the bay. Only the furry, odorous ones held fast. Al eddied in with them. Inside there was no choice at all, he went where their packages prodded him, parried backlashes with his kit. Soon he began to get the drift, he was caught in a wave of dissatisfied customers bringing perfume back. A safe place to fart. After a morning of bread and pastry, he felt faint. Summoning his waning strength, he floundered out of Chanel Five, onto an escalator.

This led to radios. Steering west, past boats, he discovered jewelry and hung treading there. A glittering saleslady smiled at him. In this high tide, she could see only his kit and coat. "Something for your wife?"

"No no."

She smiled anew. "A friend?"

"A daughter."

"How old is she?" asked the smiling bonne d'enfant.

"Around fourteen."

Her slender white hand dangled a delicate necklace before his face, while the rest of her swayed over the counter to him. "This is a lovely piece."

"Yes, it is."

"How much are those beads?" boomed a cruiser heaving to port.

The white-breasted saleslady turned almost reluctantly. "Forty-eight ninety-five."

"I'll take them!"

"Gift wrapped?"

Al flashed her a farewell smile, which she flashed back. To starboard lay a tranquil lagoon, and he set his sights on that. Books. He already had one in his kit, and he did not wish to duplicate, or seem to make invidious comparisons. Besides, these shiny new covers did not look real, more like the trappings of a TV or movie set, with sounding board inside. At least this bespectacled salesmother might know where phonograph records were to be found.

She could see Al's pants and shoes. "Third floor east— behind the ster-eos."

Thanking her, he immersed himself in a passing wave, paddled to an escalator up. Now there was no need to work at all; he let himself be carried by high tide, to ster-eos. As the lady had truly said, records were on a little counter in back, and he let himself be cast up there to rest. Today the Christmas Favorites outrated the Rock-and-Roll. Monnnk!

"Were you looking for a Christmas Album? They're on the counter there!"

"I see! I see!" Waving, he dove for nearby stairs. Down the shoot into the street, he was in the swim again. A newspaper floated by, AVALANCHE IN CASCADES. His landfalls now were the lesser shoals, with blinking lights above. They warned of jewelry and radios. He looked for watches as he sailed by; the consensus seemed to be after five. Steering south, he headed for a telephone booth he knew. Little wavelets followed him, some tossing scraps of spray or snow. The door said *spraaay*. Rolling and lighting a cigarette, he dropped and dialed without more delay.

"Hello?"

"Joan?"

"Dad!"

"Hey, how are you?"

"Fine, and you?"

"Fine too."

"When are you coming out? . . . It's Al, Aunt Dor."

"Is tonight all right?"

"Yes! . . . Aunt Dor wants to know if you'll be here for supper."

"Ah. I don't know whether I can make it out there that soon."

"Have you got my map?"

"Yes, it's a lovely one. There's one thing it forgot to say. Which way is north?"

"Hum."

"Are you on the Century 21 side of town?"

"No . . . "

"You're south. It will be a while. You'd better tell Doris to go ahead and eat whenever she usually does."

"All right then. . . . Soon!"

"Soon as possible!"

They waited five seconds and then hung up, not to waste precious time. He estimated he had at least ten miles to hike, plus one round mile to swim. In the tide again, he headed as fast as he could for the nearest Woolworth store. Plunging past the jewelry stand, he made for deserted aisles in back. A sun-bathing turtle caught his eye. The animal-keeper did not wish to sell, but he persuaded her. She had not heard of turtle food. Al showed her that, and added the two figures up, not forgetting tax. Lucky he had the exact amount; they might have had to wait for Santa Claus to bring them change. On his way out Al stopped at the candy stand, caught the glazed eye of the girl behind. Dropping peanut clusters into his bag, she turned from red and white to green; that stuff didn't look so sweet to her as it had last week. Dropping his change, she dared not stoop for it, but fished some more from her sticky drawer.

Now with two packages, one to hold upright and one to hold down beyond range of his nose, he was a participant in the shopping spree. Loaded ladies did not stare quite so hard at him, a few men stared enviously. They did not know he was shopping hotels with a drifter's eye. He drifted on until he reached his telephone booth again. Here, barring skidding cars, he had the sidewalk to himself. It was time to bring out his map, find north. This wasn't a bad map at all, once one had entered its frame of reference. There was that shopping center sure enough. There was that residential neighborhood. There, there, there we go, into a country space. She showed him where and what, and he followed like an enchanted man. To tell the truth, her airplane plant read more like half a block than twenty-five, but she made up for that with a skating rink. Trotting and walking by turns, he helped to bring her map to scale. She ignored the state police, though he could not. Soon on the trot again, he found her school, or was this the airplane plant? No, someone had spelled out MERY CHRISTMAS on the announcement board, and BEAT BREMERTON underneath. What was the significance of that white, two-storied house? A friend, no doubt. That meant he must be getting close. His turtle bag had begun to shake.

He stopped beneath a street lamp to look. The turtle was nervous too. "Steady, friend."

Ah, he remembered that she took a bus to school. "A wilderness trail," she had said. That explained the crooked line that almost jumped her map down west. The white, two-storied house was where he should have turned, so he and the turtle trotted back. Now they had a road almost to themselves, after skirting a fresh-scraped tract. He soon began to see what the problem was; they were wandering very crookedly, if not in a wilderness at least a woods. More than once he felt that they had jumped her map. Somewhere nearby ran last night's dogs. The turtle, he felt, had withdrawn into his shell. Al trotted onward for both of them.

There was light ahead. It hung from a hemlock tree, showed a gravel drive leading to a granite house. Out front gleamed a high chain-link fence. The gate was mostly closed, leaving just room enough for a man to sidle in. Al did not. Two police dogs waited on the other side. These were not the barking dogs they had heard in the wilderness, these were the snarling kind. The poor turtle was shaking again. "Steady, friends," Al said, crossing his arms over his packages. The dogs stuck their snarling heads outside the gate. He would gladly have thrown them peanut clusters, but he feared that the gesture might be misunderstood. Suppose they knew that candy was not good for them? Or in the confusion he might have thrown the turtle bag instead. He stood his ground and the dogs angrily disputed it. They were growing impatient now, not just intolerant. The larger one was halfway through the gate, snarling froth.

"Betty! Bob!"

Their ears went up, but they quickly flattened them again, pretending not to hear.

"Betty! Off!"

Growling, Betty backed through the gate. Bob took her growling place.

"Off! Off!"

The dubious dogs looked back and forth, then drew off a little bit, making room for Joan. She stood with a hand on each of them, and Al sidled in.

"Merry Christmas!"

"Merry Christmas!" he said, as they kissed cheek to cheek. He did not mention how tall she was. They turned toward the house, the incredulous dogs close upon his heels.

"Betty! Bob! Did you walk?"

"Partway."

"Did you have any trouble with my map?"

"No, not even in the wilderness."

Laughing, she took his arm, his turtle one. She did not mention how thin he was. At the house he tried to hold the door for her, but she showed that she was busy with Betty and Bob. First wiping his feet on the Welcome mat, Al stepped in.

"Hello, Al."

She stood with a smile upon her face, and he shook the hand she held partway outstretched. "Hello, Doris."

"How've you been?"

"Fine! And you?"

Her eyes, behind their tinted lenses, wanted only to measure how much he lied. At this moment any resemblance between the woman before him and her older sister, now forever younger, was obscenity. "Fine," she jeered. "Roy, Al's here."

There was a clatter of boots and Roy rolled in from the dining or trophy room. "Al, whataya say?"

"Hello, Roy!"

They too shook hands.

"Have any trouble finding the place?"

"Not a bit."

"More than one taxi driver has driven around out there all night."

"I'll bet!"

"Sit down," in a low chair beside the Christmas tree, which hung from the ceiling upside down. That was to make room for the presents heaped beneath.

"Joan, take Al's bags," Doris said.

"No, that's all right," he said, stuffing them with his kit behind the chair.

"Take his jacket."

"Thanks, that's fine too."

"Have you eaten yet?"

Al looked around. "What time is it?"

"Eight-fifteen."

"Not recently."

"Joan, fix Al something to eat."

"Dad, what would you like?"

"There are cold meats in the refrigerator. Ask Greta if there's any pie left."

"Have a beer, Al? Scotch?"

"Beer sounds great."

"Doris?"

"Oh, Scotch, I guess."

"You're lucky, Al," Roy said, patting his full jeans as he rolled out. In fact that cowboy was getting a little narrow in the shoulders, all going to waist. Eat beef!

Now guest and hostess were alone, and Doris leaned back upon her couch. Al in his low chair was almost lost. "How did you happen to find this house yourselves?" he asked.

"We were lucky," the hostess said with a little laugh.

"O. A. Tuttle of Tuttle and Tuttle was moving east. We moved in almost overnight. We've hardly begun to redecorate, of course. We want to take out that wall behind you and put in a bar." And cut a hole in the floor beneath me so that tree can grow to its full height. "Roy is going to face the gun room with oak."

"How many acres go with this place?"

"Eight. That gives us room for the horses. Roy has already laid two miles of fence. We can't run many cattle, of course."

"How many horses have you got?"

"Twenty-eight. In the summer we'll take them to the ranch."

"How many cows—how many cattle do you run?"

"Four, including Joan's. We'll take most of those down too."

"Goats?"

The hostess laughed. "No goats."

"Chickens?"

"Oh yes, loads of chickens, and turkeys too."

"Ducks?"

"A few."

Peacocks?

Roy rolled in, bearing Al's beer to him. "How's everything in Texas these days, Al?"

"Many thanks! About the same as usual."

Host and hostess sat back on the sofa sipping Scotch. "You, uh, took in the Houston show?"

"Yes."

"Have any idea how the beef prices went?"

"Well, everyone seemed well satisfied."

Host glanced at hostess, and she spoke next. "How does Joan look to you?"

"Wonderful!"

"She'd look much better if I could get her to cut her hair."

"Why?"

"Well!" Doris sipped and laughed. "Long hair simply isn't stylish for girls these days. It looks so tomboyish."

"Aha." Drinking beer, Al studied the Christmas tree.

When he glanced back at host and hostess, hostess looked ready to cut his hair too, what was left of it. "Long hair is old-fashioned for girls," she explained as Joan walked in, "just as baldness is for men."

"That's why the women are all cropping their heads," Joan said, "to make wigs for men."

Doris' silver-blond hair seemed to stand on end, but her lips could still smile on them. "Laugh while you can," she said.

Joan had found roast beef for him, and scallions and radishes, cut and arranged artistically. "Thanks, very much." She brought salt and pepper too, set his meal on a table in front of him. The library table; the newest digestion of best-selling books lay squarely in its center. In clearing room for him, Joan turned the gluttonous volume face down. It was almost too quiet now, while Al ate. The turtle was getting nervous behind the chair. Drinking deep, Al tried but could not come up with diverting talk. Eat beef! Joan smiled nearby. When his beer was gone, she would have brought him another one. "Dad?"

"Did you ask Greta about the pie?"

"Yes, Aunt Dor."

She took Al's dish, and Roy took Doris' glass. He emptied his own as he followed out. "Another beer, Al?" he called.

"Thanks!"

Now guest and hostess were left alone again, and she had ready diverting talk. "What do you think of the war, Al?"

"Ah," Al said. He finished a best-selling novel before he went on. "It's a bloody mess, isn't it?"

"Are you a chicken or a hawk?"

"Well, I'm a pretty old cock," he said. "I don't think they'll be calling on me for a while."

"What would you do if you had a son?"

Teach him to dismantle a gun. "I guess the question would be up to him."

"You mean you wouldn't want him to fight?"

"There's more than one way to fight," he said, returning her volume to its allotted place.

At a moment like this, how happy to have one's daughter walk in—even bearing apple pie. "Ah, thanks." She had thought to put heaps of ice cream on it. She offered him a choice of spoon or fork, and he chose spoon. Ever-rolling Roy brought beer and Scotch and Scotch. "Thanks!"

Roy sank sighing on the couch. "When did you get in, Al?"

"This afternoon."

"Where did you stay last night?"

"Ah, a little place up in the hills. The Hemlock Inn, I think it was."

"Don't believe I know that one. You came from the east, on Highway Ten?"

"Yes, that's the one."

"You were lucky you didn't get caught by that avalanche."

"It was close."

Roy glanced at Doris, and she spoke. "You stopped over in Spokane?"

"Yes, for a couple of days."

"Weren't you going to Denver the last we heard?"

Al shivered. "That didn't last long."

"Cold?"

"Thirty-four below."

"You sure get around, don't you," said Doris, lighting a cigarette.

"I follow the snow."

Joan was at his side. "Dad?"

"We're gettin ready to do a little travelin ourselves," Roy said, and Joan sat down on the floor again. "Want to take Joan's two-year-old to the Dallas show."

"Ah, that comes up soon."

"January two to January six."

"When do you expect to leave?"

"We'll have to get started tomorrow afternoon."

"Aha."

Doris and Roy were watching Al. Joan was watching Roy, and Roy finally spoke. "We thought you might like to come along with us, if you haven't got business here."

Everyone was watching Al. "Well, I don't know."

"We could use an extra hand," Roy said, taking Doris' glass.

"Well, thanks."

"You think it over, Al," Roy said, standing up. "There'll be plenty of room in back." He took Al's empty bottles along with him. "Another beer, Al?" he called.

"Thanks!"

Now guest and hostesses were left alone, and guest's daughter spoke. "Dad, will you go with us?"

"Well, I don't know," he said quietly, and smiled. "I've just come from there." Doris wanted to relight her cigarette, and he took a match to her. She nodded, blowing smoke.

"Don't you still smoke, Dad?"

"Not as much as I did," he said, but he took one from the china box, not to seem aloof.

"Here you go, Al."

"Many thanks!" Al said, lowering himself into his chair again.

Up on the sofa, host and hostess sipped. "You son of a bitch!" she said.

"Huh?"

Doris was on her feet, heading for the gun room or bar. Roy ran after her, slammed the door. Loud words came from there, improper nouns and verbs. The pace of the exchange attested that this scene had been well rehearsed. At appropriate intervals, glassware broke. Joan watched the door, and Al the floor. Who came out was Roy. They glanced at him questioningly, but he did not say. He threw himself on the sofa and grabbed his drink. It was quite a long silent while before Doris emerged red-eyed, with Scotch. She dropped onto the sofa and would not speak.

"Al, will you be staying here tonight?" Roy asked, after another silent while.

"No, thanks very much. I didn't think you people would be settled yet. I thought I'd find a room in town."

"We're not really squared away here yet," Roy agreed, "but we have room. There's a room above the barn that you could use, if you don't mind roughing it. We haven't gotten around to fixing it up as yet. I plan to put insulation in, and face it with spruce. We'll have to put windows in. It'll need over-flooring too, and stairs. About all there is up there now is a bed."

"Well, that sounds great."

"Huh?"

"I don't need much."

"You're staying then?"

"If it isn't any extra trouble. . . ."

"Joan, get some sheets and blankets and a pillowcase and make the bed. Take the lantern."

"Blankets will be enough. . . ."

"I made the bed this morning, Roy."

A moment of silence fell. "I'll get the lantern then," Roy said, and bowlegged out.

"Dad, will you need anything else?"

Doris belched. "Give him a beer!" she said.

Al spoke low to Joan. "A little tissue paper and a glass of water would help a lot."

"Tissue?" she whispered.

"Christmas," he whispered back.

Joan ran off.

"Ready there, Al?"

"Be with you in a minute, Roy!" Al called, gathering his bags and kit.

In less than a minute Joan ran back. She helped him arrange everything in his arms, find a free hand to take the glass. "Good night!" she whispered.

"Good night!"

"Good night!" Doris aped.

Al waved his glass at Joan.

Roy stood at the kitchen door with a hurricane lamp. He signaled for Al to go first. There was another big light out back, hanging from a spruce. Betty and Bob were on the watch. They followed hard upon Al's heels, since Roy wasn't saying yes or no. At the barn Roy paused to relieve himself. Carefully putting down his glass, Al did too. Betty! Bob! Throwing open the barn doors, "We'll probably wake up the hosses," Roy said.

Al went in first. Horses stood everywhere, nodding their heads. One neighed. Roy tripped on a hoof and cursed. It was

a stepladder he was aiming for. Once there, he tested it with
one shiny boot.

"Here, let me," Al said.

"Take the lantern," Roy muttered, shoving it into Al's free
hand that held the glass.

"Thanks!" Al started up. The water was the tricky part,
but he wasn't spilling all of it. Look straight ahead, not at
your feet. Make sure a rung is there before you step. If none,
step twice as high and hope. The trap door he opened with his
head. Climbing in, he signaled Roy good night, held the lamp
for him until he was out. The barn doors slammed closed. Al
quietly lowered his.

Hey, this was beginning to look like home again. Not only
a bed, but a dresser and a chair, of pine. Al dumped everything except the glass on a dresser top. Joan had wrapped a
bottle of beer in his Christmas paper, along with pretty tags
and string. First things first: Al opened the turtle bag. The
turtle stared out wide-eyed. "Steady, friend," Al said, slipping him into the glass. After the turtle had splashed awhile,
Al sprinkled food, not too much at first. Next he brought the
book out of his kit, carried it, the wrappings, and the beer to
the bed with him. He rolled and lit a good cigarette. Joan
had known he would have an opener; he went back for it.
She had given him three tags, one for each. "To Joan with
love from Dad," he wrote. He had bought nothing for Roy,
he found, so he inscribed the peanut clusters to both of them.
The book wrapped most easily. When he had covered Doris
and Roy's lumpy sack, he had just enough paper left to hide
the turtle and his food, tomorrow morning.

This beer tasted better than those others had. Al drained
it to the last generous drop before bearing his presents to the
dresser. In front of the looking glass, they looked twice as
much. Al himself did not. Rather hollow in the cheeks, wide-

eyed. In the turtle glass the turtle had regained his composure a little bit. He winked at Al, as though to steady him. "All right, my friend," Al said, "all right." He had not arrived up here with enough water for brushing teeth, had he so planned. What else? He cleaned his fingernails. Now he took a good look around. The remaining Christmas paper, tags, and string he placed on the dresser, next to the turtle glass. Winking at the turtle, he blew out the lamp, and found the bed. Someone had left a Christmas tag on the pillowcase, beneath the comforter. Al lit a match. Two words: "Good night." He lay back. Good night, my love, good night. In the darkness the horses clomped and the turtle bumped. "Until tomorrow, friends. . . . "

5

It was hard to say again. There were few cracks in the walls, and someone had faced the roof with dark. Rolling and lighting a thin cigarette, Al lay abed. The turtle was still asleep. Below, Roy was feeding the hungry horses. Hey, Molly. Ho, Joe. Josephine, get off my foot. Son of a bitch! Josephine clomped and neighed. Al got up. In the pale light of dawn to dusk he wrapped and tied the sleepy turtle, leaving air holes here and there. Now he had the turtle glass all to himself. Spreading a very little toothpaste on his brush, he brushed, spit the paste into the glass. Now he had himself a little mess. Kneeling, he poured it down a crack. Was that

Josephine that neighed? Roy was going to have to overfloor that floor.

"Halloooo!" It was Doris. "Where is everyone?"

"Must be goofing off!"

"I'll gather the eggs!"

"O.K.!"

Doris clomped from hen to hen, as on a booted Easter hunt.

"How many'd you get?" Roy called when she clomped back.

"Eighteen! Hasn't anybody showed up yet?"

"Not yet. I think I heard a car drive up."

"You can be sure Jewy Burns will be here today at least!"

"Yeah, and Easter too." Roy and Doris laughed at that. "Did you ever get a present for him?"

"I'll go look." Doris clomped cackling out.

Give him a beer! Al packed his kit. He did not remake his bed, but sat on it to roll a fat cigarette.

"Merry Christmas!"

"Merry Christmas, Burnsy! Have car trouble?"

Burnsy laughed. "No, not today!"

"You can start in on the cows. I've got to go back to the house and wrap some presents up."

Roy clomped out, slammed closed the doors. Al waited a minute before lifting his. "Merry Christmas!" he called.

". . . Merry Christmas."

Al went to his dresser. Tucking his presents inside his jacket-coat, he carried his kit and glass. Backing through the door like a hobo's Santa Claus, he started carefully down. Burnsy came over to hold the ladder, and to guard the stock. "You a new hand here?"

"No no, I just spent the night."

Burnsy peered at Al when he was down. "You're a friend of Mr. Warner's?"

"Joan's father," Al said.

"Oh!" Burnsy put out his hand. "I'm glad to meet you!"

"Glad to meet you too!" Al said as they shook hands. Waving, he stepped among the horses to the doors, and closed them quietly when he was outside. It was just turning light. Over by the house, it delighted him to see, Joan was feeding Betty and Bob. It looked like cold meats from here. "Merry Christmas!" he called.

"Merry Christmas!" She ran to meet him, kiss his cheek. "I was just coming to get you."

"Twenty-eight hosses were there ahead of you," he said, "and eighteen eggs."

Laughing, she took his arm, still did not say how thin it was. "How did you sleep?"

"Like a haystack, and you?"

"Like a five-year-old on Christmas Eve!"

She hadn't been so lucky as that, and he stooped to rinse his glass at a water tap. "What's the system with presents here?"

"They're going to *exchange* them any minute now." She took his glass, and he held the door for her. In the kitchen, Greta muttered at her stove.

"Merry Christmas!"

Greta muttered at the second burner now.

"Greta's a little hard of hearing," Joan said underbreath.

He would have to send his greetings by telephone. In the living room, he could see from here, Roy and Doris sat on their throne. The tree was lighted down. By now the piled presents undertop reached to its very tip, in a conical heap, like a tree almost. "Merry Christmas!"

"Merry Christmas, Al! Isn't this a glorious day!"

"Merry Christmas, Al! Sleep all right?"

"Merry Christmas! Like a horse!"

"Didn't wake you up too early, did we?"

"What time is it?"

"Seven-fifteen."

"Just right!"

"Sit down."

Lowering into his chair, he stuffed his presents in back of the heap, his kit in back of the chair. Host and hostess watched and sipped. Doris was on what looked like tomato juice, Roy on orange juice and something else. "No Tom and Jerries today," Roy said. "Have to stay clear-eyed for the road. Care for tomato juice, Al? Orange juice?"

"Give him a Bloody Mary!" Doris said, and Roy rolled out.

"Joan, have you fed your steer?"

"Yes, at six."

"Then you can start exchanging the presents as soon as Roy gets back."

Seated on the floor nearby, Joan eyed the heap. She had her work cut out for her all right. She might have to bring in her steer to help with some of those. Al hoped she would not call on him; somehow it would not seem appropriate. Man your stands, men!

"Al, here you go."

"Thanks!"

"Joan . . . "

Joan began with little ones atop, bore them to the couch. Roy and Doris put down their drinks. Seated again while Doris and Roy unwrapped, Joan gave Al a little one.

"Thank you!"

"Joan, find one for yourself."

Joan found a little one, and together they watched the couch. Doris received an electric razor from Roy, and Roy received a can of saddle soap from her.

"*Just* what I need! Thank you, Roy!"

"Me too! That's swell, Doris. Joan, aren't you going to open yours?"

Joan hurried to unwrap. She had received a colorful little bug from them. "How darling! Thank you, Doris! Thank you, Roy!" She pinned it to her shirt.

"Turn the eyes," Doris said.

"The eyes?"

Short silence fell.

"Turn both of them."

Silence again.

"Try fourteen ninety," Al advised.

"A radio!" Joan cried over the raving voice. "How do you turn it off?"

"Left eye," Al called, and silence fell.

"Al?"

Al unwrapped. He had received ten good pencils in a handy box. "With love to Dad." He smiled at her anxious face. "Thank you, Joan."

"Are they the kind you like?"

"They're just right," he said. Patting the box, he hoped he was smiling right.

"Joan . . ."

Joan went to the pile and to the couch, with two for each. Seated, she gave Al his from out in front, took hers from far in back. Now they watched. Roy got a gun from Doris, and Doris got a gun from Roy. Doris got a clock radio from Roy, and Roy got a tape recorder with five hundred feet of tape from Doris. Everything was exactly right. They thanked and thanked.

"Joan?"

Joan slowly uncovered hers, and peeked. "A turtle! It's alive! It winked at me! I'm going to call it Wink! Thank you, Dad!" She held the turtle in her palm, and they studied one another seriously. "He's beautiful! He'll need water, won't he, Dad?" When he nodded yes, she covered the turtle with her other hand and hurried out. "I'll be right back."

During this pause in the exchange, Roy and Doris compared their guns. They compared glasses next, and Roy stood up. "Al, another one?"

"No, I've still got plenty, thanks!"

Roy took their glasses out, and Joan stepped aside with her turtle bowl.

"Dad, is this all right?"

"That's fine," he said. "Later you might put a smooth stone in there. They like to sun themselves."

"I've got some pretty ones upstairs—"

"Later, Joan," Doris said, and Joan placed the turtle bowl on the table beside Doris' book. "Aren't you going to open another one?"

"I did!" Joan said, showing the turtle food. "Dried flies. Ugh! Well, they'll look good to Wink. How often should he be fed?"

"Al, aren't you going to open yours?"

While Doris watched, Al unwrapped. Inside was a shiny box. Big Marché! Inside that was tissue paper, and under that was silk. Cautiously Al lifted out. This was only half of it. Le duc de Buckingham. "Pajamas. Thanks, Roy!" he called as Roy rolled in. Roy waved his orange juice.

"I hope they're the right size," Doris said. "You can exchange them tomorrow if they're not."

"No! They look fine!"

Joan bore gifts while he repacked. Doris got a paperback edition of *Walden* from Joan, Roy a can of saddle soap, for which they thanked. Doris got a portable TV set and fifteen hundred feet of film from Roy, and Roy got a movie camera and a gun rack from Doris. Everything was exactly right.

Joan got a portable TV set like Doris' with a twenty-dollar gift certificate for Madame du Barry's Beauty Salon. Not thanking, her pony tail shook. "Dad, open yours."

Al got a small, thick pad of strong paper, with love from Joan. "Thank you, Joan."

Joan bore gifts by the armful now, and everything was just right until she came to peanut clusters and the hi-fi stereous console with FM. " '*Merry Christmas* to Doris from Roy,' " she read, and: "The color TV is for you, Roy."

Two small packages were left on the floor, and she gave one to Al. He unwrapped his while she unwrapped hers. He had received a little book of airmail postage stamps, with love. "Thank you, Joan!"

"Dad! Is this really yours? I never heard about this!"

"You said you were taking French. . . ."

"Yes! And you wrote to me inside. In French . . . To Joan with love from Dad. Look, Aunt Dor!"

Doris looked at the cover hard. "I'm afraid I don't know the lingo," she said. "Al, I didn't know you knew it this well yourself."

"I don't!" he said, as Doris thumbed through a foreign conspiracy. "A Frenchman translated that."

Doris looked at the back cover next, and that was blank. "See, Roy. . . ."

"Hey now!" Roy looked too. "Doris does all the reading in the family," he said, thumbing a little before he handed back to Joan.

"Roy's the historian," Doris said, and Roy smiled vividly at the gun room or bar. No doubt he kept his notes and tapes in there. "Look, Joan," Doris said, "you forgot one present there," behind the color TV set.

"It hasn't got a tag."

"Oh, that's for Al!"

"More!" Al unwrapped, opened the Big Marché box inside, plucked at tissue paper. Some sort of machine lay in there, with handles and wheels all over it. "Hey now!" he said, holding it up for all to see.

"It's a can and bottle opener."

"Aha!"

"You screw it on the wall or bar."

"Thanks very much!"

"Another drink, Al?" Roy called.

"No, I have plenty, thanks!"

"I'm going to get a rock," Joan said, leaving her book on the library table next to the turtle bowl.

The hostess lay back upon her couch. "You'll be here for dinner, won't you, Al? We're staying home from church this morning so that Greta can go."

"Well, thanks very much," Al said, lying back too, looking up onto the Christmas tree.

"That's an old German custom," Doris explained. "We thought it would be interesting for a change."

"Ah . . ."

"Will this do, Dad?"

"It looks just right."

The turtle climbed up on it, and Roy rolled in. "Joan, have you curried your steer?"

"I'll do it now. Dad, do you want to meet Carlos?"

"Yes!" In the hall he asked, "Which direction is the outhouse from here?"

"Oh, I'm sorry! It's right down there."

"Then I'll meet you at the pen or stall."

"Downstairs," she called.

The rest of the library was in here, in a magazine rack behind the door. Al sat and thumbed a little while. Slay for peace! Soon returning the latest bulletin to its allotted place, he washed his hands and face. Greta, dressed to kill, muttered past him in the hall. Outside, Doris was feeding Betty and Bob for him. Peanut clusters, it looked from here. Joan waved from the corral, and Al waved back. Carlos didn't want to be curried just now. Perhaps he shied at the imported currying brush Joan had received from Roy, faced with mahogany. "Here, I'll give you a hand," Al said, climbing in. Carlos, chagrined by the unfair odds, followed them into the pen or stall. "Where's the rest of the herd?"

"Burnsy put them out to pasture. Are you hungry?" Joan had brought lunch for him. "We ate at five-thirty," she explained.

"Thanks!" he said, taking the paper bag from her. "Peanut clusters?" Roast beef sandwiches.

"Aunt Dor thinks she's dieting."

"Ah, I should have bought her Hadacal at Big Marché."

Joan did not smile. "Mom sure loved those things, didn't she?"

"She sure did," Al said.

Joan went into the stall. More or less perched on a rail, he watched her brush. Her pony tail swung in time with Carlos' tail, was almost as black, but not as black as Marie's. "So this is your little two-year-old, ma'am," he said.

Joan kissed Carlos' cheek. "Isn't he beautiful?"

"Yes, he is," Al said, biting into a sandwich. Carlos, will you pardon me, please? "You sure make a good roast beef sandwich, ma'am."

"Doris was saving that for Betty and Bob, but I found it first," Joan said, and laughed.

Upstairs a horse clomped and neighed. Josephine?

Joan had stopped, mid-brush. "You'll be coming with us, won't you, Dad?"

"Would you want me to?"

"Yes!"

"Then yes."

"Oh, *good!*" she cried, and would have kissed him on the cheek had he not been perched so high. A cowbell rang. "That's Aunt Dor."

"For dinner?"

"Yes."

"Aha." Following Joan and Carlos to the corral, he tucked the other sandwich inside his coat, in case. You never know. Carlos seemed ready to follow them over the fence. Staaay, boy. Joan took Al's arm and they walked toward the ranch house watchfully, tout en causant, stooping to wash their hands at the old water tap.

The kitchen looked as though it had been abandoned in considerable haste; the occupants had left without turning off the stove and someone had dropped a great bowl of cranberry sauce. Things were different in the dining room. Old hard-hearing Greta had muttered to some effect before going to church. A magnificent turkey lay on the table, surrounded by heaping bowls of mashed potatoes, creamed onions, ruta-bagas, petits pois, gravy, stuffed celery, olives, scallions, carrot sticks, and nuts. It looked like a forgetful hobo's paradise, or the last supper of a diet buff. Roy was sharpening the carving knife. "Sit there," he said.

Al sat facing Joan. Doris, to his left, looked rather red-eyed. They waited for Roy to finish sharpening his knife, bow down his head. "Thank you, Gracious Lord, for the food we have on this glorious day," he said, and they all looked up.

They watched Roy carve, pass each plate by way of Joan to Doris, who loaded from the bowls. "Gravy, Al?"

"Yes, please."

"Joan?"

"Please."

"Roy?"

"What else?" Roy muttered as Greta might, and red-eyed Doris swilled tomato juice.

When each had his plate, they ate. No one was furious at anyone else, only too busy to talk.

"Mm, the turkey is delicious," Doris said.

"Yes, it is!"

"Yes!"

"Yeah," Roy said. "Thanks to our Future Farmer here."

Joan put down her fork with a bite of turkey on it. But for her freckles, her face looked white. "This isn't Belle!"

"Sure," Roy said. "You knew she was prime."

"You could have chosen one of yours!"

"She was prime," Roy said.

"But today!"

"Couldn't think of a better day myself," Roy said, gripping one of Belle's stumpy, nude, upflung legs. "More turkey, Al?"

"No, I have plenty, thanks!"

"Doris?"

"Please!"

Give him cranberry sauce!

"Looks like Greta's going to be eating plenty of turkey this week!" Roy said, breaking one of Belle's thigh joints.

"We can take some along for sandwiches."

That roast beef sandwich had filled him up, Al found. He did eat some petits pois, creamed onions, stuffed celery, olives and carrot sticks, such things as his diet lacked. He ate nuts. There would be mince pie for dessert, of course. He could have cried seeing Joan stare at the tablecloth.

"Joan's still a little soft," Roy said. "She'll get over it."

Joan was crying, so she excused herself.

"Sit down," Roy said, and Joan sat down again.

"Could I please have a glass of water?" Al asked, and Joan went for it.

There was hard munching silence until she came back, dry-red-eyed.

"Sit down, Joan," Doris said. "I'll take up dessert."

Doris had started to stand up, but she fell back. All three sat drinking and watching Joan clear the dishes from in front of them. When she brought in their mince pie, they ate.

"Eat your mince mie, Joan," Doris said, looking hard-hed-eyed.

Joan nibbled hard hauce until all were through.

"We can leave the dishes for Greta," Doris clearly announced, preparing to rise.

Al sprang for her chair.

"Thank you, *Al*." Give him a mie in the mye!

"What are your plans, Al?" from Roy.

"Dad's coming with us, Roy!"

"Well, doody-doody for him!" Doris called.

"Get a horse blanket from the barn and fix up his place. Get your steer ready too," Roy said to Joan. "We're rolling out of here as soon as we can."

Roy rolled into the gun room and bar, and, waving at Joan, Al went to pack too. His pencils, paper, and stamps, he found, exactly fitted the space left by his book; his bread wrapper would protect them from toothpaste and such. He saw now why she had not given envelopes: large ones would never have fit. Too, he wrapped in grocery sacks. The pajamas he managed to cram in on top; he might need them when his underwear and shirt gave out. Roy's can and bottle opener he left behind the hi-fi and stereous console set, with FM.

"Dad, what about Wink?"

"You'd better leave him here."

"Who will feed him then?"

He could not say.

"Greta won't have much to do," Joan said hopefully. "How often should he be fed?"

"Once a day. His water should be changed after feeding him."

"I'll write her a note," Joan said.

Roy rolled in with a saddlebag. "Joan, have you got your steer ready?"

"Yes, Roy."

"Let's hit the saddle then."

"I'll be right out, Roy."

Doris had her suitcase packed. "Have you got your suitcase, Joan?"

"Yes, Aunt Dor."

"Aren't you going to wear your new go-go boots?"

"No, Aunt Dor," Joan said, and Al went out to help with the steer.

Carlos did not want to go. He would prefer a plunge in the swimming pool. Roy was bent on discouraging him. Al watched awhile, then joined the poolside fun. Snorting, Carlos followed them to the rig. It was the odds that discouraged him. "You get in first," Roy said, and Al climbed in.

"All the way forward," Roy called.

Up forward, Joan had spread his blankets on a ledge for him, and Al lowered himself to that.

Carlos didn't want to go. Roy pushed and pulled to no avail, until Joan came out. Those odds again. Up forward, Roy tied his rope to a ringbolt beneath Al's ledge. "You can keep an eye on him," he said.

"Sure can!" Al said.

"Joan, you come up front."

Joan waved to him behind her back, and patted Carlos on her way out.

"Watch out for his other end!" Roy called.

"Have a nice trip, you two!" called Doris.

Roy slammed the doors on them. There was a little barred window on either side, and Al and Carlos each peered out of one. They listened to Roy start up the rig, ease into first. Gravel spat. They were moving now. Good-bye, Betty! Good-bye, Bob! Guard well that gate. What, had the rig stopped so soon? Peering out, craning their necks, they watched Roy close and lock the gate. One wondered whether Greta had a key to that. Poor Wink. Now they listened to Roy ease into gear again, spit dirt. They were rolling once more, down a crooked road. Roy no doubt knew that his backend swung.

One began to see better what Joan meant about the wilderness. The wood on this side at least was very dense, though it did not seem quite so near as it had last night. Today Wink would have worried less. Ah, there was what that pine tree looked like at day. More grandfatherly but somehow less sedate, perhaps a little addled by such a crowding progeny. There went that wooden bridge, over a babbling brook. Easy, Carlos. . . . Where were those dogs? They would surely have heard them despite the rattling rig. No doubt they were in there somewhere sleeping off the long barking night. They could never have seen them anyway in that wilderness of trees and brush. Al turned away from his window, and Carlos turned from his.

He had a kind face. Very open, frank, with large, sympathetic eyes. His forehead and nose bore a beautiful pattern in black and white, presenting his brown, sympathetic eyes. His horns curved back. Nodding, Al looked out his window again.

They were turning onto the highway now. A breadman, not Al's, stood poised in his doorway waiting for them to pass. Whataya say! Trot on, trata, you're not toting much. Now the swinging landscape swung, the poles and wires and all of that. Look there, look there, at the vehicles and everything. There's room for all on this glorious day of little accidents. Man your patrol cars, men! Blink on. We'll call you if we have need of you. Could they be discerned in the gloom in here? One open-mouthed boy could discern for sure. He called to his ma and she looked too, open-mouthed. Al lay back.

Carlos turned his head.

"Hola, young friend," Al said, and closed his eyes. He heard Carlos lie down too. . . .

When they awoke, the rig had stopped. Roy appeared at a window, Carlos'.

"Everything O.K. in there?"

"O.K.!"

Roy kicked their tires. Doors slammed when he was in his cab again. Now their doors opened and Joan climbed in. Slamming, she waved to Al and patted Carlos on the rump.

"I told them I wanted to look after Carlos," she said, kissing Al's cheek.

"Good! Hey, it's good to see you again," he said.

"You too."

"You're looking wonderful."

She did not say, of him. "Have I changed very much?"

"Oh yes," he said.

"Very much?"

"You're taller and prettier."

Smiling, she sat on his ledge. "Am I as pretty to you as Mother was?"

"No! . . . I'm sorry," he apologized.

"I'm sorry," she apologized. They looked out their windows now. "It's been two years," she said.

"Yes, it has," he said.

"You took flowers to her last month?"

"No, I was in Texas then. I took some on her birthday though. I took some for you too."

"What kind?"

"Wild," he said.

She pressed his hand, and together they looked at Carlos now.

"Isn't he beautiful?"

He would bring a high price all right. "Yes."

"Poor Carlos!"

She was crying, and she excused herself. He looked away. "I didn't want to go on this trip!" she said.

He put his arm around her. "Didn't you understand what you were raising him for?"

"Yes . . . no, not well enough! Roy said I would get over it when Carlos grew big. *Roy.* I hate him!"

"Hating doesn't help."

"I don't like him," Joan said.

"Good, neither do I."

Joan dried her eyes on a gay Christmas handkerchief. Then she turned to him. "I'm so glad to have your book!" she said.

"Lisez-vous bien?"

"Un tout petit peu," she said. "Have they been translated into other languages?"

"Oh ya," he said, "but that's usually all I hear of that."

"Do you get paid very much?"

"Some."

"Was that the money you sent Aunt Dor?"

"That was part of it," he said. "How's school?"

"All right," she said. "Are you writing another one?"

"I have to wait for the next one to catch up with the last."

"You used to be writing them half the time."

"I still am," he said. "You're taking English, French, algebra, and what else?"

"Civics and PE," she said.

"Which subject do you like best?"

"French."

"What is your school like—is it a fairly open-minded one?"

"It's all right."

"Do you like your teachers?"

"Some of them. My French and algebra teachers are fun."

"Good," he said. "What do you do except go to school?"

"Oh, I do my homework and work around the place."

"Don't you have friends?"

"Oh yes."

"Do you go out with boys?"

"No! Aunt Dor keeps trying to get me to. I think she wants to marry me off!"

"What about Roy?"

"Roy. Roy wants me to be a hoss."

He laughed. "Ma'am, is it always like that back at the ranch?"

"Yes, almost."

"Don't you ever enjoy yourself?"

"They went on a vacation once," Joan said. "Greta and I were left alone with the house. I spent most of the time outside. I took care of most of the chores myself. John and Burnsy came by every day, of course."

"Are John and Burnsy nice?"

"Yes, they're all right. They're nice." She patted Carlos' head. "Aren't you going to get married again?"

"Who, me?" he asked.

"Yes."

"No."

"Don't you go out with girls?"

"I've had a friend or two."

"You're not against remarriage, are you?"

"Oh, no!" he said.

Joan patted Carlos' cheek. "Are you a Christian, Dad?"

"What?" he asked. "Well, Jesus Christ was a great man, and I believe in Santa Claus."

"Do you believe in God?"

He patted Carlos' head. "Let's hope," he said.

"Aunt Dor thinks you're a Communist."

"Aunt Dor is always wrong."

Joan agreed. She took his hand. "You're thin," she said.

"Hell yes."

"You used to be so pretty," she said. "Now you're more . . . pretty like a clown." She smiled.

He smiled too. "Who do you think wrote all that?"

"Why are they after you so?"

"Because I'm still a free man; they don't like that."

"How are you free?"

"Well . . ."

"What do you *do?*"

He looked at her. "Well, I'll tell you," he said. "I just take the bag in my right hand and I let her go. When I come home to my daughter at night, I'm weary, but I have a story to tell. It's been quite a day. First I climb up to the very top of the stands," he said, climbing up rails. "From here I can study my crowd, watch for signs of life before I let out my call: 'Are you *lis-en-ing?* Hot . . . salted nuts! Warm, buttered corn! Is an-y bod-y hungry tonight?' I have a bite, a lady to my right. Ziiip, I let one go. Bam! Right on the nose. 'An-y bod-y else?' Ziiip, bam, bam, bam, bam! *There* you go. Fifteen cents for corn, ten for nuts. At fifteen percent,

I'm making one-and-a-half to two-cents-plus on every throw.
The money is rolling in. I dump my load and hurry down
to Commissary for another tray," he said, scrambling down
the rails. " 'Another, Gus!' 'Hey, Eighty-eight, you're doing
O.K. tonight!' 'Ya, they're eating it up!' I take my chit and
run back, to right field this time. 'Are you *lis-en-ing?* Hot,
salted nuts! Warm, buttered corn! Is an-y bod-y hungry tonight?' Ziiiip, bam! Right on the ever-ready nose. Ziiiip, ziiiip,
ziiiip! I dump my load before the visiting pitcher has time
to wind up! The crowd is roaring. Down to Commissary
again!" he cried, scrambling down. " 'Another, Gus!' 'Hey
now, Eighty-eight!' I'm off with my tray and chit, to left field
this time." He climbed sweating up the other side. " 'Is an-y
bod-y lis-en-ing? Hot, salted corn! Warm, buttered n—' Ziiiip,
bam! 'An-y bod-y else?' Ziiiip, ziiiip, ziiiip, ziiiip! Right on
the ever-lovin nose every time! The money is *rolling* in. I
dump my load and hurry to Commissary. 'Gus!' They've
run out of nuts, they don't got no more! I switch to beer.
Up, up, up I go with a double load, two chits. 'Ice-d cold
beer! Ice-d cold beer! Is an-y bod-y thirsty tonight?' They're
panting! Pop, pop, pop, pop! The beer is cold and my bottle
opener is getting hot! Pop, pop, pop, pop! Thirty-five cents
for Eastern, thirty cents for Western. At fifteen percent, I'm
making four-and-a-half to five cents a pop! Pop, pop, pop,
pop, pop! I dump my buckets and hurry down to Commissary! *'Gus!'* 'Hey, you're doing good, Eighty-eight!' 'They're
drinking it up!' I'm off with two loads and chits. Right field!
'Is an-y bod-y . . . ?' Pop! Pop! Pop! Pop! Pop! Pop! Pop!
Pop! Pop! . . . Back to Commissary. The crowd is roaring.
'Gus!' Gus is waiting at the door for me! 'Here you go,
Eighty-eight!' He forgets the chits! Up, up, up, up, up. Pop!
Pop! Pop! Pop! Pop! Pop! Pop! Pop! Pop! Pop! Pop! Pop!
Pop! My opener is smoking now! Down to Commissary!

The stairs are slippery now! '*Gus!* Gus!' They don't got no
more on ice! They've sent out for nuts! 'I'll take them, Gus!'
I take my double load and chits, up, up, up, up! 'Is an-y
bod-y . . . ?' The customers and bottles are rolling in the
aisles! The visiting pitcher catches my eye. He gives me the
signal. 'Right here, Jack!' 'Yes, sir!' Ziiiiiiip! Bam! Right on
the nose! He wants to play catch! Ziiiiiiip! Nice throw!
Ziiiiiiip! Bam! Ziiiiiiip! He's trying to beanbag me! Ziiiiiiiip,
I let one go! Bam! Right on the ever-waggin bean! He takes
aim, but I'm in left field now! Ziiiiiiip. . . . Missed! Ziiiiiiip,
I let one go! Bam, right on the ever-puzzled bean! He takes
aim again, but I'm in right field now. Ziiiiiiip. . . . Missed!
Ziiiiiiip, bam! Ziiiiiiip. . . . Missed! I'm behind the plate!
Ziiiiiiip, bam! Eat that! Ziiiiip, ziiiiip, ziiiiip, ziiiiip, ziiiiip.
. . . The other players are joining in the fray. Ziiiiip, ziiiiip,
ziiiiip, ziiiiip. . . . Miss, miss, miss, miss. Ziiiiip, ziiiiip, ziiiiip,
ziiiiip, ziiiiip! Bam, bam, bam, bam, bam! Sirens scream.
They're carrying the players off the field. They're tripping
on the corn and nuts! Ziiiiip, ziiiiiip, ziiiiiip, ziiiiiip! Have
some, men in white! I'm in left field, I'm in right! Pardon,
Carlos! Pardon, Gus! Pardon, Santa Claus! Now only the
umpire is left! 'Have some, ump!' Ziiiiiip! He runs for the
locker room! The customers are up and cheering on their
feet! The announcer is raving in his booth! The game is
called! Double-header tomorrow, folks! I dash down to Commissary! '*Gus!*' 'No more, Eighty-eight! No more!' '*Gus!*
Gus!' 'No more! Go home, Eighty-eight!' 'Tomorrow, Gus?'
'Take tomorrow night off, Eighty-eight!' '*Gus! Gus!* You
promised to put me on garbage tomorrow night!' 'No game
tomorrow night, Eighty-eight! Stay home! Stay!' '*Gus*, it's a
double-header tomorrow night! They announced it on the
speaker!' 'Go home, Eighty-eight! Stay home!' '*Gus, Gus*
. . . what'll I tell my daughter, Gus? She counts on me!'

'Tell her you're taking tomorrow off!' 'Gussss . . . !' *'Turn your coat in, Eighty-eight!'*

"I keep my hat, in case. I trudge home. My hysterical daughter lets me in. I'm *weary*. I sit down beside my daughter on the couch, wipe my perspiring face," he said, sitting on the ledge. " 'What happened, Dad?' she sobs," and Joan sat sobbing next to him. " 'I'm *weary*, daughter, *weary*.' 'What did you *do*?' 'Well, I'll tell you, daughter,' I said. 'I just took the bag in my right hand and I let her go. When I came back to my daughter, I was *weary*. I mean, I was *weary*, but I had a story to tell. It was quite a day. First I climbed up to the very top of the stands,' " he said, climbing wearily. " 'From here I can study my crowd, look for signs of life before I make my call. The customers are rolling in the aisles! "Is an-y bod-y *lis-en—*" ' "

The stands quaked under him and he came tumbling down. "Pardon, Carlos!" he called, rolling underneath, jumping smiling to his feet on the other side with hands outstretched to his hysterical audience.

"You asked me a question, I think. . . . "

"No! No!"

Al peered outside, at OASIS 88! Roy's head blacked that out. "Dinner, Al?"

"No, I have plenty, thanks!"

"Come out to dinner, Joan."

Staggering out, she waved to him behind her back. Carlos looked after her worriedly. "It's all right, young friend," Al softly said, and Carlos turned to him. Al sank to the ledge, patted Carlos' head. They were weary. "Dinnertime, young friend," Al said, bringing his sandwich out. Carlos, will you please pardon me? Carlos nibbled hay between Al's feet.

Outside, dark was coming on. When they were done nibbling, they lay down to wait. Presently harsh voices could be heard, and Roy's head appeared at the window, Carlos' again. "Everything O.K. in there?"

"O.K.!"

"Have a nice sleep, you two!" Doris called. "When Roy gets going he drives all night!"

Roy kicked their tires. Doors slammed when all were in. Al and Carlos listened to Roy start the motor up, ease into first. Rubber spun. They were moving, through the dark; the days seemed to be growing a little shorter now. Carlos still was chewing. He got more out of his food than Al did his. "Good night, young friend. . . ."

6

It was early. A dim smudge of grey light could be seen through Al's window. Carlos' window was dark, therefore he had taken Al's over. He turned his head toward Al's ledge, no doubt apologetically, and Al patted it. So they looked out the window together. Once Roy got started, he drove almost all night. The rig was not moving but parked on the east side of the highway, next to a picnic table. A large sign nearby gave illegible information or instructions, which Carlos peered at anxiously. What did it say about eating the young grass, drinking the stream water? Apparently he could see in the dark better than Al could, for he snorted and let plop with a big one. No no, he could not read the sign either. That was intuition. Partly perhaps it was thoughtfulness; Carlos had not wanted to disturb him while he was sleeping. Al patted the turned head, nodded gratefully. Together they turned back to the window.

One finally felt stupid looking out a window with longing, doing nothing about it. If they wanted to be out there, why not try to? Al moved to the back of the rig, stepping carefully. He groped in the dark for a handle, soon found it and lifted. Roy had slammed them in well, but the latch was reversible. Jumping down, Al felt guilty. He knew Carlos was turned his way. He hoped he would remember what his intuition had earlier told him, not assume that all men made up the rules, could change them at will. One can only do his best, young friend, Al silently reminded. As a sign of good intention, he left his kit in Carlos' keeping. Should Roy decide to move on soon, they would be reunited in Dallas (however briefly, one remembered). A man could only do his best. Closing the doors softly, he waved apologetically going past Carlos' window.

There was almost enough light to read by now. He left the signboard and table behind him, followed an arrow that pointed out a path. The path itself was hard-topped, but on either side the grass did look young and green where the land had been cleared. The air too was young, newly borne by a cool wind, and above the groan of a truck on the highway one could almost imagine hearing the song of a young stream. At this hour, after a long night penned in a rig, the imagination ran wild. Those looked like trees up ahead, and Al hastened up the wide path, not using the rail. Intuition, in lieu of flora and fauna, told him that he was in California now; in Oregon they had not yet logged all their parks, were still on the first cutting at least. Too, there was something about the gilded litter barrels anchored to creosoted posts; in Oregon, he felt, they still painted them bright green and chained them to trees. Let them Keep Oregon Green, baby, you're in the Golden State now.

Where else could one be sure to find company by dawn's early light amid litter on Christmasmorrow, as Al was sure to? Yet the first man he came upon was strangely reassuring. He was down on his hands and knees observing a tiny creature, it looked like a deer mouse. Something about the ill-fitting, homely uniform, the almost comic hat, Al always found touching. It went back to his first discovery that a man could care for some life other than his own. Women, many of them, seemed made that way. Young children, of course. But a grown man, that had been a revelation, which he had never forgotten. Later he had had the pleasure of working beside such men for several summers, and learning from them.

The ranger, aware that he was not alone, motioned for Al to approach quietly. Al knelt down on the path beside him. Together they observed the little creature, who observed them equally from beneath a tuft of young grass. Soon he turned his back on them and went nonchalantly about his snuffing business. "Thataboy," the ranger whispered, chuckling.

"What kind is he?" Al whispered.

"A *peromyscus leucopus.*"

In silence they watched the mouse snuff and skitter from grass to grass until he reached the path. He crouched with his white front paws upon the tar, not more than a yard from them, then sprang suddenly backward into the air. Landing rather awkwardly on his side, he quickly regained his balance and dashed to the nearest grass. There he shook himself and left some droppings. "Good boy!" the ranger called gleefully.

The mouse, having fully regained his composure, climbed a low bush and swung on its branches. Now, before his enthralled audience, he leaped to the ground and made for the path again. This time he landed squarely in the middle with a flying jump. The ranger, almost simultaneously, swatted him off of it.

The mouse landed on his back, lay still for a moment, his white belly heaving. Then he crept to nearby grass and stared out at them from there. The ranger, turning to Al, smiled intensely. His smooth, featureless face was blue-purple. "Think that'll teach him?"

"Teach him?"

"To stay off the goddam trail!"

"Aha . . ."

The ranger crawled forward a few inches, deftly flicked a dropping from the path with his forefinger. "Can you see that microscopic wire there?" he asked, indicating the edge of the path.

"Yes, I can."

"That's electronically charged." The ranger flicked it with his forefinger. "We can't hear or feel anything, but the *peromyscus leucopus* can. It's attuned to his nervous system. The *peromyscus leucopus* has a very high range, almost as high as the *sorex cinereus*. That wire is sending him continuous warnings, night and day: 'Stay back. . . . Stay off. . . . Stay off the *trail*. . . .' It takes time, it takes time. Someday we'll teach him to."

"Why do we want him to?"

"Why?" The ranger flicked at a dropping. It turned out to be a bit of dirt, and his neck flushed dark purple. "It's not just the mess, of course. That's obvious to anyone. It's a control problem. We have to control them. We place them on opposite sides of the trail as soon after birth as is possible, the female parent on one side, the male parent and young on the other. We've wired both sides," he said, indicating. "Our aim is to improve and control the species by encouraging a process of natural selection. Only the most intelligent will survive, those that react properly to our warnings. Most will never learn, of course. Like you, stupid," he sneered, as the deer mouse jumped onto the path again. "We give them two chances," he said, snapping the animal's backbone and flinging the broken body across the path. "Enjoy your little boy *now*, mother!" he called.

The ranger stood up and brushed at his knees. "Then all we'll have to do is teach the people to stay off the goddam grass," he said, turning suddenly on Al. Finding Al entirely on the trail, his color lessened a little and he straightened his hat. He wore a plastic name tag on his breast: E. T. JACKLE. "What they really ought to do," he said confidentially, "is pave the whole damn park and be done with it."

"Aha . . . "

The ranger shot a quick dark look at Al's face. "Where did you drift in from, mister?"

"I'm with that rig down there," Al said quickly, pointing to it.

"Oh!" The ranger's face spread into a smooth pink smile. "Carrying a horse there, are you?"

"No, a steer."

"Oh!" They headed down the trail together. "Headed for a stock show?"

"Yes."

They could see Carlos observing them from his window. "What kind is that?"

Veering toward the rig, Al waved. "That's Carlos," he called.

Waving too, the ranger headed for his pickup. "Make yourselves at home, folks!" he called. "Enjoy the park!"

Roy waved from his gasoline stove. "Thanks, Ranger!"

"Thanks, Ranger!" Doris called.

Waving, the ranger climbed into his pickup. His driver was an old man in a faded, homely uniform. His almost comic hat could not quite hide the most grief-stricken face Al had ever seen. He looked at Al as they drove by, and Al looked back at him.

"Better hurry it up there, Al!" Roy called. "Your eggs are cold."

Approaching the stove, Al gave a little wave to Joan, and she waved back. "Thanks, Roy!"

"Here's some hot coffee, Dad."

"Joan, have you fed your steer?"

The table was gummy with cold egg and bacon grease, so Al squatted nearby, on the trail. His coffee was hot, and he could imagine he was eating raw oysters on the soft shell. His paper plate he burned in a fireplace, after reading the signs. Doris threw around some more for him, and he burned those too. Roy finished cleaning his stove. "O.K., has everybody brushed their teeth?" he called.

"Yes," Doris said.

"Let's get rolling then. We can shave on the road." Roy led the way to the rig. "You're riding up front, Joan," he said, holding the door open for Al. "Watch that rear end, Al," he said, and Al stepped all the way forward.

"Toodlydoo!" Doris called as Roy slammed the door.

Carlos looked up from his fresh hay. Al patted his head, and he went back to eating. There were no hard feelings between them. Let those others jeer and slam all they wanted, let the signboards say what they would, friends still stuck together. Let Roy lay rubber all over the trail. Let his electric razor buzz on forever. They still had one another, and hay. That hay did look good, for the teeth in particular. Al opened his kit. Now he wished he had preserved his vitamin A bottle, for water. It still would have fit, even with all his presents.

No, it might have broken and spoiled his paper. Something told him he would have need of that soon, if *possible*. He spread a very little toothpaste on his brush, worked it thoroughly. He could not spit in Carlos' hay, so he spat out their window, mostly. "Sorry, Carlos!" he said, wiping paste off his rear end. "Don't worry, Roy! I'm watching!"

Seated on his ledge, he tried to go over the recent experience again from beginning to end. At first he could not do it, for already he could hardly believe it himself. He knew that he had to. If one allowed himself not to, soon there would be no writers left in America. So he forced his memory to retrace every detail, from that first violent smile to the last tragic look of the driver. When he had finished he lay back exhausted. "Carlos, even you wouldn't believe it."

Ruminating, Carlos looked up with worried, sympathetic eyes.

Al closed his own. When he awoke, Carlos was gazing out his window at the American flag. It was floating high in the air above a big building. An Oasis? No, this parking lot was smaller, more crowded, mostly with red or blue wagons. Here and there loomed a rig, but nothing quite like Roy's. Roy called through the window behind them. "How's it going in there?"

"O.K.!"

"Come on out for a breather."

"Thanks, this is fine."

"Come on out," Roy said. "Carlos needs some time to himself."

Al glanced at Carlos, who glanced back at him. Patting Carlos' head, Al breathed deeply before stepping outside.

Doris was teasing her hair. "We're going to drop in and visit Roy's boss, Vern Brown," she said. "You'll like Suzy too. She's High Church, but very right underneath."

"Thanks, I'll wait here with Carlos."

"You better come along with us," Roy said, looking around the parking lot. Several wagons still showed unopened Christmas presents on their Kleenex shelves—and AMERICAN BEEF IS BEST on their bumpers. "It wouldn't look good."

"It sure wouldn't," Doris said.

Al looked back at the highway, then at Joan. In response to her imploring glance, he followed them up the trail. Vern Brown's house was long and low, of reinforced concrete faced with gilt. Oh, it was dazzling in the moon's brilliant light. It was windowless, like a modernday church. In fact, there was a little steeple on top. The narrow door had a peephole, in the shape of an eye, which blinked open at their approach. There was no visible doorknob or latch.

A butler or bouncer opened for them; he wore a black suit. He held the sliding door as they filed in. Since Roy and Doris wore rodeo shirts, he went for Al's jacket or coat. "That's all right," Al said, behind Joan. Joan gave up her sweater.

"In the meeting room," the husky man said.

He pressed one of several buttons, and a door glided open at the far end of the hall. It was thoroughly soundproof, for now there was din. High and delicately arched, the door framed a tall, white-haired lady as in a shrine. Her white paratrooper's suit fit her slender body tightly all the way down to her bare feet. Standing up on her toes, she reached her arms out toward her guests, ethereally, as though a higher power prevented her leaving her niche. "Roy! Doris! Joan!"

"Hi, Suzy!"

"Hi, Suzy!"

"Darling! . . . Darling! . . . Darling! . . ." As they filed in, she embraced and kissed each one in turn. Al she did not kiss, but neither did she appear to notice his beard. She took his hand warmly in both of hers and looked into his eyes. "We're so pleased you could come!"

"Thank you!"

Smiling, high on the balls of her feet, she led them through the crowd. Smiling observers made way for them. They were headed for a stout-torsoed man in a wheelchair or go-cart. He had a massive head, with a strong neck to support it. A fur robe, probably buffalo, covered his lower parts. Whatever was under there, he showed very large boots down below. He could move his powerful arms.

"Hi, Vern!" Roy called, waving.

"Hi, Vern!"

Vern Brown did not kiss, but his face glowed and his blue eyes shone welcome as he warmly patted their backs. He patted Al's shoulder blades. Suzy Brown stood beaming nearby. "There's room over here, darlings," she said, leading the way.

Three chairs awaited them. Al moved aside, but Suzy Brown took his arm in one hand and Joan's hand in the other. "Joan, the children are playing games in the barn." She showed Joan to a back door that led directly outside. The top button opened it. Al and Joan exchanged little waves as it closed.

"Scotch, Roy? Doris?" asked the hostess, returning.

"That sounds fine!"

"Beer, Mr. James?"

"Ma'am? Thanks!" Al said, as a maidservant appeared at his side with a cold one. He raised it to Doris and Roy, but they were busy observing. Ice tinkled everywhere around them. Everyone else was smiling at everyone, whether in black suits or cowboy. A few had their suit pants tucked into their boots, to go with their bolo ties. One of these, a man of full voice, called across the room to Vern Brown.

"Vern, did you see what Bates had to say in the *Times* yesterday?"

"Yes!"

This produced hubbub. Doris glanced at Roy, who shook his head bitterly. She did all the reading in the family. Opportunely, the tinkle and slosh of Scotch on the rocks claimed their attention. Al looked away. For an instant he thought he spotted Will Watson among the suits, but on second look changed his mind. This man's shades were noticeably greener. Doris' own looked rather too pale in this company. They would betray her when she turned red-eyed. At the moment she was in no danger of that, for her eyes shone almost as brilliantly as Vern's as she arched toward her drinking companions. "Isn't this delightful?" she asked, sipping.

"Sure is!" Roy sipped too.

"What is the occasion?"

"This is the Third Annual Christmas Party," Doris said, leaning closer to confide in a whisper: "They never receive on Christmas Day. You know Suzy."

Suzy danced up on her toes, a Scotch in one hand and a beer in the other. "How are we doing, darlings?"

"Fine!"

"Fine!"

"O.K.!"

"How's everything up north, Roy—under control?"

"You bet!" Roy said.

"You saw what Kinkaid wrote in the Sunday *Post-Examiner*?"

Swallowing Scotch, Roy looked hard at Doris.

"Yes!" Doris said.

Suzy nodded archly, her eyes shining. They rested on Al.

"Darlings," she asked, "do you mind if I steal this interesting man for a minute?"

"Well, all right," Roy agreed.

"Hurry back!" Doris called.

Beckoning to Al with her head, Suzy Brown led the way to a settee or love seat against a wall where a window once had been. Seated, she beckoned to a manservant bearing Scotch, traded glasses with him. "Al, another beer?"

"Thanks!"

"I'll join you," she said, beckoning to a maid. "Excuse my drinking with both hands," she said as they exchanged. "I'm a little up in the air. I learned the other day that an old friend had committed suicide." Sipping beer, she gazed into her highball glass. "I hadn't seen him very often recently, but we were once very good friends. I think I understand why he did it. He was an extremely sensitive man, too easily hurt. At the same time, he was a very stubborn man underneath. Some men are less willing to bargain than others." Her handsome, hawklike face turned to Al, and he nodded. "What do you think, Al?" she asked, examining him. "Could a man be justified in taking his own life?"

"Oh, I think so," Al said. "If he weren't getting anything out of life, or contributing anything, and found himself hurting those around him who were, he might be doing the best thing." Nodding total agreement, Suzy Brown leaned toward him, and he said in full voice: "I would never consider it for myself."

Sitting back, pushing her glass away from her on a table, she shook her head briskly. "Let's talk happy!" she said, smiling. "I've heard so much about you that I've been dying to meet you! We like to have a representative gathering. Ortu there is half Australian aborigine. Augie Sloan over there is

a Catholic Jew. John Henry Jones couldn't come today, but
he sent a message of apology. Are you writing?"

"Not just now."

"I've wanted to read your books for the longest time,"
Suzy Brown said, reaching for the other half of her boiler-
maker, "but I simply never seem to get the chance."

"They're a little hard to find."

"My son has read them," she said. "He's one of your most
ardent fans."

"He's a lonely boy," he said.

"What? Oh, he reads all sorts of weird stuff. Henry James,
Faulkner, Beckett, Gowan. Is it Gowan?"

"I don't know," he said.

Rather pettishly, Suzy Brown waved for a barmaid. Vern
Brown, rolling by, waved a big arm. He was headed for a
low door which glided open before him. The clack of a tele-
type came from in there, and the whisper of tape recorders
and probably film projectors. A television camera swung into
view, swung away just as the little door glided closed behind
Vern Brown's electric go-cart. "V.W. has a call from his
boss," Suzy Brown explained, handing Al a fresh beer. "Have
a Scotch too."

"Thanks!"

With so much in common, they sat back to enjoy. Suzy
Brown stared wistfully into her glass. She did not allow her
thoughts to revert to her departed friend, however, but remembered her guest. "Such a waste, such a waste," she murmured.

"Excuse me?"

"So much talent going to waste!" she said, shaking her
white head sadly. "Take you yourself, for example. All that
writing and writing, and you probably haven't even got a
shirt to your name—"

"Oh yes," he assured.

"Al, have you ever tried pamphlets?"

"Pamphlets?"

"Thought-provoking pamphlets on historical, economical, sociological, geographical, political subjects? That's the new field in writing, you know. That's where the audience is—not just in English, but in all languages. The government alone spends untold millions of dollars annually on pamphlets, not to mention the many private agencies. You should think about that, Al."

"No, I never hire out as a writer," he assured her. "When I need money I prefer to work with my hands—outside."

"I can understand that," Suzy Brown said, nodding thoughtfully. "Yes, I can understand that. You would probably prefer something like park service. That's mostly outdoors, and they have an excellent training program. It'll look good on your employment record too. Would you be interested in that, Al?"

"Not right . . ." he began, but he could already hear the echo. Leaning forward, brushing a perhaps imaginary bug from Suzy Brown's sleeve, "What was the question?" he asked.

"Would you like park service?"

"They've done some fine work over the years. . . ."

"Well, you think about it, Al."

"Oh, I will."

Vern Brown drove by, waving, and his wife made ready to join him. Tilting her beer, she turned to her guest *en buvant:* "Al, what about that book you wrote last year?"

"Last year?"

"Have you found a publisher for it yet?"

"No, I haven't."

"If you have an extra copy of the manuscript, I'm dying to

read it," Suzy Brown said. "Maybe I could interest one of my publishing friends . . ."

"Thanks very much—I have one or two others I've promised to try first."

Dark-faced, Suzy Brown picked up her Scotch. "You'll have to meet my son," she said standing up, and Al stood up too. Saluting, she sailed away on the high balls of her feet. Scotch, vodka, and gin were sloshing over the glassrims, and spilling onto the bolo ties. The powders, gasses, and sprays came table d'hôte, as a matter of course. Al found himself rather light-and-heavy-headed, in need of fresh air. Steering for the back door, he could see Roy and Doris engaged in animated sign language with Ortu, whose bolo tie dangled in his gin like a primitive fishing line. The top button still opened the door, for just long enough to duck out.

The sun hung over the barn like a primitive symbol, and Al headed for that. There was a paved trail for V.W.'s go-cart, maybe wired. Al's legs were almost beyond his control, but he managed to stay on. The barn door presented familiar problems. He pressed the top button, and an eye appeared at the eyehole.

"Yes?"

"I'm looking for Joan James."

"Wait a minute." The eye withdrew. "Joan James!"

"She's down with her steer," a voice called, drawing laughter. "Who's asking?"

"Some old stud."

"Bring him in," the voice called.

"Thanks, not just now," Al said, but the door was open and left and right guards brought him in.

"Studio One." They shoved him toward it. A sign on the door read "TV INTRAVIEW—in progress," and the door glided open. The room inside was hot with bright light and laughter, loud applause from the audience. A grinning host in black suit and tie sat alone at a table in front. His real mustache made him look older than those clean-shaven or bearded, not including some of the girls. The host did not rise but waved Al a mock greeting.

"We have a guest celebrity today!" he told his applauding audience. "Come in, come in!"

"No, thanks, I'm camera shy," Al said, waving, but two guards or tackles took his arms.

"You're on screen," the host warned, waving him forward. "Remember Lee Harvey . . . O.K., shoot, Jack," he called over his shoulder. A blast of hot light flooded Al as flanking guards led him to a chair, sat down on each side of him. "We're honored to have with us today a real live author," the smiling host said to his audience, adjusting his tie, tugging his shirtcuffs. "Welcome to 'TV Intraview,' Mr. James. Audience, let's give a warm welcome to Mr. Al James. (What does that Al stand for, Mr. James—Alvin?) Mr. James is the author of several brilliant novels whose titles I can't at the moment recall. Alvin?"

Shielding his eyes from the light, Al shook his head. "Albert," he said.

"Ah well," his host said, "perhaps they'll come back to us later. Let's begin first with some general questions. Mr. James, what do you see in store for the writers?"

From under his cupped hand Al peered at the audience. "Let's ask the readers."

"Oh no!" his smiling host said. "We're asking the questions, Mr. James! First let's call on you to list some books worth reading!"

Al spoke to the audience: "Have you tried Geoffrey Chaucer's *Canterbury Tales?*"

The host's hand went up, but no others.

"George Orwell's *1984?*"

Only the host again.

"Ignazio Silone's *School for Dictators?*"

Only the host.

"Albert Camus's *Resistance, Rebellion, and Death?*"

No one had read that, and the host's face flushed deep purple. "Mr. James is a comedian," he told his listening audience. "He mixes jokes with pure fantasy in a futile attempt to mislead us. Nothing is documented, nothing is cleared with the Censor's Office, he asks us to rely on his word alone. As for the books he just mentioned, each one of them should be banned from our libraries, and soon will be. Rather than waste time on extinct 'literature,' Mr. James, suppose you tell us something about your own writing methods."

Al looked out through his fingers. "Well, I'll tell you," he said, leaning forward. "I start out from wherever I am. Usually that's somewhere down low. As with anything else, you know there are higher places above and you hope to reach them. The first half of a novel is like any other kind of climbing," he said, climbing onto his chair. He had regained control of his legs. "Sometimes you simply can't make it, you have to come down again," he said, stepping down to the floor. "At other times things go better," he said, climbing onto the host's table. "You find a good stride and you keep with it," he said, stepping onto an old toolshelf above, which supported him. "The first half of a novel is always the hardest," he continued, climbing onto a crossbeam. "You're not sure what you'll find at the top, if you get there, though there's sure to be something." He was on a narrow diagonal beam now and climbing. "To reach the halfway point is a wonderful feeling," he called from the hayloft, seated dangling his feet and facing his audience. "You may be shaken by what you see from there, but at least you know now you'll get somewhere, one way or the other." Thank the carrier pigeons, Vern Brown had not made a room of his loft. Leaning back, Al lifted the trap door and was quickly through. "You keep going," he called. The rickety ladder was no trouble at all, without his kit, presents, and glass. He gained the main floor in a matter of seconds, even without Burnsy to steady him. The guards were in Studio One, still craning at the ceiling. There was a back door to this barn, which responded to the same tiresome button.

Heading downhill, he did not walk on the trails but on the dry grass; it was faster. When he reached the parking lot he slowed, whether it looked good or not. Joan was in the back of the rig currying Carlos. Flip-flop, flip-flop—he stood watching a moment, making good his promise to Roy. "Hello in there!"

"Hello!" Joan called, and Carlos turned to look with her. "You too?"

"Yes, I thought I'd come down for a breather."

She went back to her brushing. "They seemed to be having a gay time up there."

"Yes, they did."

"I hate all this!"

"Let's try to think of a better word. . . ."

"I despise it!"

"Good, so do I." He watched switching tails for a while. Then, "Are you all right?"

"Oh, yes."

"Why don't you stay here with Carlos," he said. "I'll go up and see how things look."

"Be careful," she said.

"Never fear."

They exchanged little waves as he left her, climbing slowly up the trail. To one side a ground squirrel gazed at him from

out of his hole. Something about the sly look of the animal
made Al suspect that his tunnel ran under the trail. Had anyone else thought of that yet? He hoped not. The glass eye
blinked up ahead, and he waved as the door glided open.
"Thanks!"

"You again."

"That's all right," Al said as the guard grabbed for his coat,
almost popping Al's top button. Waving, Al adjusted his coat,
and the guard tended to his own buttons. Suzy Brown was
no longer in her shrine. She was seated on the trunk of Vern
Brown's go-cart, kicking her pretty toes in the air. Some sort
of meeting or forum was in progress. Everyone was seated,
on the floor, go-cart, or chairs, except for the speaker. Roy
and Doris sat on the floor; they had either been crowded
off their chairs or fallen off them. Roy was staring hard at
Doris, who stared straight ahead very red-eyed. Once she got
going no son of a bitch could stop her.

"I'm Janet Hillhouse. My field is the junior and senior
citizen," the plump speaker was saying. "We've been experi-
menting with a new hormone drug designed to bring such
people closer to the acceptable norm, help everyone find his
rightful place in society. It's still too soon to draw firm conclusions, but so far the results have been most encouraging.
Just last week one of our eighty-year-olds married one of
our teen-agers in a beautiful church ceremony. Perhaps you
heard what Helene Drake had to say about it on channel
nine. . . ."

"Yes!" Vern Brown's eyes shone.

The beaming speaker waited for the enthusiastic audience
to quiet. "Of course, we can't expect to bring respectability
to everyone overnight," she concluded. "But we're trying!"

"Yes!" Vern Brown said, evoking widespread applause.

Beaming, the speaker sat on the floor. Another lady nearby

got up from her chair. The floored lady grabbed for it, but was beaten out by a spry oldster behind her. The new speaker was thinner, her smile sharper. "I'm Patty Green. My special province is Gypsies," she cried in a high, quavering voice. "I have been zeroing in on the Evil Eye in particular." She paused, and snickers encouraged her. "I am going to go in and rid those poor people of their silly superstitions. I plan to get started on this as soon as possible. So if anyone knows where any Gypsies are, please let me know!"

"Yes!"

"My number," she cried above the applause, from the floor, "is 365-281-0500!"

"Yes!"

A tall young man in black suit and boots rose from his chair. Straight-featured, level-blue-eyed, he surveyed his audience coolly, waiting for silence. When he had complete attention, he smoothed a lock of silky blond hair back from his prominent forehead. "I'm Gaylord Smith. Homogenetics," he stated quietly, "is a relatively new science. Except for a few German authorities, the literature is sketchy, and for the most part misleading. Therefore I have devoted most of my energies to field work. Except for the aforementioned authorities, I have confined my reading to a study of genealogies, my own and others. My studies have led me to the acquaintance of, thus far, some one hundred and fifty young men and women with genetic histories almost identical to my own. The young men, all between nineteen and twenty-six, are built as you see me." He paused, throwing one leg ever so slightly to one side. "The young ladies," he went on, "are a little shorter. Blond, full-breasted, wide in the pelvic region but not too wide, with deep vaginas, they are all between sixteen and twenty-three. Once a month we young people get together and have a party. As the lady says, it's still too

soon to draw firm conclusions, but you can be sure there
will be some—in most cases," he added, with a little toss of
his hand and a flick of his hips.

"Yes!"

Nodding coolly to applause, the young man eased himself
onto his chair. A black sleeve shot up stiffly behind him. It
was not this man's turn, but he had something urgent to say,
and the lady whose rightful turn it was graciously deferred.
This man was tall too, though middle-aged. Standing stiffly,
he spoke not to the audience but to the soundproof ceiling:
"My name is Bill Hartman and my field is closely related to
this young man's." His shining gaze still uplifted, he placed
a fatherly hand on the young man's shoulder. "Genocide is
an even newer science, my friends, still largely unexplored.
So far I haven't approached my subject as scientifically as
this young man, but I attend lots of funerals. I take my children to them too." Some spittle or foam was running from
the corners of his mouth, but he made no attempt to remove
it. "The fear of death," he went on in a rapt, liquid voice,
"is our first hurdle. Once we overcome that, we'll be on
our way!"

His shining eyes dove to Vern Brown. Vern Brown did
not glow quite so warmly as usual, but he said, "Yes!"

Beaming proudly, the speaker fell out of sight in the same
sharp, stiff way that his arm had shot up. It shot up once
more, acknowledging applause.

Now the audience quieted down in deference to the lady
who had deferred her rightful turn. A buxom woman with
a motherly smile, she wagged a scolding finger at the man
who had so impatiently interrupted her. "Mr. Hartman, you
should be ashamed of yourself!" she said with mock indigna-
tion. "You've stolen my subject." Beaming at the applause,
she raised her hand for quiet. "I'm Filomena Boyles. There's

little more that I can add," she said, speaking seriously, "except that my concentration has been on the literature. In addition to the well-known German studies of the thirties and forties, it may interest you to know that some very important ongoing work has been undertaken by the good old U.S.A. and Russia and the Moslems, among others. At present this material is available only to qualified specialists"—she turned to flash a bemused, motherly smile at Mr. Hartman— "but in time we hope it will be released to the layman."

"Yes!"

The stiff arm shot up. "Let's hope we release ours before the Roosians and Mooslems release theirs!" the liquid voice cried.

"Yes!"

"No seconds!" Suzy Brown cried over cheers. "Next!"

"My name is Willie Wayne. My father is of normal size. My mother was four-feet-one. My older brother is of normal size. My sister is five-feet-nine and married. Her children are of normal size. My grandmother on my mother's side was five feet tall. My grandfather on my mother's side was three-feet-ten. My grandmother on my father's side was of normal size. My grandfather on my father's side was six-feet-three. My name is Willie Wayne. My father is of normal size. My mother—"

"Next!"

"I am Ortu!" Grinning happily at the applauding audience, Ortu raised his arms, crossed his wrists above his head, and waved his fingers. His feet performed a kind of jig below. Now his hands began to work the air above his head in a sensual, milking motion. Head tipped far back, his hands rounded softly about an imaginary breast or bottle, gently drew that to his gaping mouth. His full lips closed upon the teat or neck, blissfully sucking. Seemingly it was full to overflowing, from the length and loudness of his lipping, but even so Ortu stripped the last precious droplets with one tender thumb and forefinger, licked his lips and chin of droolings. From that soft receptive posture he suddenly jerked rigid, right arm flung one way and hips the other, eyes staring vacantly as at a rerun vision. He held that catatonic pose while almost everyone gave a standing ovation.

"Yes!"

Crossing his eyes and ankles, Ortu sagged floorward. The standing audience, but for one old lady, followed.

"I am Pris Lovejoy and my interests are closely related to Ortu's." She jerked into his same rigid stance and the crowd went wild at her feet. Now she relaxed, thumbs hooked in jeans, dainty right boot tapping the floor. "Cool it, kiddies," she said, and the audience fell silent. "My father was a missionary of normal size, and married," she said, her eyes twinkling. "My primary field is subliminal proselytizing. My secondary field is the American Indian. I know it sounds goofy, Jack," she called to an imaginary heckler in the back of the room, "but a gal has to start somewhere. I chose the Indians because I never know what the hell they're talking about, and they never know what the hell I'm talking about either. If I teach them something, nobody can accuse me of cheating, right?"

"Yes!" Vern Brown called, eyes shining.

Tapping her foot, waiting for the uproar to die down, she winked at him. "Those redskins have all sorts of nasty little habits," she went on, turning back to her audience. "They like to stand all alone on tops of mountains. They can't drink worth a damn. They listen to their mothers. Pretty soon they'll be mixing corn flakes in with their peyote. My aim is to straighten those kids out, teach them to do things comme il faut. I figure if we can teach them something, we can teach anyone. Comme il faut!" she said, jerking into position, her right hand flung up in a stiff salute to which the audience responded. She gazed down on them. "And if any joker thinks I'm kidding," she said in a lethal whisper, "let him try me."

"Yes!" Vern Brown said, all awry in his go-cart.

"Next!" Suzy Brown called as the old lady coiled herself up on the floor.

It was Roy's turn; jerking arms helped him upright, for his broad hips were dislocated. "I'm Roy Warner," he announced in a manly voice. "My specialty is current history. I've got one of the largest collections of films and tapes in south King County. Some of these people are mighty slippery. When you're trailing a man through the woods you don't want fingerprints, you want film and soundtracks!"

"Yes!"

"What about boot tracks?" someone called.

"I've got plenty of those too!" Roy promised.

"Yes!"

"Next!" Suzy Brown called, as Roy acknowledged back slaps. "Doris?"

Doris was rather red and heavy-lidded, so Roy slapped her face a good one. She slapped him back and stood up swaying. "Son of a bitch. . . . I'm Doris Warner!" she called loudly. "I'm no specialist, but I'm a lishener. I didn't catch everything that last lady was saying, but I heard what she said about the Roosians. She mentioned ginicide. Well, I believe in giving credit where credit's due. Now, the *only* thing I like about those Commies," she said, enunciating clearly, "they don't go for this democracy bit!"

"Yes!" Vern Brown's eyes gleamed brilliantly.

A wave of fervor followed. "Next! Next!" Suzy Brown

was calling, but no one responded. "What about you, Mr. James? We haven't heard from you yet."

Al waved to her from his corner.

"What's the matter, Mr. James? Haven't you anything to say?"

"Chaqu' un à son goût," he said.

"No!" Vern Brown shouted, and a hundred faces flushed deep purple. Vern Brown pointed. Al waved as a hundred pairs of fixed, gleaming eyes turned upon him. One tanned man in a distant corner caught his attention, and Al glanced back, *en glissant.* The crowd was closing. Standing with his back to the wall, Al held his breath against odorless sprays and gasses. Here and there gleamed needles. One man—Will Watson—aimed for the back of Al's neck, but Roy's new movie camera got in the way. Others aimed for his hands and arms. Good that he had kept his coat, had pockets. You never . . .

"The party's over, darlings!" Suzy Brown called above the clamor. "Don't forget George Washington's Birthday."

"Yes!"

Now faces glowed a little cooler, a few returned to smiling. Furious Roy and furious Doris pushed through the crowd, Al close after with turned-up collar. Sharp boots trod his heels but did not matter. Good that he had bony elbows. One pushing lady staggered, momentarily holding off pursuers. In the congested hall that tan man moved in close behind; Al nodded thankfully. The doorman hit him full in the face with Joan's sweater, no doubt well sprayed. Al gave that to Doris. No matter how grimly she and Roy tried, they could not shake loose from Al and his shadow. Those four slipped through the narrow door like a quartet of buddies.

Outside, the children were already waiting. Well-trained,

they did not approach but lounged here and there in small packs, leering. A few spoke of writing and writers, or waved comic books. Al waved too, obliquely at his friend getting into an old Chevrolet without license plates. The man waited there until Al and his escort reached the rig, then coasted downhill and across the highway to an unnumbered dirt road leading to somewhere not named. Roy summoned Joan, and Doris threw her her sweater. Al climbed in and forward without being ordered. He wondered if anyone had thought to give Carlos a breather, but he did not inquire. Carlos looked very well groomed, yet restless. Ah, Joan had cleaned up his floor, and a bit of dry grass was caught in one of his hoofs. Perhaps those electronic signals were making him nervous— was he supposed to stay on or off of that trail? He seemed relieved when Roy slammed the doors. Doris hooted something after, but they paid no attention. They were looking up at Vern Brown waving them a glowing farewell from his go-cart. Suzy Brown stood high in back, on the bumper. She looked ready to bail out at any moment. From here, Vern Brown's big head looked like a saniplastipacked parachute. Geronimo, darlings!

Tooting his horn, Roy made tracks to the south. Vern Brown tooted after. Al noted that his friend's dirt road disappeared among trees, his dust had already settled. His smooth tires left faint marks which the ground squirrels were already obliterating. The highway was crowded. Taking advantage of a hill and a curve, tooting Roy passed five or six wagons. They tooted back in falsetto. Glancing at one another, Al and Carlos shut their eyes; maybe what they didn't see wouldn't hurt them. Yet they could not go to sleep at this pace. Burying his head in his arms, Al forced himself to retrace the recent experience, from beginning to end, one purple face to another. . . . "Carlos, would you believe it?" He felt Carlos nuzzle the back of his neck, at the hairline. "Thank you, young friend," he said, for he was crying.

Animals have more hope than men. They don't know. Do they care? Men care, and know. It's almost too much for them. They want to stop. *Don't* stop, *don't* stop, whatever the lure. Who knows who then will care?

The rig jolted, swayed, squealed to a stop. Doors opened and slammed. Doris was screaming, outside Carlos' window. Outside Al's, Roy was hung up on his side-view mirror by the straps of his movie camera. Screaming Doris took off through the brush, her heels kicking up dust. Strapped Roy was cursing. Track on! Track on! Now Doris tripped on a tuft of grass or a gopher hole, lay writhing on the ground screaming for some son of a bitch to come help her. Finally free of the mirror though still badly entangled, Roy charged cross-country. He tripped too but managed to right himself. Arriving at Doris' side, he stood over her, catching his breath, disentangling himself from his camera. Or was he taking her picture? Doris kicked him hard in the shin and he stooped for her, threw her over his shoulder. He staggered back to the rig, Doris kicking and scratching.

"Get in *back*," Roy ordered Joan, and Joan obeyed quickly. Slamming the doors well, she joined Al on his ledge. They did not speak, but sat listening to the cab thumping. Doris was bent on spraining both her ankles, or breaking Roy's. They could hear Roy grunting. There were three sharp slaps, followed by silence. Some time later, the rig started up, ground into gear.

"Roy?" Al asked.

"Yes."

Gravel flew as they leaped onto the highway. Taking advantage of a climbing, tortuous mountain road, Roy set out after wagons which had passed him. This time there was no tooting, but brief glimpses of shocked white hands gripping steering wheels. Faces were obscured, for darkness was falling. A light snow was mixed with it. Joan and Al held hands tightly. If nothing happened they would soon be in Nevada, where the gambling men still had it. Then the Old Baby State, where the babies were tiring. Then New Mexico, where the cowboys were losing out to the national boys. Then . . . "Do you really want to go to Dallas?" he asked.

"No!"

Al reached for his kit. "Then let's get out of here before the holiday traffic hits."

Pressing his hand, she stood up to kiss Carlos on the cheek. Al touched it. Together they made sure that his lead rope was tight. They knew he turned his head as they moved to the back of the rig, but he could not see them well. Al opened only one of the doors, held it with one hand to prevent its banging. Seated on the sill, he drew Joan down beside him. "We'll wait for the next curve," he told her. "When you hit the ground, roll away like a ball."

"All right." She was shaking.

"Ça va bien?"

"Sí."

"Se habla español tambien?"

"Sí."

"Ya?"

"Ya."

"Ya!" he said, and they rolled out into the darkness.

They ended up on the side of the road within a few feet of one another, as the rig's red-lighted rear end disappeared around the curve. "O.K.?" he called.

"O.K.!"

He helped her to her feet. "Let's hurry then." Crossing the highway, they ducked among dark bushes and trees before headlights could find them. They did not stop climbing until they were well above range of the highest. Finally pausing, they threw back their heads, breathing deep. A few large snowflakes cooled their faces. "Any broken bones or bruises?"

"Not yet," she said, and he laughed. It had been a long day for both of them. Since the terrain was quite steep, they walked around the side of the hill until they reached a small canyon. There were no hemlocks back here, so he chose a young pine. He showed her how to recline on a bough, using higher boughs for arm support. The niches were not as convenient down near the bottom, but he found her a good one. He found himself another nearby, with one arm branch. Hemlocks were better, of course. Leaning back, closing his eyes, he relaxed tentatively. The temperature felt just right in here. Yet there was one thing he had forgotten in his hurry. He was starving. Tomorrow—

"Are you hungry?" she asked.

"What!"

"Roy and Doris had loads of sandwiches, so I stuck a few in my sweater. I thought you might be hungry. Are you?"

"Now that you mention it . . ." She gave him two, wrapped in wax paper. Tomorrow he would have to hunt up a water bottle for sure, but meanwhile these sandwiches were moist. These were deviled egg, and Greta had put her heart in them. He lay back, relaxing. Just five days ago at this time he had been dumping chocolate-coated ice cream bars between the pathé travelogues, and eating cold corn for supper. Not bad for your first night, 88! Maybe tomorrow would be better. You never lose hope. . . .

Joan sighed too. "This is wild," she said.

"Yes, it is," he said.

Down below, the snow was beginning to pile a little bit.

JOHN-JUAN

For Yvonne

The fast runner
runs ever faster
into the future
in quest of
present records.

Note: The first half of *John-Juan* was written sporadically from the summer of 1962 to the fall of 1963, the last half intensively during the winter of 1964.

D. W.

1

He arrived in town with his pajamas, his slippers, three NōDōz pills, and an uneasy feeling that he had known himself in better times. Normally he would have guessed that he had driven, what with those pills and that sense of having been slammed in alone too long, but when did a man drive off without his pants and driver's license, and he had no key. He might have delivered the car somewhere, of course, but in this attire? Furthermore, his legs, back, shoulders, neck, even his hands, had a marvelous tone; only his mind was tired. His feet perhaps were a little sore. He was not asleep: in a dream he would have clothed himself and been long gone from here by now, with safer thoughts. Awake he had less fine control. Nor was he drunk. He could not drink, these days, that much, he felt. He was cold-sober wide-eyed on foot in town, and the citizens were aware of him. They stared, not at his pajamas but at his watch. He had his watch.

It seemed to him that he had lived in Texas once, during a war, and that the language he now heard was spoken with what they had used to call a Texas sluh. Yet the words he heard here now were not so well rehearsed. Yet, again, he noted the high-heel boots that boosted little men up toward big empty hats (here and there a baseball cap) and noted fine wide leather belts, and it seemed a high proportion of Cadillacs, but with a giddy assortment of license plates which could not have told him much even had he brought his glasses on this trip, though since when had he worn glasses? Complexions, masculine, ranged he thought familiarly from white to rosy red to sallow outdoor man to citified Indian, and back and forth again. The pale ladies looked right in raven hair or bleached, with large dark eyes and dark brown teeth. Children were all their own, camouflaged in dirt and noise, free sample packages of wasted energy. In fact the adults too had preserved just enough of that vivacity, that eager communicativeness, to give them slight preference over those other Texans he perhaps recalled. Yet right off he could not make out what the hell they were talking about.

"A memento, pod?"

"Sir?"

The man, in little league baseball cap, had delivered him from a dozen overexcited boys, a muscular girl of four or five, a basket case on roller skates, several uncherished dogs, trained shock troops for who could imagine what reserves? They, the little old leaguer and John (George?), had found sanctuary in the vaulted entrance to a bank now closed and densely barred. John-George himself was seated on the top-most step, the old leaguer erect on the next lower one shielding him as best he could from spies. His blue cap bill pivoted left to right several times monotonously as though following a very slow exchange in the bullpen directly behind his back, his narrow eyes were live with plays, his little ears lay tight against his skull, his sharp nose was up, but when finally he allowed himself to look at John-George full face his gold-rimmed smile glittered reassurance, solicitation, guilelessness.

"Padre instead desire me *the time o' day*, pod?"

"You said?"

"Tender instead—laminable, dad—desire me—*the whore?*"

"Again?"

"Tinny instead—*the watsh*, pod?"

"Aha! Tinny instead the watch!" He liked that talk. They weren't making many good words for civilians these days; he remembered all about that. As with the horseless carriage during that war—military scientists drove the jeep while the populace brought up the rear in secondhand rattletraps. Conscientious mechanics worked these over as best they could, aligned and relined, bored and rebored, day and night. The greater the depreciation, the higher the price men paid, and went on trading among themselves until everything fell apart. When children and poets and old men in ball caps found the remains just lying around, they suddenly were new again, as Ford once meant, for life. But even children and old men can be mass produced, and the last poet will die not at twenty-five but at the moment of birth. Then the word will die a pushbutton antimissile-missile death. And the word is the world, instead, he thought, finding some comfort in the smile beneath the cap. He wanted to thank the man for saving him from the troops, but this man was tinny in love with a *watch*. It was an unusual one, the kind that pins to the clothing, pajamas in his case, and over the heart, tells not just the whore but also the day and the month. Somehow it did not seem to him the kind that he would have bought himself. With what? His slippers were not so bad at all, but his pajamas looked like hand-me-downs twenty hard years ago. If true, he was an ankle taller than his father, or whoever it was. "Padre instead *you admire my watch*, sir?" he inquired.

"Hmm, is *slow*."

"Ah?" Perhaps he was about to discover how many time zones he had come. "How much instead, you think? An hour, a day, a month?"

Hands flew up. "Keenan *knows*."

"Keenan?"

"A memento, pod." Tapping John-George lightly on the crystal, he crept downstairs to scout, flipped his cap backward on his head before he peeked out, flung sidewise his stiff left arm to caution John-George and bar the troops. After a tense moment his excited cap bill announced success, in pantomime, to his skinny neck. He returned to John-George's feet with a flying grin. "Is abierto, pod!"

"Keenan Abierto, sir, you say?"

Shrugging, his scout grasped John-George's watchside arm, high up, turned to peer over his shoulder several times before he rose on tiptoe to John-George's ear, breathed, "And a lay!"

"Sir?"

"And a lay, for the love of God. Come on, let's go, let's vamonos!"

They were in the street again with the beseeching troops, all of whom his scout soon outmaneuvered skillfully, except that basket case. No matter where or how they moved, that old soldier could not be lost. He had tied onto John-George's pajama leg with his strong front teeth. His breath was warm, his roller skates were in real need of grease. "Unmomento, suh!" It was a muffled cry through rending cloth: in pity and horror John-George slackened pace.

"Sir?"

"*And* a lay!" cried his scout, flogging the grey head with his baseball cap. "Screw off!" Wheels ceased grinding, John-George's pajamas clung limp and spitty to his leg.

"Unmoment—ah!"

His scout had dropped a coin in the old soldier's mouth.

John-George thought to give the soldier something too: not NōDōz pills. He was ready to hand down his watch, though he would have pinned to the soldier's khaki shirt, all there was left of the uniform. No chance for that. By now other troops surrounded them, all crying, barking for their fair share of bounty due, and his cursing scout lay about him left and right. Taking John-George almost roughly by the watch, he flogged them a path to an open door. The troops deployed. Inside the shop, his scout encountered the proprietor in a most respectful way, shoulders sagging, cap lumped in fist. "Good evens, Minster Dumas!"

"Buen-as tar-des, Zur-do." The proprietor's deep fat voice seemed to speak for itself, as all his inert weight balanced cross-armed on a glass countertop he had already cracked. Beneath his broad-brimmed hat two intent round eyes waited to be leveled at whomever the voice addressed; the portraits they snapped would be developed by the mind in its own good time. John-George, fingering his beard for the first time since reaching town, felt it to be a rough two days old. He believed he had known all along that he was bald.

Shutters flicked. "Bon soir, monsieur."

"Sir? Bon soir. . . ."

"Minster Dumas, tango for instead an pod that tinny an watsh muy *slow*."

"Un mo-men-to, Zur-do." Those portraits were developed by now: the eyes took four more, muy quick. "Bon soir, monsieur."

"Bon soir, monsieur."

"Vous parlez français, monsieur?"

"Un tout petit peu, monsieur. J'ai eu la freshman course, je crois."

Portraits by time exposure now. "Qué es, qu'est-ce que c'est, la *Frenchman course*, monsieur?"

"C'est le premier an de l'école, monsieur."

"Ah, oui. Oui . . . the frenshman course. Pablo Dumas, University of Los Angeles, nineteen forty-seven, evenings course, at your service, sir. Father of Montreal, mother of Mexico—English, French, and Spanish spoken here."

"Ah. A question, sir, if you please."

"At your service, sir."

"How many people live in this town?"

"People? Personnes ne vivant pas dans cette ville, pero se dice que hay vientiuno mil habitantes, sir."

"How far would you say this town is from Dallas, sir?"

"Dallas? Enfin, peut-être onze cent kilometers, mas o menos."

"How would you say the name of this town in French, monsieur?"

"In French! On ne peut pas traduire cet nom, señor."

"Merci beaucoup, señor."

"Rien de tout, je vous en prie."

"Minster Dumas!" John-George's anxious scout unpinned his watch for him, adroitly with his free left hand. "Tinny for instead an watsh muy *slow*."

"Zur-do." M. Dumas' stiffly pleated forehead folded slowly into his hat. "This type was born in the Rio Grande, monsieur, and has never swam to either side. Il parle seulement Tex-àne, c'est à dire Tex-ass talk." But he did extend one arm to accept the watch. "Sir, you want it *right away*, n'est-ce pas?"

"S'il vous plaît, monsieur—"

"Très bien. Zurdo, sirva al señor una taza de Nescafé entretanto, por favor."

"No, thanks, very much—"

"A memento, pod." His scout poured two large cups from the pot at M. Dumas' side, handed John-George the fuller one, sugared, stirred, so black it bruised the eyes to look at it. "Muy *hot*."

"Très bon." M. Dumas took up a magnifying lens close to hand, screwed it firmly into his right eye. He had a little pocket knife chained to his vest, with which he pried loose the back. Removing his hat, he groped a string that turned on the big overhead light, before he examined the watch. Now he blew on the works and injected a shot of oil from a nearby can which would have worked wonders on roller skates. Gently he rotated the watch so the oil would spread. After holding the watch briefly to his ear, he snapped the back tightly back on again, leveled his left eye at the working electric clock above the door. "Precisely one hour slow, monsieur."

"Just one?"

"Précisément." M. Dumas' big fingers delicately adjusted the time, extended the watch to John-George. "Tout prêt, monsieur."

"Merci beaucoup, monsieur." Precisely 18:05 P.M., sixth day, fifth month, what year, what calendar?

Returning John-George's half-empty cup to the counter, his scout looked anxiously toward M. Dumas. "Cuantos *much*, Minster Dumas, for the love of God?"

"No es nada, Zurdo. Rien de tout, monsieur, je vous en prie."

His scout sprang to John-George's side, held the pajama top taut for him to pin. "Solamente one Texan dollar!" he interpreted in a pleased aside. "Muy *cheap!*"

"Sir . . . ?"

"Muy *cheap.*" Nodding, winking encouragement, he tapped John-George's pocket or his breast.

"Aha." Pinned, John-George emptied the pocket for him. "Voilà, señores."

"Pod?"

"Monsieur?"

John-George placed the rattling box upon the counter between them.

"Monsieur, qu'est-ce que c'est?"

"Es NōDōz, monsieur."

"NōDōz?"

"NōDōz!"

His scout gave M. Dumas a look which M. Dumas returned in full, an amateur snapping a professional who was in the act of snapping him. Together they leveled at John-George next. M. Dumas was first to develop his prints. "Sir, you wish to *hock* your watch?"

"No, I hadn't thought—"

"Zurdo, vea usted si Señor Bustamante es todavia abierto, por favor."

Patting John-George's arm, his scout ran to the door for him. Flipping his cap backward on his head, he looked carefully outside for him. "Ay, pod," at last, "is closed," he said.

"Zurd-o, toma el señor a la casa de Señor Bustamante inmediatamente, por favor. Zurdo will take you to Mister Bustamante's house inmediately, sir." M. Dumas snapped two last candid shots of John-George before they left. "Hurry, *sir*," he said.

"If it pleases you, señor," and out the door.

The sun was just now sinking behind the Texas Liquors Store, but doing what it could to make the moon look warm: let all partners take comfort in that, a promise that in the morning they would have their star again. The troops themselves seemed not to care; they were all too intent on making the old soldier cough up that coin, by turns tickling and taunting him. But he knew well how to hold his tongue, and lay rocking on his rollers with a tight proud smile. Thus he repaid largesse tenfold, affording his leaders that many skate lengths' start to hock a watch, instead. John-George's scout took full advantage, ducked into an alley so thickly paved with yellow mud and ordure that all but the best-oiled wheels would quickly clog. Over the squelching suck of his own slippery tread John-George could too plainly hear the cruel clambering of troops in a rage to escape from a bottleneck. To his relief, Zurdo led the way into a wider, cobbled street: an old soldier would think twice before rolling there. Leaving a few obscene tracks to the right, John-George and scout reversed field to speed on tiptoe the other way, the farther side, gain the next corner before the puzzled troops picked up the scent. "A memento, pod," Zurdo gasped. "You run muy fast!"

"Ah. I used to aim at the four-minute mile, je crois."

What had happened to that? Tonight he panted after his panting scout, not holding the watch but clutching his heart. Yet he still had some kick left when his scout announced Señor Bustamante's house. They lunged in a dead heat against the door, facing the oncoming troops while they buzzed their host. There were two buttons to push, both operative: John-George's rang a bell, but Zurdo's set off an alarm inside. It wailed three times, about three seconds each. As the last faded out, running steps could be heard in the house, now a door, a scraping chair or box, a high voice through a hole above their heads.

"Quién?"

"Zurdo."

"Quién más?"

"An watsh."

"An what?"

"And a lay, for the love of God—open in!"

"Un momento, por favor."

"No más mementos—las tropas come!"

The door did open in, wide enough for Zurdo at least, and he held it so that John-George could slide through without scraping anything. Behind the door a young man with a weak mustache greeted them guardedly, a wooden chair in hand. "Quién más?"

"An watsh!"

"De verdad? Andale."

A man who did not lose poise even when not satisfied, he followed them down a long hall or court to another door, where another pale mustache whispered through a somewhat lower hole. "Quién?"

"Zurdo y un otro."

"Un momento, por favor."

The hole was closed, two voices could be heard inside, a zephyr consulting a thunderhead. Soon a reluctant key.

"Entres ustedes."

"After instead," Zurdo begged, but chair legs prodded them hospitably in. At that, their first doorman appeared to have preceded them, though on further look the second was of course his twin. This same pattern was faithfully carried out in quadruplicate or quintuplicate by the other men who remained seated at a large table in the middle of the room, each smoothing a very pale, very blond mustache while roughing up John-George with dark protruding eyes. Their heavy black locks had just been combed; they shone beneath the light of a three-balled chandelier of pure tarnished gold. The table was round, yet one man sat at the head of it. He was the one whose heavy hair suggested the possibility of scalp beneath, whose blond mustache was perhaps longer and firmer by some slight degree—at least it stayed in place without his stroking it. His stomach had been around some good many years longer too, but in the midst of such company one needed little imagination to see him young and slim, as he clearly saw himself. He had a young man's foot, in a blond leather boot which he held cocked beside his chair, ready for anything. While the others chose beer, wine, or whiskey to ease their thirst, he took whatever was close to hand, disdaining favor or fuss of any kind. He was the rumbling one. "Nacogdoches, muchachos, pense para un momento que tuvimos un refugiado de la bomba! Mary, turn the glassbrain television off, turn on the radio. Get the twelve-forty news."

Mary, partially hidden in an easy chair facing the television behind his back, crossed her big legs with a great waving of skirts. "Santa Ana," she muttered, but she did press the remote control button which was perched high on her lap, losing her sound if not her sight. A wave of her other hand sent a graceful young girl gliding to the radio. This girl knew her stations, knew her parents as well; she made her adjustments with a truly angelic neutrality. Back-to-back silence waited for the tubes to warm to rock-and-roll.

A fist crashed down, bottles leaped. "Try the birdbrain seven twenty then!"

Country style.

"O.K.! O.K.!" the big man roared, and cackling Mary returned to her set.

"Perdone, señor, we've all been a little nervous in this house today. This morning Jim sighted a flock of bluejays heading south, this afternoon Mary found a rattlesnake in the patio. Each of these events is uncommon here, in spring. You left Texas in a hurry, suh?"

"I'm afraid I did."

"Well, those things happen, suh. I notice you got out with your watch at least," he said, twiddling it. "Fifth month! Jim, check that date! I mislaid mine up there some years ago one night. I was a little drunk. I don't visit up there very much these days. I wait." The staggering remnants of his teeth aimed a barrage of spray at John-George point-blank, while his war-torn eyes estimated the effect. "I like Texas. I'm a native up there myself," he said, lightly touching his mustache. There were four fingers and a thumb on the hand he held out now, all still intact, and four stout gold rings. "Call me Joe."

"John-George."

"Minster Bustamante . . . !"

"One moment, Zurdo. Jim, did you check that date?"

"It's right."

Clapping John-George on the back, Joe said, "Tex, what are you drinking tonight?"

"That beer looks—"

"Betty, brew up a pot of coffee for Tex. He's a little tired from his trip. Open up a fresh can for him."

"No, thanks very much—"

"It's instant Lone Star, Tex. Jim, pull up a chair for Tex. That's a boy." Jim dropped the chair he had greeted them with, and Joe's sharp boot toed it up close for his guest. His slap on the back helped John-George to sit. "I like Texans. I'm a native up there myself. My mother, God bless her, was on a shopping trip. Ana María Alvarado Cortés de la Cruz, may she rest in peace. She met my father here in town of course. Sam Bustamante junior. He was a Pontiac salesman out of Houston—very fair," he said. "Betty, was that can full this time?"

"Daddy, almost."

"Texarkana, Jim! Get the inspection number from Betty, send him a congratulatory telegram. That address is San Antonio 21,052, isn't it, Sam Two? Tex, do you get up that way much?"

"Not very much. Not since the war, I guess."

"What war was that?"

John-George, having surprised his triplicate image in the chandelier overhead, looked once again. It was as though those shiny balls reflected themselves, after being rudely dented, punctured, cracked. He was in bad need of sleep, of course. "The one before last," he guessed.

"Well, Tex, you should see it now. As I said, I don't get up there much these days myself, but I hear S.A. is doing really great. Over half a million people all together there in the town, with a postal zone for every one of them. Imagine: all those Texans just sitting up there waiting, Tex. It makes a native sad to think of, doesn't it? Betty, is that coffee brewed?"

"Daddy, right here." She stood shyly behind their backs, waiting to be noticed with her steaming cup.

"That's a girl, set it right there," Joe said, chasing a boiler maker with a little mescal. "Say now, doesn't that look good? Sugar, Tex?"

"Please, and milk."

"Betty, bring Tex some sugar. Open a fresh bag of Lone Star for him. Where were we, Tex? Up in San Antonio? Half a million Texans just waiting up there to bite the dust? No, that Texaco map doesn't show S.A. that big. It's a little out of date." He nodded at a map on the facing wall, next to a calendar photograph of the Alamo, also out of date. At least the month was wrong, and squashed fly corpses hung rotting from the Alamo's walls and roof. "I like to go by the *National Geographic* map," Joe pointed out. "No roads, no dams, no population figures of any kind, just rivers, deserts, mountains, lakes, how it used to be." The *National Geographic* map hung to the right of the Alamo, with little plastic cereal box toys, pilgrims and ball players, rockets and cars, guns and guitars, pinned, no doubt strategically, here and there. "How it will be again," Joe predicted, crossing himself. "Betty, did they put in the right sugar this time?"

"Yes, Daddy. White."

"Amarillo! Things are looking better already, aren't they, Jim? I like Texans, Tex, even if I did misplace my watch. I can't understand why those others have it against them so. I'm nonaggressive myself. I just believe in being well prepared, then when someone is attacked I can launch a second front. I'm anti-imperialist too, but when the bodies happen to be placed in your river, what do you do? you take advantage of a natural bridge. You wait for the dust to settle up there, then you move in. You don't subjugate anyone— there's no one left. Oh, if you happen to find a few sick ones around, you mercifully put them out of their misery. And who's to challenge your right? Who else will want such a blasted place? You're just taking it back again, because you happen to be a native up there and you happen to like Texas how it was when you misplaced it one hundred and twenty or thirty years ago—except this time no damn cowboys and Indians." Closing one flaming eye, Joe gazed into a bottle of Lone Star high in the light of the chandelier. "Then you find you a nice warm cave, throw out the rattlesnakes, haul your supplies, and declare your independence from Mexico. Viva Nueva Texas, boys!"

The boys drank to that, while grunting Mary bucked her chair a few inches closer to "What's My Life?"

"More coffee, Tex?"

"No—"

"Minster Bustamante . . . !"

"Drink up, Zurdo. I don't *have* to work, Tex," Joe explained, twiddling John-George's watch with a ringed forefinger. "I just do it for raising funds." He let the watch drop, felt of John-George's coffee cup. "Friend, why didn't you tell me your coffee was cold! Betty, bring Tex a fresh cup of coffee, good and hot this time."

"No, don't—"

"No, I guess we won't need it, Betty. Save it for morning, hey, Tex? I guess you must be pretty tired from your trip. Our house is at your disposal, suh. Betty, make up a fresh bed for our guest."

"Minster Bustamante!"

"Will you be staying the night, Zurdo, or is your family expecting you?"

"Minster Bustamante, I try and bring an watsh for instead!"

"Pete, this beer is warm. Get Zurdo a few cold cans from the refrigerator to take with him instead. Here's a little mescal and bourbon for your wife, God bless her heart. Jim will show you out, old friend."

Zurdo accepted the bottles open-armed, waited smiling, nodding near the door while the cans were brought. His bright eyes rested on John-George for an instant, as if in thanks, but he did not attempt to speak. Jim only had to say "Andale!" to him, and Zurdo was out the door before Jim could lay on a helping hand. Tinnying so many bottles and cans it was not easy to see how he would put on his cap when he hit the street. Somehow he would, muy certainly.

"Betty, you have that bed ready yet?"

"Daddy, yes."

"You laid fresh white sheets on it?"

"Daddy, yes!"

"Tex, Betty will show you to your bed. Now if there's anything any of us can do for you, don't be afraid to mention it. Betty, lay out a fresh set of pj's on Tex's bed. Sam Two's should do. Sleep well, my friend."

He did not stand up. The others at the table joined him in lifting glasses and bottles and nodding good night, not half trying to hide little smiles of satisfaction with themselves. As soon as their audience had left they would burst into extemporaneous talk, congratulating one another on how very well they had performed tonight. Only Jim did not take part; he stood at the door between their small world and the other he had just ushered Zurdo out to. An onlooker could feel both wonder and concern for him. He probably knew all the lines better than any of them did, knew the response of the audience far more intimately too, yet there he stood stiffly aside with nothing at all to say for himself. Like all ushers, official greeters, announcers, broadcasters, undersecretaries, in fact all liaison men everywhere, he guarded a door he could not pass through, either to become a part of the act or to gain some saving distance from it. He could tell you what show was playing now, who was in it, when the next show was scheduled to start, and when it would end. One question more would someday be answered by him. When time came for the theater to burn down, he would be the first to sniff smoke. Interesting to see whom he would think to save first, the players, the audience, or himself. For his part, John-George was more than ready to leave the scene early, though this meant carrying with him the germs of disturbing ideas that might finally be laughed or explained away in here, yet would run all out of control when they were let loose in the outside air. He had been already on the run when he came in —he felt even less self-confident now. The world is no longer a stage but a tube, and we are the reflections of images in it.

But he was being channeled somewhere new, to a darker world where he would have time, if not to restore himself at least to hide. In the hall Betty smiled at him and took up his hand, and with that his day began to take shape, for this was a moment he felt he could trust. Whatever else had gone before, this was a hand he could trust. Was he sure of that? He seemed to follow her freely enough, but why with this guilty sense of perhaps? Sometime he had heard it said that a man carries with him only the good things from his past, buries the bad. What of a man who found himself carrying nothing at all except flickering hope?

"Here's your room."

A tiny one, crowded with a single narrow bed that did look white and fresh against the dust. No window, but at the other end was hung a heavy cloth or canvas that served to separate this from some larger place, as on a post office box whose last holder had lately given both box and town up in disgust. On the floor you could still see the disgusted streaks of his fingertips. The lone piece lying whitely in there did not belong to him—God only knew which box they were cramming his own mail in.

"Excuse me, I'll be right back." She stepped lightly aside, playfully tossing his hand away.

"No, if it's for pajamas, please don't bother. Mine will do."

"Daddy said—"

"Tell him his guest didn't wish."

"Well, will you be comfortable?"

"Yes."

"Well . . . don't you take off your watch?"

"Yes, I suppose I do."

"Here, I will." Closing the door, she came to him where he stood in the center of the room, or the narrow standing space between wall and bed. This near she looked not so very young, he could see how her body swelled in ways not shown by her loose childish dress, and her eyes revealed more than he himself at the moment seemed to know. Yet her hands played upon him with a child's straightforwardness. "It's cute!"

Dangling between them on her stiff little forefinger, it was all of that. "May I take it to bed with me?"

"What?"

"Oh, come *on*," she said. "Please! Oh, you!" She had started to drop the watch inside her blouse, but now pressing a hand to the gap up there she bent forward to slip the watch up under her skirt instead. He was allowed a good glimpse of what she had under there—no pants, but above her plump thighs a thin, very pale mustache which she must often have stroked with pride. He watched the little pink mouth spread round and wide to swallow his watch with flattering appetite. Now the curtain dropped, Betty backed bowing, laughing to the door. She waited until she was in the hall, to sing, "I'll be just next door if you need your watch!"

"That's all right."

Too weak with laughing to close the door, she wriggled her fingers at him. "What time do you want me to wake you up?"

He tried to show her a fatherly smile, though he felt he did not have it straight. "That's all right," he said again, and firmly closed the door. Now he rested against it, not for long. He was wide awake, his bed looked all too fresh for him. Beyond the canvas there were other beds, as he had guessed, and windows too, all opening onto the rattlesnake patio. He had little difficulty slipping between bent window bars, and he dropped to the tile below on tender slippered feet. Betty was in fact just next door; he faced her through an open window three feet away, but she had her head thrown back listening to his watch. Had it stopped? He could not say, from the expression on her face. He had no idea whether it was shockproof, supposed it was hermetically sealed at least.

He backed in semidarkness until he reached laundry tubs. Climbing in, he was able to vault himself onto a wall that separated the Bustamante from the next-door patio. Now he edged the darker way until he came to a chicken nest or roof, tarred and feathered each night anew. Moaning radios absorbed whatever squelching sounds he made. He hurtled some sleeping hens and a cock that did not crow. Dogs barked but not at him, at night in a patio. The roof gave onto an alley dark enough to be impenetrable, but as soon as his feet hit mud he took off in what was if anything the less popular way. At the corner he came upon a clearer choice; the town lay left and he ran right, in the foul ankle-sucking scum bordering a ditch of stinking soup on which floated a slice of hard-boiled moon. Now he seemed to hear the splash of troops not far behind, and perhaps the stealthy screw of greasy wheels. He bore left, probably west, hoping to find dry land somewhere.

He had not known they had a transcontinental fence in such good repair, a high wire fence, so finely meshed as to have been erected for the defense of mice, joint venture no doubt of the ASPCA and the Department of the Interior. By the time he veered from it at the sudden grassy edge of town he no longer feared pursuit, yet his flying slippers did not stop until they reached the jagged, painful shadow of a concrete stadium, all cracked and crumbled from standing thirty to forty years in the center of an oval parking lot. Had he made the four-memento mile at last? Hands on hips, he caught his breath. It was quiet here! and deserted but for a few furtive cats or dogs and joyous bats. He picked his stumbling way along the wall. The main gate swung open to the ticket booth, but the cheap and easy way was through a narrow

slot with an arrow pointing down and out. He sidled in, to
the moon's roundhouse. She was using only half of it tonight. After a brief exploratory trot he chose a good bench
on the shady side, not too low, but not too high up. Stretched
on his back, he remembered the stars and felt that they remembered him. A cool breeze, too gentle to raise the dust,
wafted him a faint odor of stale dung and beer and blood.
Turning on his side, away from the light, he contributed a
fresh pint or two of instant steaming Nescafé. He thought
to wonder what kind of teeth he had, whether they would
require a brush, but by now he was too sleepy to find that
out. He was beginning to feel right at home down here, without his watch.

2

He awoke not on his side but hard on his back, one eye shut
and the other blind. Cupping a palm over the staring one, he
began to see; that black handball he gripped inside was in
fact the perfect image of the three-quarter sun just now rising above the foot of his bed. Held so hard in his hand, it
slowly disintegrated in a serene explosion of light. Ah, those
fine fissures were tracks, of all the stars he had recorded during a wide-eyed night. What were those darker arabesques
that hung in his way now like a tatter of madwoman's lace?
Bat paths, of course. Good enough. He might never see with
that eye again, but he possessed one complete night. No, he

did not, for it was on fire and he lay watching it burn outside in. He held on as long as he could, until the last bat escaped through his fingers in a hurry of smoke. Now he tried to find his night again in the whorls and creases of his palm, but could not. However marvelous in themselves, they were not right; but they would serve to remind him at least. This, for a man with almost no memories at all, was a start.

He found what the problem was when he began to clean out his eyes: a tough yellow crust sealed the lids of his left, while a fine white powder propped open his right. Black eyelashes fell from the one; these he cleaned and aligned on the bench near his head, for they were glossy and young. Extracting a pure residue of NōDōz from the other eye, he sprinkled the lashes lightly with it before making a quick dash up the side of his bed.

He had chosen the right side, with a perfect view of space. For as far as the squinting eyes could see there was nothing save dirty sand laid flat by centuries of feet and hoofs and wheels, yesterday's bruises hiding permanent scars. Here and there a dismembered creosote bush seemed to mark the way to the end of the world. Halfway there stood one black cow or horse, with a lonely grey bird perched on his sagging back. Where else? The animal, it was a horse, did not even bother to switch his tail. John-George took his fill of free air before climbing back down. Then two brisk laps around the track, and ready for anything. He did have his teeth, and paused to suck on his gums, scrape with his tongue, spit a weak coffee into the drying black puddle beneath his bed. Refreshed, he left the sun's roundhouse boldly by way of the ticket booth, headed toward town at an easygoing pace.

Either no one had slept, or he was encountering the morning guard. They did look a little fresher, better disciplined, than the night before. Each patrolled his own sinuous beat carefully sidestepped by everyone else, for it had been assigned to him alone. Anyone could deafen whomever he cared to though, the air was free and each man had his quota of sales to make before bankruptcy was declared tonight. Fresh creosote branches, señor, a tin can with a handle on it, a flabbergasted Rhode Island Red? Defense bonds for tonight's attack? I see you in your pajamas, *sir*. Yet they did not waste much of their good time on him, as though they could not entirely trust him without his watch. Only at the Texas Liquors Store.

"An eye-opener on the house, señor?"

"Haven't had breakfast yet."

"On the *house*, señor."

One ushered him in while the other poured.

"It will kill the germs of the night, señor."

Wilt the tastebuds first.

"You like it, señor?"

"Mmm-ahhh."

"Fresh tequila from Tampico. One Texas dollar per liter or quart—fifty percent discount if you have your own jug."

"Ah, mine's at home."

"First will you sign our guestbook, señor?"

"With pleasure, señores."

"With name and address, please."

John-George, John, George.

"Señor, a testimonial?"

Stronger than NōDōz, stronger than Nescafé.

"Mil gracias! See you tonight, señor!"

"Tonight!" Now he knew better how to go, now that his beat had been assigned to him, out the door and to the right, up on the curb, into the street, keep to the shade, avoid the heat, until the office was in sight. He was a little late. Joining the anxious line, he leaned forward with the rest to observe what the early ones up front received. One man got three! At such a rate, would there be any left? A sigh went up whenever one turned away with empty hands. Poor man, it is so sad for him, but it gives us fresh hope. But why is this line beginning to move so fast? Have they run *out?*

"Sir, your name?"

"John-George."

"Is that J-o-r?"

"No, that's G-e-o."

"I'm sorry, sir. Return at half past twelve, when the airmail delivery arrives. We receive it directly from the airport, sir, by truck."

"Oh, good."

"Be here early, sir."

"Thank you, señor, I will."

Outside he found himself not moving quite so well this time; that eye-opener had set off a series of internal eruptions that threatened to open his navel up. He was starved, and everyone was offering him delicacies he could not in all conscience accept, without his watch. He engaged one or two in talk, Qué es, señor, qué es, mmmmsnuff, managed thus to inhale a little of the burn if not the bulk. Each child sucked a length of something good. Hm, qué es, my son, he inquired of a tiny one, who swallowed it. Slugar cane. He took his slippers off and offered them, My slippers for a tortilla, señoras, but they only sniffed for they all had husbands with daintier feet. Stopping to slip them back on again, he stood shining their toes by turn on his pajama legs, smiling and nodding at whoever looked. Most of them smiled and nodded politely back. Many stopped. He soon had a smiling, attentive audience, but no inquiries or offers of any kind. When one began to strum his guitar, John-George stole away on shiny toes. They did not comprehend. He slunk on until he came to a Woolworth store. Here in the window foot-long hot dogs, hamburgers, cheeseburgers, steakburgers, Texas style, were on display; to him they would have looked all too real even without the Texas flies on them. He singled out the fattest, healthiest fly, mired deep in the juicy dog, imagining himself to be. That's right, relish is always good. Yes, mustard too. Now, *meat*. A tap on the shoulder startled John-George, the fly hove off.

"Ten o'clock, amigo. Time for a coffee break."

The man who guided John-George through the swinging Woolworth door had the air of a steady customer, one who did most of his shopping here and liked to acquaint newcomers with his find. He maneuvered among the counters in a relaxed, proprietary way, inspecting rapidly the arrangement of goods on either side. No question but what the man had taste, he chose the cosmetic-jewelry route over the bric-a-brac–chinaware, eschewed candy for desk supplies, veered left off toys. Returning the smile of the ladies' wear clerk, he glanced at John-George from the corners of his eyes: Man, with a few more accounts like mine, wouldn't they be making it? Holding John-George's stool at the lunch counter, he said aloud, "They all speak English here," and, "Two javas, on the double, Concepción."

The menu spoke a kind of English too. John-George drew loose his eyes from the "Hot Dog Caliente, $3.25," while his stomach mumbled humble Esperanto to his host. The man feigned not to comprehend, although his neat dark suit and hat, his small black mustache, his full blue bow tie, bespoke an internationalist. He did pass John-George the sugar and milk. John-George poured in both up to the brim, bent to draw off the top.

"You're a Californian, gringo."

"I am?"

"Your label shows." His host straightened the collar of John-George's pajama top.

"What does it say?"

"Amigo, don't you know?"

"No," lowering his eyes, "I'm afraid I don't."

"Sleepwalker of Hollywood. Amigo, please, no offense. I would have known anyway. Your forehead is all burned on top. In New York and Texas all men wear hats. There's never that much sun in Oregon and Washington. With straight shoulders like yours you're not from the South. Inland everyone wears shoes and socks. Please, amigo . . ." His glance at John-George's shiny slippers contrived to be an admiring one. "Concepción, sweeten us up." Watching her pour, he advised, "You should use a nailbrush every night before bed, Concepción." Removing the sugar and milk from in front of John-George, he slid a skinny leather case in its place. The kind of man who could carry such a thing inconspicuously, he threw back its lid with a flick of his sleeve, proffered a brush to Concepción. "During the day you could use it to brush lipstick off your coffee cups."

"Ha, we sell those brushes here."

Reversing the brush, "With name embossed?" What about that, CONCEPCION?

"Aya," she said.

"Three pesos," he said, and to John-George: "That's twenty-four cents. What, no sale? We'll nail her yet." Spitting on a napkin, he wiped lipstick off the lip of his coffee cup, handed it to Concepción red spitty side first. "You could use a new toothbrush, amigo. What do you call yourself?"

"Who, me? John-George."

The internationalist hunted through his case for quite a while, finally held a pink toothbrush up, with JUAN embossed. "Only seventy-two cents."

"Aya."

Eyeing the nape of Juan-George's neck: "Between times you could brush your hair with it."

"Aya."

"You could use it to brush the milk droplets out of your whiskers too."

"Aya." Juan-George used a paper napkin for that, but did not hand it to Concepción.

"Amigo, how long did you say you've been in Mexico?"

"About a day, and a night."

"How did you sleep in Mexico?"

"Very well."

"Amigo? You lodged out of town?"

"A little, yes."

"You'll be less tired tonight. What will you need, sleeping pills?"

Hot Dog Caliente, $3.25.

"What else?" Smiling his teeth, fingering his blue bow tie: "Amigo, please, I'm your friend. What else do you use? Can you remember that?"

"Please pass the sugar and milk?"

You only had to ask the amigo's friend, he swiped both from his next-stool neighbor who was just now reaching for them. But slid the leather example case instead. "You're from the East, gringo."

"How'd you guess?" asked that other one.

"Your beard—it inclines to the west when you're facing south. It's the prevailing winds. On the West Coast it would be inclining east. In the Deep South they wear them extra long to hide the face. Inland they don't wear beards anymore, they want to recognize a stranger at once. You'll want a good military brush, amigo, to smooth that out. How do you call yourself?"

"Hannibal Poe."

"Amigo? Will you be in town a week or two?"

"Fraid not," said Hannibal Poe, smoothing his beard to the east. "Got to get back to work."

"Concepción, sweeten us!" called the amigo's friend, and, "What do you do with yourself out there, amigo—paint?"

"That's right," Hannibal Poe mumbled from behind his hand, stroking south. "I paint."

"Amigo mío, I thought you did! Sometimes they'll fool you though, out West. Not out East!" The amigo's excited friend fumbled his case, fondled his bulging bow tie with fingers of his other hand. Now his left hand held a paintbrush up. "I have BEN," he said.

"Verdad?"

A quick trade: "And METH."

"Verdad?"

"I have MES."

"Verdad?"

"I have MARI."

Hannibal Poe looked to his wife this time. "You have?" she asked.

He had. "And HASH."

She muttered, "Verdad?"

"Also COD."

"Verdad?"

"I have COC."

"Hannibal . . ."

"Verdad?"

"There's more!" It looked like MORPH. He was displaying his wares in fast succession now, so fast that his giddy audience could make little sense of the names embossed. Juan-George probably just imagined he made out a PEYTE. "Here's a handy set," said the amigo's friend, holding up a matching pair in black and white. "Just the thing for man and wife." HERO and HEROIN.

The Poes seemed a bit impressed. They sat close together, eyeing the brushes and sipping their milk. Juan-George expected the amigo's friend to make note of droplets on the easterly beard, but he did not. He tugged at his bow tie until friendly words came out: "You only have to name it, amigo. Amigo mío, what do you use?"

"A broader brush." The thumb and forefinger of one hand spread out as wide as possible, wide enough to paint a house.

"Amigo? Nothing else?"

"Well, windows and woodwork. . . ." Thumb and forefinger drew together halfway, while Hannibal Poe finished his milk. "Ready, kids?"

The amigo's friend seemed to notice for the first time the blond boy and girl to Mrs. Poe's left, stuffing Hot Dogs Calientes into their swollen cheeks. His hand went for a yellow tube he had in his case, but he let it drop. "What do you use, amigos? Paste?" Retrieving his property from Hannibal Poe, he slapped shut and latched the lid. Up on his feet, he adjusted his sagging blue bow tie in the mirror behind Concepción, who had bent forward to add their coffees up. Now he unsnapped that lid again, came out with a shaving brush. "Amigo, you'll want to scrape that fuzz first chance you get, dummkopf," he said, handing it to Hannibal Poe with the coffee check. "How did you call yourself again?" The amigo's friend did not wait to hear; Juan-George glimpsed the brush before joining him. HARRY, it read, and Hannibal Poe had paid $6.50 for it.

They left the store by their same course, but this time the

amigo's friend showed less high regard, seemed almost to disdain the goods. He did glance cursorily at the brushes, probably to make sure that they were still unembossed. He did not hold the door for Juan-George, hit it hard enough for both of them. Outside he hit the sidewalk hard, in the way of a self-made man who had not waited to have his beat assigned to him. Wise hustlers made last-minute changes in their plans; these did not always take into account Juan-George trailing just behind. He was grateful when the amigo's friend drew up at the Texas Liquors Store, grateful too when the proprietor stepped inside and softly swung the door. Leaning hard against the glass, the amigo's friend surveyed the scene. "Amigo," he said at last, "it's a little quiet today in Mexico. Shall we cross on home?"

"On home?"

"Texas. Please, amigo, no offense. . . ."

"You live up there?"

"No no, not all night. I just keep my office there. The rent is higher and they give you a smaller box, but you get more numerals. You get a combination too—mine's JAG. That way, you have no key to tote. All you need to remember is your memory. Please, amigo . . ."

Juan-George smiled reassuringly, for his friend had given him, if not a memory, at least a clue to one. He had a combination too. His own identity hung on just such a shibboleth. If he could remember it, all he would have to do would be try the doors until he found the one that opened out, then reach inside. Whoever they had written letters to, that would be him. Suppose no one had written? He felt his heart miss a beat at this. Suppose his clerks had made mistakes? His heart flipped twice. Suppose they gave the same combination to more than one? He did not allow himself to think long of that, for he felt it to be a mathematical certainty and he had no time to waste. Something big was happening. His fingers were spinning dials, he was wild in love with the alphabet. "Mine's BJJ!" he blurted out.

"BJJ?"

"Yes!"

"Amigo, you're sure it isn't PJS?"

"No, BJJ!" Be John-Juan, it said (spin *twice*), for he had needed words to remember it by. Be John-Juan. Who had he been? "I used to have CJH," he said.

"You did?"

California Jams Heaven. "I am—I'm a Californian!"

"Amigo, we knew that. . . ."

"Please, friend, no offense. . . . Tell me, can you trust your clerks?"

"Implicitly. My inspectors too—they keep a close watch for me, always check to make sure I receive no mail that would do harm to me."

"Does anyone else have JAG like you?"

"Like me! Not here in town, they don't! Maybe in San Antonio."

"Offhand, how many post offices would you say there are in California, friend?"

"Amigo? I haven't been there in quite a while. I can find out for you. Will you be in town for a week or two?"

"No, forget it, please. It would take too long anyhow."

"Amigo, please . . ."

"Take *me* too long." California Jams Heaven—Be John-Juan—combinations to memories he felt he was not ready to open yet. Meanwhile he believed he could take a hint.

They had reached the fence, and his friend knew which way to go to find a hole in it. Most others went in their direction too, but some did not. Two men leaned against the fence to talk, thus it was not electrified. The one on the Texas side was short, the one on the Mexico took off his hat. As they talked they watched one another's boots gently kick the fence. Further along, a dog wet on it from the Texas side, but most of the benefit was received by Mexico. Fair enough, for Texas had all the river here, ten feet behind the fence. Birds perched on top of the fence. Interestingly, they all sat facing south. Thus Texas had a regular borderline, freshly sprayed in white. Black and red ants could be seen crossing it, carrying who knew what back and forth beneath the fence.

"Hold it there! Pull over here. Unload everything and spread it there." It was a uniformed officer. A big man with gun, he waited for signs of compliance before he smiled. Then there was no real suspicion in his attitude. If anyone had cared to shoot it out, that would have been another thing. Meanwhile he was only here to guard this hole, protect all mice inside. John-Juan's friend grasped his arm, drew him aside, for the man in custody was Harry Poe.

"What's that first name on that registration there?"

"Hannibal."

"Where were you first born, Hannibal?"

"New York."

"Where you heading to?"

"New York."

"What do you do out there?"

"Me? I paint."

"Painter, hey? This your picture on this driver's license here?"

"That's me, officer. I grew this beard down there in Mexico."

"How long she take?"

"Ten weeks."

"O.K., we'll be with you in a minute, Harry. Unload

everything and spread it there." The officer stepped in front of another car. "Hold it there!"

When Harry Poe opened his door his shaving brush rolled out with him. A battered white potty rolled out with Mrs. Poe. Commenting underbreath, they picked them up and after a moment's indecision set them over there where the officer had told them to. That was a start. Harry Poe's big car was full. John-Juan and his friend stood back to watch how he unloaded the rest of it. He had to unload the children first, feet foremost; they too were full, and for a while it was all wedged backsides, fat thrashing thighs and dirty kicks. They made it though, and now you could see a little light up top. Harry Poe skimmed a layer of blankets and pillows off, stuffed them backhanded out the door for Mrs. Poe to spread on a bed of motor oil or grease. Came a layer of suitcases next, some fumbled, some almost caught. She erected a makeshift stall of them around that pot and shaving brush, spread the bedding as a roof. Now Harry had orange crates, mostly of canned goods, dishes, pans, and Mrs. Poe set her kitchen up. He handed the radio out, but she wasn't ready yet. She wanted her hotplate first. There, that completed that. *Now* she was ready for her radio, and her phonograph, placed them side by side in the family room. Standing at the door with hands outstretched, she frowned over her shoulder at her new house. What did she lack? She was waiting for something, certainly, but all she received was Harry Poe.

"That's enough," he muttered. "Let's hit the trunk."

"Hannibal, the officer said—"

"The hell with it, let him look at it in there. It's only one layer spread out in there."

"Amigo, shh, the place is bugged," whispered the amigo's friend, too softly for anyone but John-Juan to hear.

The uniformed officer was just sauntering by. "How we doing there, folks?"

"O.K., officer. Just about to hit the trunk."

"We'll be with you in a minute, folks." He had to step fast to order a driver to hold it there before he parked all over Mrs. Poe's porch. Now he had to make sure that driver understood where to spread it, but he returned as soon as he could. He leaned on Harry Poe's door, but did not seem curious about that layer in there. He would rather smile at the girl in the living room. "Well, blondie, guess you'll be glad to get home and see your boyfriend again?"

She tittered at him.

Mrs. Poe, in the laundry, laughed. "I'm afraid she left her boyfriend in Mexico."

"Amiga, shhh. . . ."

The officer sprawled even more slackly over Harry Poe's door, caught up his smile almost as soon as it fell. "That right?" He winked at the staring boy.

"She means José!"

"Amigo, no!"

Smiling, the officer stood himself up on his feet. "That right?"

Titters confirmed it was.

The officer stretched. "Carry on there, folks. We'll be right out." He sauntered smiling off.

"Amigos, he's going after the orangutan!" They all looked up, and cursing Harry Poe hit the trunk hard with his head. "Amigo, shh!" They watched the officer saunter to a glass cage in back, peer inside before he opened the door. He opened it just a few inches at first, then stiff-armed it wide and high enough for a pair of long, uniformed arms to swing out. "Amigos, he's heard and can understand every word that's been said!"

The orangutan was wearing dark glasses beneath the visor of his officer's cap. His holster and gun swung low on his hip like a sidelong cock in a horsehide jock. They must have lowered the specifications for him, he was scarcely of shoulder height, but heavy-set and long on ears where short on neck. He was mostly shaved, what you could see of him. He only glanced at the other cars, swung sidelong for the Poes'. One arm went in, jerked forward the front seat, jerked at the bottom layer in there. "Everything—out!"

"Amigo, quick!"

Harry Poe moved around to the other door, slowly and with warily lowered eyes. "Easy there, Jocko," he murmured, but Jocko had already started his swing among the other cars. Harry heaved four big boxes out, and Mrs. Poe let them lie where they fell, in the vestibule. Slapping the front seat straight, he went round back to hit the trunk: there was one layer in there he had almost forgot. He helped Mrs. Poe tote the orange crates to the family room, but dropped the ammo box right there and sat on it.

"How we doing there, folks?"

"Everything's out," muttered Harry Poe, wiping his hands on an old khaki shirt.

"Be right with you, folks."

Here came Jocko now, sidearm swinging at double time. He went for a front door first, flung wide, jerked that seat, hung low in there for sniffs. He swung all grey-nosed to the trunk, could hold the door high high in the air even while doubled so low at the waist, or belt, that Harry Poe peered over his head with ease from the ammo box. Withdrawing, he did not pause to wipe his nose or scratch, but began at once a swinging tour of Mrs. Poe's house. "What's that?" His shod toes kicked out at the suitcase stall, and Mrs. Poe lifted a corner of the bedding up, for him to snuff. "Everything—out!" he said, squatting low. The suitcases he un-latched himself, left Mrs. Poe to attend to that other and the shaving brush. He had jobs enough to do for the Bureau of Inspection and Security. His harried hands groped Mrs. Poe's underthings in the way of a man who knew well what he was looking for; he felt twice of some; some he used for wiping dust, under the guise of snuffs. He glanced up once, at Mrs. Poe, at her daughter, back down again. Harry Poe's shirts he held aloft for all to see how pitifully inadequate were the sleeves. He didn't even bother to unfold those crazy long pants; but did take hard note of their obscene flies right out there in front. Pushing to his feet, he left the suitcase for Mrs. Poe to repack and latch.

"What's that?"

Mrs. Poe did not reply. He was only making conversation anyway, he knew he was in the kitchen now. Stooping, he rummaged disconsolately through the canned goods for a while, as though hoping to find an opener. Pots and pans he was disdainful of; he already had an official hat approved by the Secretaries of Defense and State. His eye was on the family room, those orange crates. Squatting once more, he lifted a baseball bat, a hunting knife, a water gun. He held up a cowboy suit, this time did unfold the pants: except for that awkward fly, they were a bit all right. He folded them neatly, tucked them back before hitching himself over to the other crate. Now he seemed to have softened a little bit. At least he lifted dolls with real gentleness, laid them carefully side by side upon the floor, all heads pointing north. For a moment it almost seemed he sought a change of clothes for them. Ah, he only wanted to get at the Parcheesi set, the tiddlywinks, the jacks. He did not play these games himself, but a glance at the girl hinted he could be taught. Lowering his eyes, he reached one arm into the living room for the radio, placed it beside the dolls. He did the same with the phonograph. There, that looked much better now, if what was wanted was a family room.

But back on his feet again, the little twitches around his mouth stiffened themselves into a grimace as he entered the vestibule. Grunting, he skidded those three big boxes into the living room with his hands and feet. After he had caught his breath, he kicked the biggest first. "What's that?"

"Towels and sheets."

He had no time for such, gave the next a harder kick. "What's that?"

"Hannibal?"

"Damned if I know," Hannibal grunted from the ammo box.

"Betty and Bill?"

"That's books."

Jocko was quickly asquat, but his fingers plucked at the rope ends with a strange unhurriedness, trying for the tricky one. There was no need for haste; those books would still be there when he got in. Finding a loose end at last, he gave it a little tug, drew it with great care out of its knot, then suddenly flung the rope away from him. Turning up all four flaps, he studied, but not for long, the newspaper spread on top. He knew, he knew. One hand dipped in, brought out books. There was a frown about the eyes as he examined both their spines. Turning them over, he thumbed rapidly through the strange tale of *Black Beauty The Wizard of Oz*. Now he picked up others one by one, squinted, thumbed. *The Murders in the Rue Morgue* he already knew. Not *Heidi* though. This he began at the beginning, the title page, the copyright page, page 1, plucking with those leisurely fingers of his which he licked each time, until he came to the middle of page 23. He opened *Webster's Dictionary*, licked, thumbed, licked, ran a forefinger here and there, but soon gave that up too. However, he did return to *Heidi* long enough to scrutinize that spine once more, as if committing to memory before adding it to the pile. He piled in rapid handfuls now—*Babar The Greatest Story Ever Told, Babar's Children Bambi and Boise, Babar's Friend Stephen Little Frankenstein*—he was looking for something in particular. But he paused with *The Fanny Farmer Cookbook* in his hand, glanced at Mrs. Poe. He knew, he knew. That one he placed in a separate pile for her. *Babar's Guide to Mexico* had him puzzled though; he glanced from one to another at everyone, finally gave it to Harry Poe. No, on second thoughts he added it to that other pile, since he was not sure. He might not have been so quick to change his mind had he known how near the end he was. In fact he had reached bottom now, for he did not count that newspaper folded there.

He had one more box, box three, to kick. "What's that?"

"Betty and Bill?"

"That's pictures and paints."

Aya. Squatting, he looked knowingly at Harry Poe: they were getting somewhere, finally. His fingers plucked just a little faster at those ends, he was getting the hang of them, found the sliding one third try this time, jerked hard and flung it far aside. All flaps went up, both hands plunged in. He did not even need to open the watercolors set, but glancing sidewise at Harry Poe placed it where he had been about to place *Babar's Guide to Mexico* for him. Pictures, though, were not to be treated casually, these were to be given undivided attention to, one by one, some to be held in front of the nose not just for sniffs but for close appraisal of texture, length and breadth of strokes, others to be held at least four feet away, better to get the total view. More than one delighted him: a fine split-level house, with a smiling face at each window on the first and second splits, a big front door, with knob, an antennaed roof, a chimney with black smoke curling out of the chimney top, a path and a green tree in front, a big smiling sun up in the sky. Equally good, a red smiling cat, with whiskers and tail and everything—you could make out the green mountain in back, beneath the frowning moon and the smiling sun. Also, full-page, a big old tree or antenna with birds singing on it under the smiling moon alone. And a split-level house with a smiling face at each window on the first and second splits, a big front door, etc. And too, a big smiling mouse with the whiskers, the ears, the antlers, the tail, and everything in place. After viewing twenty or thirty of these, Jocko had to look admiringly at Harry Poe. There was something to this painting thing after all; he kept an open mind toward it. Meanwhile he stacked those pictures neatly, edges straight, on top of the water-colors box, picked up another folio.

These were drawings, mostly in pencil, crayon, a few pen and inks. Jocko approached them with the same open-minded respect the watercolors had aroused in him; he nodded once or twice as he shuffled them, but careful observers could not help but note the enthusiasm slowly ebbing from around the eyes and nose even before he began to frown outright. There were one or two houses here, but for the most part this was portraiture, portrait after portrait taken from the life, of Mom, Dad, Betty, Bill, alone, in groups, some full-length and clothed, some bodiless, some in the nude. Very good like-nesses, yes, no doubt, but with it seemed an almost morbid preoccupation with certain private parts. Bodies, whether clothed or not, had little bald belly buttons in their midst, with not one modest hair to hide behind. Many had bare tits above. One picture in particular held Jocko's eye, a self-portrait obviously of Harry Poe. Here were not just the belly button, the tits, but, dangling below, the hairless, self-centered cock. Each time Jocko turned to it his nose would twitch, his jaw would jut; his hands shook noticeably. Each time, on-lookers held their breath: was he going to confiscate? No, it seemed he wasn't ready to take that step. Letting drawings drop just anywhere on the floor, he lurched to his feet, ap-proached Harry Poe. One foot shot out. "What's that?"

"That's an am-mo box," said Harry Poe, but he made no move to get off of it.

Jocko's right hand swung to his holster, and for a moment it looked as if he were about to commit public indecency; but he thought twice. So did Harry Poe. Rising from the ammo box, he left Jocko to work out the combination of key and lock.

Jocko, squatting, studied both keys very carefully, for they were identical. Having finally chosen one, he inserted it painstakingly in the lock, tried it left, then right, again left and right. That wasn't it. Patiently he turned the key upside down, inserted it. Still no luck. Now he inserted the other key and a twitch of pride went across his face when it sprung the lock. His expression changed after he had thrown back the lid, for what Harry Poe had was old tools in there. For a moment Jocko's left hand hefted a monkey wrench, then he let go of it, climbed to his feet. "Everything—back!" and he swung sidelong for his cage again.

"Not him, the other one! Watch the other one!" whispered the amigo's friend, for John-Juan to hear. "He's about to give Harry a shot of the turista sickness, a farewell dose. Watch!" Sure enough, while everyone packed, the smiling officer dusted Harry Poe's steering wheel with a little brush he had. "Now he'll give the girl a dose."

"Ready to go, blondie?"

Tousling her hair, the officer dusted Betty's purse for her, and she tittered at that.

"She won't be back to visit her boyfriend soon," whispered the amigo's friend. "Won't they all be glad to see New York again! That's right, hold onto that!" he hissed, watching Mrs. Poe return that potty to the car. "The assholes will be crying for it soon enough!" He nodded enthusiastically as she tucked it under the front seat this time.

But now, adjusting his tie, he picked up his example case. "I sold them that brush myself, with ADIOS embossed. Amigo, you'll want to watch yourself; they'll tag your wallet if you don't look out."

"Wallet?"

"Amigo, no wallet? I thought you probably had it in your money belt."

"No money belt."

"No . . . ? Don't even try, don't even think of it!" Shaking his head, the amigo's friend stuck a pink toothbrush in the pocket of John-Juan's pajama top. "See you around, Mex," he mumbled, giving him a final pat.

John-Juan watched him saunter to the cage, swing his example case onto the counter and hold it there. He had started to spread everything out, but the officer waved him on. The careful man took his time, rearranged his brushes with patient hands, lowered and latched the lid, adjusted his drooping blue bow tie in the window glass. Then, after a little farewell salute to the amigos, he headed for the office with his combination in his head. John-Juan waited until his friend was out of sight before he turned BJJ toward town again.

3

Now with a toothbrush peering from his pocket he felt himself somewhat overdressed. If the other denizens had such things they did not wear them ostentatiously. He frisked himself, to make sure he had no money belt to put it in. None, of course. Almost he was ready to discard the brush, slip it casually through the fence, but at the last minute he could not: AMIGO was embossed. Neither could he think where he might make use of it. It was too early to return to the Texas Liquors Store. Besides, he had at least one prior appointment that he must keep. He tucked the brush beneath his arm and hied himself.

Turning onto a familiar street, he found the office soon enough. He was early: one clock said twelve, one said twelve-fifteen perhaps. He joined the patient early line, had time to examine boxes to his left. They all took keys. He began to understand all too well what his friend had meant, for if his own box had required a key the odds were good that he would not now be carrying it, while he did have his combination in his head. He pondered what to do with it; perhaps he could request that his mail be forwarded. From where to where—from BJJ to General Delivery? Even his friendly clerk would smile at that. He had raised his window now, and this afternoon John-Juan was sixth. Things looked good: the five before him were all having luck.

"That was J-o, wasn't it?"

"J-o. That's right."

With so much mail still to be distributed, it took his clerk quite a long time to look through it all. When he had looked through once, he started at the beginning again, flipping letters only a little more rapidly. Finally he shook his head, but still his fingers flipped. "I'm very sorry, sir. There doesn't seem to be anything."

"Aya."

"You could try the four o'clock from Mexico." But he looked at John-Juan rather doubtfully, not wanting to seem to hold out too much hope.

"Fine, thanks very much."

"Sir, sometimes it's late."

"Oh? Many thanks."

"The other day it didn't arrive till night."

"Aya . . ."

"The post office might be closed by then."

"Aya," again.

"Sir, why don't you wait for the morning mail! That way you'll save yourself an extra trip."

"Thanks! I'll wait!"

"The first delivery arrives at nine."

"Thanks!"

"We open at eight o'clock."

"Oh, fine! And thanks!" John-Juan turned away from the window with a little wave of thanks, believed he saw his clerk give a little nod in acknowledgment.

"You can read my letter, sir, if you wish!"

It was one of the lucky five, number two or three. Her letter had been the biggest one. Now she held it up high for him to see, all unfolded out; a full-page letter it was, in type, and single-spaced. He could see the envelope too, and the

airmail stamp on it. Aya. She fluttered the letter and smiled
so invitingly he could not feel nosy about taking it. "Out
loud?" he asked, and seeing her nod enthusiastically he began
to read. " 'Dear Mrs. Ramírez,' " he read. " 'This letter will
come as a surprise to you, *do not* tair it up. You have been
chosen by a devote freind to receive a Crown of Glory such
as few ladies in our time have been flavored with—' "

"Not here! Not here!" she whispered, almost snatching
her letter away from him, and folding it. "That's what I
thought it said!" She grasped his arms so suddenly and hard
his toothbrush dropped.

"A memento," he said, holding back for it.

"Aya! Please pardon me!" Now she took his other arm,
hurried him out of there. "This way," she warned, in time
to let him make a sharp left turn without dropping anything.
She turned left again, then right, in the same fast, considerate
way. No one even tried to follow them. At a prewarned time
they stopped, in front of a house much like and linking all
the rest, but lavender, with a fine wrought-iron door that
matched the window bars. She had a purse, but she did not
fumble in it. Her key was in the right-hand pocket of her
dress, where she knew it had to be. John-Juan caught the
swinging door, but she prodded him graciously ahead of her.
Slamming the door, she waved at a little table in the hall, with
a lovely cloth on it, and he placed his toothbrush there. It
was that kind of house, with a place for everything, everything in its proper place. Following Señora Ramírez down
the hall, he caught a glimpse of the TV room, even the rabbit
ears had an uncommon grace. In the kitchen-dining room
eight to ten children sat up straight at a huge sturdy table,
their eyes and their dark hair agleam, all of them ready for a
beautiful young woman to serve their dessert. It was bread
pudding probably, but in her hands it looked like whipped

cream cake. At the loaded sideboard there was a cleared space for her own plate, at exactly the right height for her to eat standing up.

Señora Ramírez stood to one side, better to show off her guest. "Sir, I haven't the honor of your name," she said.

"John-Juan, señora."

"Niños, please have the honor to make the acquaintance of Mr. John-Juan. Dolores, please meet Mr. John-Juan." Dolores curtsied, smiled, and her whipped cream cake had a ripe pomegranate topping it. "Arturo . . ." Señora Ramírez introduced each one of them, Arturo, Alfredo, Francisco, Juan, Juanita, Louisa, all of them, and each stood up from the table to bow or curtsy for John-Juan. There were nine, including Dolores; he kept a close tally of his own bows.

"Please sit down, sir! Sit down!" Señora Ramírez finally begged, waving at a large divan against the wall. "Have you had your lunch?"

"Señora, not recently."

"Sit down! Sit down!" she cried, waving at the divan again. "You'll want a little mescal first! The children are almost done."

"Excuse me, sir. . . . Pardon me, please. . . ." The children stood up and filed out of there, licking whipped cream from their lips. Eight of them. Dolores stacked their dishes before curtsying. "Please pardon me, sir." She left the room, after John-Juan had bowed, taking that pomegranate along with her. By now Señora Ramírez had his mescal placed on a little table beside the divan, was bringing nuts. Her own glass was on the same sideboard Dolores had partaken from, but a higher shelf. "Sir, salute your health!"

"Salute yours, señora."

Returning her generous smile, he sipped, swallowed in

time to whisper thanks to her offer of nuts. Thankfully he watched her turn to the sideboard for her mail, select that letter from two others she had received as well, probably in the nine o'clock. "Where do you live in the United States, señor?"

"California."

"Ah, I will visit there someday. They say it is beautiful!"

"Yes, they do."

"My letter is from Phoenix, Arizona. That's out that way. Have you visited there, señor?"

"Not recently."

"They say it is beautiful in the winter there!"

"Yes, I hear."

"My oldest son, José, works there, in the factory. Sir, those are your nuts there."

"Aya?"

"His wife, Anita, is North American, she was born up there. She writes a lovely English, doesn't she?"

"Aya, she does."

"Anita writes much too good for me. Will you have the goodness to read it out to me, señor?"

Accepting the unfolded letter from her hand, he said, "With much pleasure, señora."

"Let me give you a little mescal first, señor!"

"N . . . thank you very much."

"These are piñon nuts." She gave him hers. Under her gracious smile he took a sip from his brimming glass, to clear his throat, then nibbled nuts, for voice. " 'Dear Mrs. Ramírez,' " he gasped, but then: " 'This letter will come as a surprise to you, *do not* tair it up. You have been chosen by a devote freind to receive a Crown of Glory such as few ladies in our time have been flavored with. Let me ask you a simple question first: Would you give up one hair of your haid in echange for a unique, distenctive full-fashion wig? Of course you wold! All you must do is this: within three days simple pluck one hair from your haid, prefer one of the longest ones, and mail it to the lady whose name and address you find at the top of the list herein attacked. Then cross off *her* name from the list, add *your* own name and address to the end of it, and send a copy of this letter within three days to six of your best freinds. *No men.* You may send by either air or regular mail, whichever you like best. In twenty days you will receive 46,656 hairs, and you will be surprised where some of them came from! Select the 15,000 you like best. Mail to Chainwig, Drawer 1, Los Angeles 46656 (it will cost you from 20 to 30c by Parcel Post) and within three weeks you will be the proud owner COD of a unique, distenctive full-fashion wig, for far less than you ever gessed!' "

John-Juan glanced questioningly toward the sideboard, sipped mescal when Señora Ramírez breathed "Aya" at him. " 'It's as simply as that,' " he breathed back. " 'No strings attacked. This chain was started on December 25, and has not been broken since. You *must* send your hair and your letters within three days, or you will brake the chain. *Do not* brake this chain. "Do onto others as you would have them do onto *you*." (Matt. 7:12) This is allowed by the United States Post Office and is legal. If you brake this chain you will have one year's bad luck—' "

"Aya!"

"Aya," John-Juan agreed, and Señora Ramírez poured for them both. " 'To be absolutely safe,' " he read, " 'cross out the top name on this list at once (after first mailing your hair to her):

> Sandra Jones
> Pittsburg, Ill.

Dorothy Flugan
342 E. 1st
S. City, Iowa

Mrs. Charlotte Flugan
Flugan, Iowa

Jo Anne Butts
Harvarton, Idaho

Filomena James
1717 Moursund Boulevard
San Antonio 81, Texas 80081

Anita Ramírez
411 W. Jones
Phoenix, Arizona

and add your name to the bottom before sending *six* copies
to your freinds. Don't forget to send 15000 hairs Parcel Post
to Chainwig after you have chosen them! They will fashion
them into a full-fashion wig for you at cost.

I am looking forword to my unique, distenctive wig, as I
know you are to!

Your devote freind,
Anita Ramírez

P.S. José sends you all his love. He will write you a letter
someday soon. (Mama, don't copey this.)' "

It was the end. Seeing expectation in Señora Ramírez' eyes,
he turned the other side to view. There was nothing there at
all. Together they drank mescal until she could smile again.
Now she was ready to take her letter back from him, and he
watched to see what she did with it: put it on the sideboard
on top of her other mail, unfolded out. "Please pardon me,
señor." With her back to him, she studied it. In the quiet he

could hear her hands smoothing it, a little roughly it seemed
to him. He watched her fingers touch her hair, fall heavily to
her sides. "Aya, so much, so much," she said. Her shoulders
sagged, but she straightened them as she turned back to him
with brave smiling face. "Anita has more time than me."

"Señora . . ."

"Thank you for your very kind help, señor."

"Señora, you . . ." She had a magnificent head of hair.

"Look now, it's two o'clock! How long I've had you wait
your lunch. Bring your mescal to the table, sir!"

"Gracias." He staggered obligingly to his place, sank onto
Señora Ramírez' stoutest chair. Already she had three dishes
there, which she described as canary beans, fried rice, and
squash seed soup. Where to begin, with such a choice? She
added another, small and grey, a special treat. Cactus cheese
—he began with that. She had known how good cold sand
could taste to a famished man! Better still, her other dishes
turned out to be far more than she had claimed, choice
strained steak, with thin-sliced steakbreads to sop the juice.
Señora Ramírez watched ecstatically how he did; she had not
believed that any gringo could eat his lunch and hers in time
for the four o'clock. But he was only hurrying because he
had not forgotten that whipped cream cake.

"Bread pudding, señor?"

"Señora!" Laughing, sighing, he attacked her cake from
the bottom up, saving the cream for last. Nor could he have
only imagined the flavor of pomegranate juice as he sucked
his lips, so sweetly sharp was it. Sighing, he looked up:
Señora Ramírez was beaming, there was no more, he had to
stop.

"Señor, will you finish this last drop of mescal? I'll leave
you for a minute, with permission?"

"Señora, of course!" He could lift his brimming glass to

her at least, while trying to see if he could lift himself. She was back before he found out, holding something in front of her at shoulder height. It was her hair for Sandra Jones, a thing impossible to carry offhandedly. It led her to the side-board, where her free hand fumbled for a clean envelope. The first time she tried to tuck her chain hair in, one end sprang out, the root. Starting all over again, she planted with greater care, root first, and that proved right.

"Aya, I think I will have to send a note, she might not look. Will you write the English for me, señor? I can copy the address out."

"Of course!"

She had clean notepaper for him and a brand-new ball-point pen—ATOM BOMB, Hecho en Mexico. She showed him how: you banged it on the table, then it worked. You held it high up near the top, for it was a dirty one. Waiting for orders to evacuate, you watched black ink fall out.

"Señor, how do I start?"

"Dear Mess Jones," perhaps?

"Good!" she cried, and now inspired words gushed forth with almost the speed of ink: " 'Dear Mess Jones, Enclosed please find my hair. I hope you will like it well enough. Your devote freind, Anita Estella de Clemente Ramírez.' Señor, how is that?"

Very wet. "A memento, por favor," while he dabbed at a drowning freind. Together they held their breath while he went back to dot his *i*'s, emboss his *t*'s. Now he extended dripping paper and pen, at arms' length, for her signature.

"Señor? 'A E de C R,' " she splashed, and returning the pen with the envelope: "Señor, do you want to copy the address out? That way it both will match."

"Quite right, señora. 'Sandra Jones, PITTSBURG, ILL.' Will you want to write your own address in the corner, señora?"

"Where? Don't bother with that! They won't send it back. Thank you, señor!" She spread letter and envelope on the sideboard while she looked for stamps. These were in a Nescafé bottle, and she glanced sidelong at John-Juan while selecting one. He was already shaking his head before she asked: "Would it be wise to send this by airplane, señor? We would have to write 'Correo Aéreo' on."

"Aya," he said.

"How far is Pittsburg away from here?"

"From here? Perhaps two th— Pittsburg? Say one thousand miles, more or less."

"Aya! So far?" She poked her stamps. "Bus isn't so bad anymore, señor. It's safe. If we take this in time for the four o'clock it will be in Texas by the morning, señor."

"So soon!"

"Señor . . ."

"Señora?"

"Did you plan to go to the four o'clock?"

"I had thought of it."

"You could run this letter over there with you, it would probably be dry by then. That way I could write my six copies myself, after I wipe this pen. You wouldn't have to worry about that."

"My pleasure, señora!"

Quickly she selected a stamp, licked, banged it conclusively onto the envelope with her fist. At a time like this, there could be no second thoughts. The folding of the note was next, and she had the heart for it. Fold quickly once, peer in the crack, fold twice, stuff inside the envelope. Her hair sprang out, but not the root. She jabbed it back in and licked. Doubt was no match for heart as she bore the results to him. "Hold it by the edge, señor."

"Aya," and parallel to the floor.

"Do you plan to start soon, señor?"

"Señora . . ."

"Señor?"

"Have I time to brush my teeth?"

"Pardon me, señor! There's time, there's time! This way, if you please, señor! That clock is almost right."

There was time, and he could walk! He let her fetch his brush, then followed her into a cubicle crowded with washstands, wet rags, wet towels, and other effects, all personal. Enough hair in one brush to make at least half a wig. Left to himself, he let out a little mescal first, before testing his AMIGO brush. Finding the new bristles stiff, he thought to soften them with cactus soap. Gritting teeth, he brushed. Canary beans had no chance at all, scarcely more did squash seed soup. From the drain amphibious cockroaches scurried up to lunch when he rinsed his mouth; they too had to make the four o'clock. He ran water, not too hot, giving them a good start down the subterranean route. There's time, there's time; he banged his brush. Not wanting to get his only pocket wet, he tissue-wrapped, headed out the door ready for anything.

"Niños, the señor is leaving! Come shake good-bye! Hold it by the edge, señor, it's almost dry."

He did, but saw that the picture on its stamp was of a carrier who toted his pack upon his back, supported it by a leather strap wound around his head. Too, the man wore no clothes above his waist, almost none below, no footgear of any kind. John-Juan felt awkward carrying so, by the edge and to one side, while the children lined up to shake goodbye. He noted a flicker of mirth in Dolores' smile.

"Niños, the señor is in a hurry to make the four o'clock!" Señora Ramírez tucked a small tube into his pocket as she led him to the hall. "It's Glisterine," she said, "hecho in New

York." She held the big front door for him: "Come back to visit us again sometime, señor!"

"I will!" He was already in the street and running well.

"Be sure to drop it in the *slot*."

"I will!"

"Don't hand it to the Administrador!"

"The man who passes out the mail?"

"No no! The one who sits behind his desk reading the *National Geographica!*"

"I won't!" Waving a last farewell to the family grouped inside the door, he headed back to the office along what seemed to be the same route he had come, though longer now and more complex. Without Señora Ramírez to show him how, other runners got in his way, deflecting him. Many took note of his letter to Sandra Jones. Sir, are you going to the four o'clock? This way, this way! They ducked into alleys, questionable doors, beckoning John-Juan to follow them. But he would not be led off his course, for all their guile. Only one of them for an instant tempted him; she wore high heels and carried her little backside in a tight orlon sack, which she would have him believe was a special delivery pouch. Whether or not he had memory, he had wariness. Was it this, or luck, or Señora Ramírez' dedicated tutelage that got him to the office with seconds to spare? The line had formed long ago, but the clerk hadn't raised his grating yet. At sight of John-Juan his hand froze on the latch.

"Señor!"

Waving his letter, John-Juan drove for the slot.

"Ah! Ah!"

John-Juan slid his letter in, sticky side up. Behind a glass partition, in the office space, a gentleman peered over his *National Geographica*, half rose to his feet, slumped down again as a clerk approached the slot with a sack. It was four o'clock! John-Juan, catching his breath, watched how the man packed, besmearing Sandra Jones with his thumb. The PITTSBURG at least was intact.

"The line is over here, señor!" It was a boy of no more than seven or eight.

"Thanks, thanks!" John-Juan fell in behind the boy.

"Señor, would you like my place?"

"No no. . . ."

Their clerk had let his grating fall with a crash, and was waving with both of his hands. "Who? Me?" People stepped out of line, but he waved them back, shaking his head. John-Juan shuffled toward him. People drew farther back. Bending his head to the grate, waiting for John-Juan to come close, his clerk addressed him underbreath. "Sir, do you want to rent a *box?*"

John-Juan spoke quietly too. "A box? No no, thanks very much."

"It's only four dollars a month."

"Not just now, thanks very much!"

"I could give you three-o-one."

"Three-o-one? Well . . . no. But thanks!"

His friendly clerk shrugged. "I thought I would mention it, sir. Will you be here for the nine o'clock?"

"Yes! Thanks!"

"Come early, sir! There's always a long line for the nine o'clock."

"I will! I will! Thanks!"

"Señor . . . ?" It was the boy of seven or eight.

"Son?"

"You may have my place."

"No no, you don't understand. . . ."

"Will you be here for the nine o'clock?"

"Yes!"

"I will save you a place!"

"Thanks! Many thanks!" Pivoting, waving, he plunged out the door. Behind him he thought he could hear that grate slide quietly up. Not wishing to spoil everything, he ran down the steps without looking back, and in the street he held his fast pace. For one thing he felt himself ready to use that tissue at last; Señora Ramírez' fried beans were already mumbling good-bye to him. Where to decently deposit them, in town, at four o'clock? As far as he could see, on the run, this problem had never before come up, not in English certainly. He could not confront just anyone: Where do you crap, señor? Mil gracias! He began to think longingly of that greasy ditch that bordered the fence, but which direction was that? Had he known so much, he might well have gone all the way to the moon's roundhouse.

"Pod!"

It was his scout of last night, trotting not so straight, sidewise in fact, his cap on askew, and carrying in his hand the bottle of bourbon Señor Bustamante had meant for his wife. When he flourished it at John-Juan the last drops splashed out. "A memelnto, plod!"

"Not now, Zurdo. . . ."

"Plod, slow up! Minstler Dumas is waitling for you!"

"Later!"

"He wants to know if inslead *hocked* your wlatsh!" Zurdo had somehow lurched directly into his path, grabbed his pajama top high up with one desperate hand, never loosening his grip on the bourbon bottle with the other though, and letting his nose hunt the watch. "Plod . . . ?"

"I misplaced it down at Señor Bustamante's house. . . ."

Zurdo's frantic right hand felt of John-Juan's pocket for him. "Plod, qué es?"

"No es nada, Zurdo. . . ." But Zurdo had out his brush,

was seeking to unwrap it for him. "No!" Just in time John-Juan snatched it back, and Zurdo groped in his pocket again. "Nada, Zurdo!"

"Plod? No es NlōDōz?"

"Na—"

But Zurdo had hold of the tube, and in his intoxicated state he cried out with relief: "Plod, I show inslead the way to Señor Bustamante's hlouse!"

They tugged at the little tube, as well as they could with thumb and one forefinger apiece, watching it stretch. It soon popped, of course. Zurdo staggered dangerously back, dropped his bottle with a crash as he fought to stay on his feet. Passersby dove for the fragments of glass, but Zurdo seemed not to notice as he raised his hand up to his nose: his dazed, reproachful eyes could see only John-Juan. "Pod . . . qué es?" Stiffly he lowered his hand to his side, wiped, with downcast look, the sticky mess onto his pants. John-Juan took the opportunity to duck past him, knowing that shock would not last. Running, he cleaned up his tube as best he could, folded it double at the break, and stuffed it far down in a corner of his pocket away from his tissue and brush. Now he too had a handful of Glisterine to be rid of. He wiped as he went, but not on his pants, on nearby walls, awnings, perhaps one lady's skirt. That was strong paste. In less than a block several dozen men, boys, and dogs had picked up the scent. Zurdo could be heard crying, more clearly than before but making little more sense: "Pod! I sorry, pod! Is it broke?"

Was it broke! But glancing back, John-Juan felt pity at sight of him floundering so, flailing his arms, totally unaware that his hat pointed crazily off to the left, and crying, "I sorry, pod! Let's go, let's vamonos!" as if he were still trotting out front like a scout, when it was all he could do to keep up with the rest of the troops. John-Juan was in a real hurry now, could not wait. In fact he had begun dropping little foggy hints behind, which he hoped might obscure the Glisterine scent. Either sharp noses were heeding them or he was simply too fast tonight. Many runners gave up after a stride or two, many only waved as he passed. No question but what he was well known in town: on more than one face he caught a quick flash of something very like civic pride. Passing the Texas Liquors Store, he saw the proprietors start for the front, but then bring themselves to a halt with humorous, admiring shrugs. At Woolworth's, he almost ran into Concepción, just leaving work. Her first impulse, when she had recognized him, was to give him a friendly smile, but that soon faded out. What, couldn't she take a hint? No no, she had probably spotted his AMIGO brush. He quickened his pace, for this was no time to pause for explanations, apologies.

"Paaaad!" It was a harrowing wail from the Woolworth's gutter, where Zurdo lay sprawled full length, or trying to drag himself up over the curb, beseeching John-Juan with one outflung hand while seeking to retrieve his cap from beneath trampling feet with the other. Every shred of good sense in his command told John-Juan to keep running, faster. Two more steps would have taken him around the next Woolworth corner. Yet he got only half that far before he broke stride, found himself reversing field, charging head low into the appalled ranks of pursuers. He broke a path through them, not without pain, and commiseration. Children were literally upended, men were staggered, dogs escaped mayhem only by tucking their tails in. How long the trip seemed to take him; fifty miles cross-country would have seemed no longer. Only Zurdo's pitiful cries kept him going. He arrived almost too late even so, for Zurdo's cap had been kicked halfway to Woolworth's, and a passing boy's fingers were grasping, just as John-Juan plucked it. Beating it against his knees and some others, he fought his way to Zurdo, who lay now with his face at least partly protected by a shallow cavity in the sidewalk. John-Juan had no choice but to place his little league cap on backward, which was not entirely unfortunate. It could offer little or no protection, but it did look cocky. At very worst, it would serve as circumstantial identification.

"P-od?"

It was hardly a cry, little more than a question, murmured to the pavement. Surely Zurdo, from such a lie, could not have seen him: either everyone was "pod" or John-Juan was his only amigo. No time now for conjecture. He patted Zurdo's head without a word, feeling that in some cases ambiguity is kindness. The troops too seemed uncertain. Now with John-Juan brought to bay, their eyes asked What had they wanted with him? He no longer wore his watch, and he was farting. They stood back a little, as if waiting for him to start running. That few seconds to himself proved valuable. Had he run from them, back the way he had come, they would have trampled Zurdo all over again. . . . He ran into them.

This time there was less pain and less confusion; he had taught the troops to break ranks more gracefully. A few still were clumsy, but most stood well back with outstretched hand, or called, "A momento!" Almost it was as though he had become their leader, they were awaiting orders. He waved Not-now, and farted. The troops he passed stood at attention. Now some fell in behind him, dogs mostly, but the majority turned away to look at Woolworth windows. They did not appear to be miffed exactly; they simply had their own interests and sensitivities. Yet once around that next Woolworth corner he came upon raw new recruits already

lined up for enlistment. Qué es? Qué es! Dónde? They fell
in step with John-Juan's followers, who did their best to stiff-
arm them aside, discourage them. Nada! *Nada!* John-Juan
slackened his pace, by way of confirmation, then shot off at
top speed thanks partly to jet propulsion. Glancing over his
shoulder, he was surprised to see two men far back there
stagger; he had not known he was a ventriloquist. When a
block later he looked again, he found that many of the newer
troops had already deserted, but there remained a determined
handful led, not too surprisingly, by that same old soldier on
roller skates. A conservative man, he had had his wheels
greased since last night. This made him not only faster but
quieter, that much more disquieting. Even last night he would
have been more than a handful, without Zurdo to bribe and
belabor him, and then at least a man had known where he
stood by listening for the screwing wheels. John-Juan disliked to do it, but at first opportunity he ran up the steps of
a crowded Mercado, turned down an aisle almost too slippery
for slippers.

"Suh! Un momento!"

John-Juan faltered but an instant. Had there been time he
would have given the man anything—his pajama top, his
AMIGO brush, his Glisterine, even though the old soldier
probably needed this last about as much as he needed NōDōz.
Perhaps here in the Mercado he would find something he
liked better. The counters were high, but goods were also
displayed on the floors, and one man carried over his shoulder
a great pile of scarves whose tassels dangled low enough so
that a child of two or three could have reached them.

But that man joined the army! Going out the back door,
he was close after John-Juan, with some others. "Señor!
Señor! You need a serape!"

"*Nada!*"

This man was game, but he was too heavily laden. Besides, dogs tugged his tassels. At the edge of town he finally had to give up running, but never yelling. "Sennnñooorrrrr!" The howling dogs echoed him.

Now there were only four or five remaining, one dog among them who seemed of all the strongest competition. For a while he stayed close to John-Juan's heels, snapping, barking, but then, as luck would have it, he had to pull off the road. He had to rest-stop worse than his quarry. By the time he was straight again he had lost all ambition, or incentive, and he trotted back to town with the air of one who does everything with a purpose. Civic-minded.

Now there were three—two. One in particular seemed to challenge. In fact he was beside John-Juan, running shoulder to shoulder. John-Juan spurted forward, and that man spurted too, falling into step with him. Now the man spurted ahead, and it was John-Juan's turn to follow. When John-Juan came abreast, the man turned to welcome him, smiling and nodding. They took some turns that way, four or five apiece, each time jumping ahead a little faster, farther. Each time John-Juan caught up, the man would congratulate him again, nod and smile at him. When it was the man's turn to have caught up, John-Juan would nod. Soon the other took his hint, and fell into a steadier stride, not so fast now. They jogged along in this way, matching one another's pace exactly. The man even looked a little like John-Juan, and not just because he wore pajamas. He was tall and thin, lanky, and quite bald on the forehead. However, he did not wear slippers. Sandals, and his feet were darker. He smiled more easily. John-Juan, since there was no getting rid of the man, soon drew out his AMIGO brush and began unwrapping. The man looked discreetly elsewhere.

"Señor?" John-Juan waved his tissue.

Smiling and nodding, the man at once began to brake speed. They coasted gradually to a stop at the roadside. The man dropped to one knee there, scooped up a handful of sand and watched it run out between his slender fingers, as if testing for something. It could have been gold or silver, the reverent way he sifted it. Waving at the man, who did not look up, John-Juan retired behind some mesquite, not wishing to disturb him.

When John-Juan soon returned wrapping his last sheet of tissue around his AMIGO brush, the man rose to smile and nod his greetings. Brushing the last grains of sand from his palms, he glanced sidewise at John-Juan questioningly.

John-Juan tucked his brush into his pocket, waiting for the man to make himself clearer. "Señor?"

The man flexed his leg muscles, first one leg, then the other.

John-Juan did the same. "Señor?"

They were off and running. This time the man did not bother with testing him, but fell into a long loose gait which John-Juan found surprisingly easy to copy. It was beginning to get dark now, but the moon was already shining brightly and the narrow strip of macadam glowed straight and clear, like a fluorescent arrow pointing to somewhere important, a few downhill miles ahead of them. There was little to draw attention from it; the occasional bushes lay like soft grey masses on the desert, their thorns seemingly retracted. Here and there a beer can did gleam by the roadside, and the Señor would stoop for these without breaking stride, drop them in his pajama top. When he had a shirtful, he paused to dig a shallow hole in the sand with his hands, for burial. Soon John-Juan began working his side of the road, and the Señor smiled and nodded encouragement. This, the east side, was easier in that fewer cans were to be found here, but stooping always to the left was hard, might soon grow tiring. The Señor, anticipating this, exchanged sides with him. They went on in this way now, exchanging sides whenever one had a load to bury, thus lessening the monotony, the possibility of overtraining. Too, beer cans grew scarcer with each mile they put between themselves and the border.

Finally there were in fact none of beer, no cans at all unless an occasional V-8 juice can, or Vienna sausage. These themselves were so rare that a finder could usually carry one for a mile or more, using it as a receptacle for Kleenex, before coming upon another. Thus he could devote full attention to his Kleenex picking. The Señor had a way with that; he could scoop it with his can and almost simultaneously pack it tightly with a stick he'd found, never himself touching any mucus, excrement, or lipstick. Whenever he had a load he could bury it can and all, for by then he had always found an empty. John-Juan himself was less skilled and lucky. Partly it was his side again, the east side had no sticks that he had noticed, there were fewer cans, more Kleenex. He had to bury it in handfuls. The Señor, seeing him grow sticky-fingered, traded sides again, and also found a stick for him— on the east side! Smiling, nodding reassurance, he paused to watch John-Juan scoop a wad or two before himself resuming. Things were going much better, though John-Juan could hardly qualify as expert, far less immaculate. Too often a wad would elude his can, or fall out before his stick could jab it, he would have to run back and make another pass or two. He did not like to leave any. But it was of course embarrassing, to squat there scooping, jabbing while the Señor sailed on ahead of him. Many times, when he was squatting far behind and hoped his back might hide it, he would use his fingers. Shit, he thought, this west side isn't any better. Had the Señor known this stretch that well, and let him have it?

As for this so-called stick he'd given him, did he think a gringo didn't know a twig when a gringo saw one? No no, the fault was all John-Juan's, the truth was he didn't know what he was doing. And up ahead the Señor was taking a very long time with burying, as though all at once it were difficult. When he had finally finished, he darted to the west side and kicked a No. 2 can closer to the road where John-Juan would be sure to see it.

Sides to him made little difference. He could scoop with the left or right hand equally, and maintain a steady pace irregardless of distribution, shape, or quality. If he had not come upon his next can quite when he was ready, it did not matter. He would only glance ahead and keep on packing. That was his secret, it was in the packing. Another man would have been content merely to get a wad in, let it go at that until he had another, but the Señor was always, always jabbing. His hands seemed tireless. Once, he jabbed so much at a wadded mess that his stick came out all green and dripping diarrhea, but he did not try to hide this. He bent forward to shake it, low down, held daintily by the fingertips, at arm's length, quite humorously, like a thermometer. By coincidence, or perhaps contrivance, it was at that moment they encountered their first car of the evening. It came on from the north very fast, with blinding headlights, but the Señor paid it no attention. He stayed there by the roadside shaking. John-Juan called out, "Señor!" but the Señor seemed not to hear him. Now the big car was almost upon them, and in the intense illumination John-Juan could see the Señor's eyes gleam narrowly. When the driver let fly a wad at him, he fired back his stick, with wonderful speed and accuracy. It stuck to the white trunk lid, less than six inches from the yellow Texas license plate. That was all right; even on the east side the Señor could find another.

Behind them now, when the exhaust had settled, they could see wads decorating the roadbed like dirty paper flowers. John-Juan was prepared to run back for them, but the Señor was already running southward, scooping one-handed and with the other—there was a stick in it—waving John-Juan onward with the unhesitating, unerring logic that comes of long experience. Were they to retrace their steps each time a car passed from the north, they would never get to where they were going. John-Juan hastened after the Señor with a sudden new thought in mind. Where were they going so hard, so usefully to be sure, but so fast and late?

4

Perhaps the Señor knew what time it was, and where, when they topped a long rise in the road and left it. He turned to point back at Polaris perched upon the border, nod his head in satisfaction. Either it was setting, or they themselves were. They buried their half-full cans, placed their sticks on either side of the road where a man could find them, then started out cross-country, east. They had anyway not had much work to do for hours now, not even Kleenex; it was almost as though someone else had worked this territory recently, since the daytime traffic. In point of fact there had been some footprints, sandaled. With little else to do, John-Juan had had time to study these, as well as what could easily have been fresh burials at what seemed plausible distances, measured by the Señor's standards. If they did in reality have such helpers, there was no further evidence of their presence. They had not passed by. Nor were there any tracks or signs at all out here on the open desert. It was as though the Señor and John-Juan were the first to pass here, this season anyway. Tracks are finally erased, of course. Even down here they must have some kind of winter, presumably the wind did blow here. It could well have blown in recent weeks. This was fifth month, wasn't it? The occasional weak grasses did not tell, not in the dark. The grey mesquite clumps looked less and less like shrubbery, more like great brains who knew when it was time to sleep. The Señor himself seemed to go out of his way to avoid these.

No, it turned out that he was simply seeking firm ground for them to run on. Sand was apt to be soft around a mesquite, from driftage. The way he chose, their steps left scarcely any marks at all. John-Juan's left heel did make small scars at times; he had lost the other. Was that perhaps why the Señor chose their way so carefully, because John-Juan wore slippers, might find soft sand more difficult to run in, with one heel missing? It seemed that to the Señor himself firm and soft would be of small importance, with sandals, and this roundabout route was certainly longer, much more tiring. But there was at least one other motive equally likely, if less subtle: he just did not wish to leave any more tracks than necessary, worried less for John-Juan than he did about him. Or why not a combination—he showed concern for tracks, John-Juan, and everything? This was another new thing to think about while running.

It went on like that for hour upon hour until suddenly two things happened simultaneously: they saw the first light of the sun and they saw a village. As usual, John-Juan guessed, there was an end to everything. He knew that they would not have seen the village so soon but for the sunlight; the moon was gone now. There again, an end, and a beginning. Like yesterday. Yet the village itself seemed always. They were entering its outskirts now, at a notch or two faster than they had been running. This was less a village than a number of dirt huts, freely scattered, no one quite like another but depending on the quantity and content of its own dirt for contour. Some had thatch-batch roofs, of cornhusks. The streets—there were none. The ground around was "clean" but wet in places and very trodden. At least a hundred hairless dogs, which had been barking fiercely, slunk hangtail through the ruptures that served these huts as doorholes. The people inside eyed the runners sleepily, over the little fires they crouched near cooking breakfast in their pajamas. The Señor maintained a smart pace, in spite of this reception, and headed directly toward a hut located more or less in the center. It too was different from any other, but no more splendid. It did have a kind of garden nearby its doorhole, and the lady crouching inside cooking breakfast in her pajamas was beautiful.

The Señor, not exactly bowing but bending double to clear the hole and land on his knees below the smoke level, drew from his pajama top an unbroken bottle, which he presented to the lady. John-Juan, staring hard as he knelt beside him, had nothing suitable. The lady herself seemed not to notice, but gracefully placed the bottle in back of her with some others while all the time turning pancakes. She seemed to have prepared at least enough for everyone. "Just in time, señores!" she said in smiling English.

The Señor smiled and nodded.

"Shall we eat first, then talk, señores?"

Already smiling, John-Juan too nodded. It would have been more than impolite, impossible, not to nod and smile at sight and smell of her cornmeal pancakes drowned in syrup. She served them stacked in coffee tins, with wooden sticks for lifting. The sticks had their own fine flavor. She used her unbroken bottles for serving water—not including the Señor's, however; cleaner ones. The water she dipped from what appeared to be a natural spring scooped out beside her. So her hut was after all the best one, or this entire village was a marvel. John-Juan recalled the wet spots here and there outside, but at the same time more than enough bald dogs for mundane explanation. She herself did not partake of anything until John-Juan and the Señor had been served and reserved, then she took but two small pancakes with a quick, conspiratory smile which implied that she was dieting. She munched very slowly, allowing her guest no grounds at all for fearing they had deprived her, allowing them full opportunity to admire her lovely teeth so straight and brown. As she chewed, her serene face was a study in delicate, intermingling creases, each one beautiful in itself and in harmony with the others. Her straight black hair was caught casually behind her head by a ribbon of green cornhusk. John-Juan saw that the Señor too studied her with intense, unconcealed pleasure as she sipped her water. When she was finished she dabbed her unsullied lips with her pajama top, stacked their dishes, and offered little brown cigarettes from a sardine can. Cornsilk, John-Juan found when she had lit them, three on a mesquite ember.

"He comes from the north, Señor?"

The Señor smiled and nodded.

"He ran all the way?"

Both men nodded.

"Is he fast?"

The Señor alone this time.

"Is he serious?"

The Señor smiled and nodded, most definitely.

But the lady interrupted him, with a keen glance at John-Juan. "What sort of man have we here?"

The Señor shrugged.

"He looks a little old for the Peace Corps, doesn't he?"

He shrugged again.

"What, is he a Director then?"

The Señor shook his head.

"Are those his own pajamas?"

The Señor nodded, but the lady caught his uncertainty.

"The Señor is a mute, sir. Perhaps you can answer my questions better?"

"I'll do my best, señora."

"Are those your own pajamas, sir?"

"Yes . . ."

"Where are you from, sir?"

"California."

"Is that a toothbrush in your pocket?"

"Yes, señora."

"Are you serious?"

"Yes, señora."

The lady turned to the Señor. "Do you approve these answers, Señor?"

The Señor smiled and nodded his strong affirmation, as before.

The lady also smiled, most beautifully. "Sir, you have your nomination."

It was that easy. John-Juan accepted the warm hand she offered him, watched her other hand gently take his cigarette and throw it in the fire. "Well now, where shall we begin?" she asked. "Señor, you say he ran all the way with you?"

The Señor nodded that he had.

"And fast?"

Yes, he had.

"He helped you with the cans?"

Yes.

"The Kleenex?"

Yes.

"He found a stick?"

Glancing at John-Juan, the Señor nodded yes.

"He discovered no unbroken bottles?"

Glancing again, the Señor shrugged and shook his head.

"Sir?"

John-Juan shook his head. "None that I can recall, señora."

The lady fell silent for a moment, studying, while they waited. "Señor, time is short," she said suddenly, with firmness. "What is your opinion: could last night's trip be considered to satisfy the requirements for dual training?"

Surprised, the Señor rubbed his forehead, nodding.

The lady's smile was radiant. "Sir, the Señor is our most experienced coach. I have every confidence in him. I trust his methods and judgment implicitly. You are ready to solo immediately!"

John-Juan, her burning eyes on him, her hot hand in his, bowed his head. "Thanks, señora."

"Señor, let's not push our new recruit too fast!" the lady gently chided the Señor, and laughed. "Our young friend is dusty. He'll want a little time to brush his teeth and rest his ankles."

John-Juan lifted his eyes to her kind smile. "Thank you, señora."

"We'll give him the ten A.M. southbound route."

Bowing again, "Thanks, señora."

"That will give me time to pack an extra lunch."

"Thank you, señora."

Extending a hand to each of them, she rose gracefully to

her feet, at the same time pulling them up. Now they could make out more clearly the shapeliness of her body beneath her pajamas, and appreciate her impressive height, almost as great as theirs. Perhaps greater—up here it was very smoky. "Señor, will you show your star pupil to the second runner's quarters!"

Nodding, bowing, the Señor ducked out the doorhole, John-Juan close after. Behind them the lady laughed merrily at sight of pupil all but overrunning coach with zealousness. The Señor seemed not to be offended; at least he smiled as he straightened up already sprinting, glanced out the corner of his eye at John-Juan trailing him by half a step. Those corn-meal pancakes were a little heavy, or John-Juan did finally need to rest his ankles; he was now less sorry that the lady had thrown his cigarette away. He could not quite catch up with the Señor but held himself well to the left of him, so that from a distance they might seem to be running side by side. Too, he felt that he naturally made a good appearance, he could run, he knew that, and had had ample time to compare himself with the Señor, correct any little weaknesses of technique, of carriage. He had always run with his toes straight forward—he could tell that—and luckily that quarters was a nearby one. Plunging after the Señor into a doorhole, he tried to disavow a grunt by coughing.

There was no smoke in here, but they fell kneeling anyway. Nor were there any signs indicating this was the second runner's quarters, except a slight austerity. There were but two unbroken bottles, one coffee can. Aya, the water supply in here was a half-full ravioli can, turning rusty. In one corner (there were several) a pile of cornhusks had been fitted out for resting ankles. Now a young boy stumbled in with cornstalks, a few sticks of mesquite. He dumped them sleepily in a scatter beside the firespace—John-Juan could stack them—and left at once, more stared at than staring. With shaking head the Señor brusquely set to stacking, the cornhusks first, by size and greenness, the mesquite sticks slapped down hard beside these, according to circumference. That was how you did it. From his pajama pocket he drew a bit of straw, teased it with his cigarette, cupped it in his palm, blew on it until it flamed up—a safety match. He held it to a cornhusk, firing that up, tossed on a stalk, now a greener one, a slender mesquite stick, all in a crooked, flaming pile at which a Boy Scout would have frowned with envy. Back on his heels, the Señor could smile again and nod. He could take time now to point out to John-Juan his accommodations, starting with the bottles, serving sticks, and pancake dishes. He indicated the half-full ravioli can, as if John-Juan had not already seen it. And nodded at a wooden box, whatever that was. The cornhusk bed itself he did not refer to, but patted John-Juan's ankle. By now it was getting smoky; he cast his arm expansively at everything in the hut and left it, too fast for questions.

John-Juan did have one. Without a watch he had no idea what time it was, how long before the southbound 10 A.M. Rather gloomily he unpacked his toilet articles. Zurdo had made a mess of things. By the time John-Juan had tidied up, that tissue was scarcely fit for tinder. He spread paste onto his brush directly from his pocket, and did not rinse, conserving ravioli water. The Señor's fire almost went out when he spat on it, but then turned stubborn, and even smokier. Well, at least he had a place to leave his brush and Glisterine, next to his unbroken bottles. AMIGO! He eased himself to the noisy bed to rest his ankles. His feet had swollen too large for him to remove his slippers, but this way would look better in case anyone came by needing him for anything.

One thing, or even two, he had forgotten. Ten seconds'

rest had left him a little stiff, but in less than five seconds
more he was out the hole and running. The villagers were
more awake now and observing him more closely. It amused
some of them to join his game, look everywhere around
them, as he did. Where was it? Where was it? Every hut he
glanced into had smoke and people in it. From one he thought
he saw two lovely eyes peer out, most proudly. That bol-
stered his self-control, but he was getting desperate. He had
gone twice around the track, it seemed, before he spotted a
hut somewhat larger than the others, roofless. Closer exami-
nation suggested other differences. Still he had no idea if this
was meant for second runners, but had no time just now for
protocol. Inside, further shocks were waiting: they had a
trench in there, circular, which one had to leap over so as to
squat with back to trench and wall, tight between two other
pajamaed squatters, while making loud, rude apologies to the
tense old lady across the way. He was in far better tone than
she was; within five seconds flat, without waiting to try the
cornhusks, he was out the door cutting crazy figures in search
of the second runner's cell.

He might never have found it had not a visitor, his first,
been awaiting his return. She stood out front, one hand
shielding her eyes, the other waving. There was a smile on
her face as he drew up, tying his pajama cords, but she spoke
with firmness.

"Sir, I thought you might like to look over our layout
here."

"Thank you, señora."

Leading the way, she said, "I ought to have thought of it
before, I guess."

He did not say, but fell in behind her as she headed briskly
in a direction diametrically opposite to the one which in-
stinct, or habit, would have suggested to him. She pointed

out the post office, the barbershop, in passing, but did not stop until they neared a hut somewhat bigger, higher than that other. The ditch was wider. Even way out here, the telltale air of man was stronger. Actually, it was more like cow or horse, or centaur. How had he missed it? The lady wasted no time on explanation, far less conjecture, but turned and headed fast for the outskirts of the village. On the way they passed the cornhouse, a mud barn of heroic proportions, which she was justly proud of. She said it took two shifts of twenty men to stack it. All together, more than sixty men and women were employed in the refinery, and the lady wondered if they had time for a very quick tour of that, in view of John-Juan's interest? What could he answer? The stink around here was unbelievable, even to a man with his fresh memories, but she was prepared to show him the entire refining process, step by step from the beginning: first the men all trampled it, then the women ground it between a small stone and a large one. Younger women poured the meal into wooden boxes, which younger men carried to the grainhouse. The chaff was swept by men into larger boxes, to be used for dog food, fertilizer, and underbedding. Little wonder those dogs were hairless, but John-Juan himself was feeling easier. He could return the lady's smile when she finally spread her arms out, finished. "Everything is useful!" she said. "Would you care to see the tortillería?"

"Please, señora!"

They left the refinery at once and headed, fast but always walking, past a lesser building which emitted a vastly more agreeable aroma, a din of clanking bottles. The lady's shoulders winced at the sound of a broken one, but she did not stop to investigate. She led him to the large doorway of a very clean clay building in which fifty women of all ages knelt on the almost spotless floor slapping with all their strength mounds of masa into the size and shape of babies' asses, then patted them. (Corn and water, John-Juan found out.)

"No, we each make our own pancakes, sir!" the lady said, not sure whether to take John-Juan seriously. "We used to make our own tortillas too, until six years ago. Nowadays the younger girls simply will not learn unless they are closely supervised. You know how they are, they would rather walk around and comb their hair. I opened this factory with some misgivings, but it seems to be working well. The younger girls seem serious. Perhaps after a generation or two from now . . ." She did not finish, but turned from the door to look off into the distance with a rueful smile. But: "Look, you can see the fields from here! See how the young corn is already coming up! Thank the Rain for coming to us last week! That's our first crop, sir—or our fourth, depending upon how we look at it. You see, we never lack. We always have the Rain, and if not the Rain the Sun, and always the precious Earth." She knelt to scoop a handful up, with that same reverence the Señor had shown last night. But this earth did not slip through the fingers the way that other had, it seemed firmer, not just more trodden, more alive, as though each handful had been patted as long and lovingly as those fifty ladies were patting their masa inside the house. "Feel it, please!"

John-Juan knelt to scoop a handful too. It was pliant, warm, and seemed almost to throb with life.

"Can you feel its blood beneath the flesh?"

"Yes."

They lay their handfuls down, patted them back into place. As they stood up the lady's radiant smile shone on him; he was surprised to find himself returning it. It seemed the Moon had no say against the Sun. The lady herself was not surprised by any of this, but she did laugh and shake her head. "Sir, there's no time for visiting the fields today. You'll see them tomorrow morning when you take your exercise. Hadn't we better be getting over to the locker room?"

"All right, señora."

She led again, in silence until they had passed the refinery. Then, "Everything will go well if we can get them to stop eating the dogs," she said.

"The dogs?" He had forgotten them, but saw now that they lay everywhere in whatever shade there was, doing their best to avoid a burn, keep out of the Sun, or sight.

"It's something the conquistadors introduced," she said. "A generation or two ago we had almost shamed it out. There has been much backsliding since. It's hard, it's hard. The dogs are most delicious."

"Señora?" She *seemed* to know.

"Yes. I ate of dog when I was twelve; it was my uncle who enticed me on to it. My father tied its tail around my neck. I wore it there for thirteen months. I have eaten meat but once."

"Ah . . ."

"Texatycyl?"

A man was trotting, or staggering, past them with an immense pack upon his back. Not turning his head, he gasped, "Señora?"

"Qué es?"

"Mackerel," he gasped, and staggered off.

"Texatycyl has the Thursday eastbound route. We eat fish, once a week. It helps to keep our minds off the dogs a little bit." Now they had stopped before a hut. The lady pressed John-Juan's hand encouragingly. "I will wait here, sir," she said.

He ducked through the tiny doorhole, into a hut entirely

bare but for one old wooden crate or bench. The Señor and three others were sitting on it, though the one on the left end was all but off. When the Señor rose to greet John-Juan, that end man bucked his neighbor sidewise, rather sullenly, until he was all on again. Every one of them was as bald as the Señor, as John-Juan himself. He began to see why when the Señor set to work on him. First he took off John-Juan's pajama top, then strapped on a harness that chewed the scalp. To this he strapped a tiny pack, in back—John-Juan's lunch; he could smell the fresh corn in it. The canteen hung on that. After tugging, testing straps, the Señor nodded and smiled approvingly, waved him to a certain line neatly drawn by toe just inside the door. John-Juan stood a little this side of it, while the Señor readied another man. Soon that man moved over to stand a little behind John-Juan, quite naturally. Their new second runner had caught on fast. When a third man joined them there, only that end man remained on the bench, squarely in the middle now. He started to rise, but the Señor waved him back. No no no, he shook his head, then nodded pointedly at John-Juan. The man slouched on his bench even more sullenly as the Señor placed their pajama tops, folded up, on either side of him; he spat on the ground as the Señor turned away. The Señor seemed not to hear, but winking at John-Juan he stepped to the head of the line in the place that John-Juan had saved for him. Ducking, they trotted through the hole in single file, took their positions before the lady side by side. Her manner was not unfriendly, but to the point. "You all know what your assignments are. The Señor will help you to get started, sir."

"Thank you, señora."

She was obviously pleased with everything. Her manner softened noticeably. "I'm known as Mantilla," she said.

"I'm known as John-Juan."

She smiled again, and he right-faced in unison with the rest, trotted off led by the Señor. Their way was here and there, mostly west, among the huts and the quiet dogs. The few idle villagers were mildly curious to see a new man in the second runner's spot, but they were soon left behind. In fact the runners had already passed a sign in many languages, one of which had read: "You are now leaving Sonorla, friend—come back again sometime!" John-Juan could not recall seeing anything on the other side, coming in, but he did not want to look now with two Sonorlans running so close in back of him. Yet it seemed he could only hear one trot. He did glance back, saw that the fourth runner had dropped out of line. He was running backward, bent double at the waist, erasing tracks. From here that sign looked like a mesquite bush.

The westward trip was a rather uneventful one, except that the Sun was extremely warm on John-Juan's back. He not only felt himself turning red, he could smell his cooking lunch. That was all right; it would cool while he was running south. The man he worried for was whoever had the northbound route, his pack to the Sun. No, on second thought, that route turned back when it was almost night; by then the man's refried corn would be cool enough to eat. It all worked out. The Señor himself had no lunch to be seen, and he was still wearing his pajama top. Was this an idiosyncrasy of his, did he like to shield his lunch—or did he expect to be back in Sonorla for that? Where would he eat—in Mantilla's hut? John-Juan did not let his mind dwell on this. He was glad to see what looked like the highway up ahead.

It was, and the Señor slackened pace. They soon drew up at the roadside, stood for a moment looking north and south at the mess. For the first time, something seemed to be disconcerting the Señor. He nudged John-Juan's arm, waved to-

ward the south. Then he stood high up on his toes, his right
arm stretched above his head, his slender forefinger arched
and jabbing stiffly down at the ground. Then he sat down
at once, unstrapped an imaginary pack, drew out an imaginary lunch. Munching, he watched John-Juan's face, and
John-Juan nodded intelligently. But the Señor still was un-
satisfied. He went over everything again, more slowly. When
he looked up at the end, John-Juan nodded hard. *"Lunch,"*
he said.

The other runner, who had been squatting watching all
this, grinned and shook his head. "He means go until lunchtime," he mumbled a little disparagingly, "then start back
again. We don't go all the way to Mexico D.F. in the summertime."

"Oh? Thanks very much."

Shrugging, the other heaved to his feet and started trotting
north at what seemed to John-Juan an almost leisurely pace.
The Señor was looking east, at the distant back of an approaching man. John-Juan stood hesitant, and the Señor
waved abstractedly toward the south. He himself squatted
now: he was waiting for that man to erase his tracks on the
homeward run. John-Juan started off at once.

On his own at last, he found himself suddenly with lots of
time to think, and lots to think about. When a man took a
route alone, was he supposed to handle both sides at once?
He wished he had thought to observe the northbound runner
more carefully, had not let himself be offended by the man's
attitude. He tried hard to visualize whether the man had ever
once crossed the road, in the short while he'd watched, but
he could not say definitely. He dared not look back. . . .
Just then a car shot by, settling the question logically. He
would work one side at a time, only switching over when a
hand got tired, then work the other side on his way back.

His burial mounds would tell him where he had been, in case everything was in a mess again.

Actually it was not so bad down here, compared to the border run. The same number of cars passed by, of course, but by the time they got this far their supplies were running low. They had to wait until Mexico D.F. to load up again. Then on the way back, the same thing again—they ran out again. No doubt that was why runners never went all the way to D.F. in summertime: motorists threw faster with all the windows down. Aya! He had not been told exactly where to stop. What were the man's words again—Go until it was time for lunch? Go until lunchtime, that was it. It didn't help. The man had meant to be obscure. John-Juan had had a bad feeling about him anyway. It seemed his first impression had been right. How was a stranger supposed to know how they measured lunchtime down here? Did they go by the Sun or by appetite? That was the dilemma the man had left him with. It wasn't the Señor's fault. Thinking of the Señor, what would *he* do? Run! John-Juan decided to go until it was turning dark, something comparable to the northside route. Nobody could complain about that. Even if he were to cut it a little short, he doubted that there would be complaints. This was his first solo, wasn't it? He would look sillier if he came in late, and he did want to try to get back in time to eat breakfast in Mantilla's hut.

With thoughts like these, the time passed fast. Yet he took pains not to let them interfere with his work. It wasn't so bad a job at all, once you got the hang of it. Those wads did pack, and it hadn't taken him five minutes to find a stick. He already had an unbroken bottle cached back there, marked by a Kleenex cross, waiting to be dug up on his way back. The sand was very warm and soft, just right for burials. In fact the only things a man had to worry about were the cars and Sun. For a while, when the Sun lay due south, John-Juan had to depend on his hearing to warn him of traffic. He was blind, everything, road, sand, sky, was black, only the Kleenex stood out. Then the Sun eased off to the right, and John-Juan began to see red, most of all when he looked at himself. When at last he could look at the Sun, it had turned big and cool in the west. Even the Señor, he believed, would have stopped. No man could have got far anyway in garbage like that.

He found a good mesquite to eat behind, out of range of the exhaust fumes and wads. Sighing, he unstrapped, drew out his lunch Mantilla had packed for him. He already knew what it was, but she had prepared it differently. These were folded tortillas with whole kernel corn inside, corn sandwiches or tortilla tarts. Three. One of them was shaped a little like a heart; had she intended that? Surely she had known the Sun would have cooked them to a turn, that they would have cooled enough to eat by the time he stopped. It was a sign of how much she trusted him. He ate with more than ordinary appetite, saving the heart-shaped one till last. Done, he probed the bottom of his pack. He had half hoped she might have put a cigarette in there, but she of course had done what was best for him. She was right. Burying his corn-husk wrappings, he started for home at once.

The trip home was in many ways remindful of last night's, but now he had the added challenge of watching out for his burial piles, to tell him when it was time for changing sides. He also had to remember to watch for that Kleenex cross, not just scoop it up without thought of the bottle buried underneath. He found it there, unbroken still. In fact soon afterward he found another one! He was just tucking this second one in his pack (he should have saved those husks) when a runner dashed past him heading south, apparently on the 10

P.M. Had he noticed John-Juan's lack of husks? Did he think John-Juan was loafing there, having a drink, under the pretext of adjusting his pack? Even if he knew better, when he got home would he hint as much? John-Juan plunged on, wincing each time his bottles clanked.

He was gripped by a sudden new horror worse than any of this! Would he know where to stop, where to leave the highway and head for home? Or would morning find him floundering in panic up the northside route? Sweating in the cool night air, scooping and packing like one in shock, he tried to visualize the turnoff point as he had seen it a few fast hours ago. He had had plenty of time for studying; how the fuck had he frittered it? Oh, he could picture the Señor squatting all right, see that other buddy fucker jogging lazily north, but otherwise it was all fucking road and sand. Why hadn't he left himself a fucking mark? Everything looked all fucked up in the moonlight anyway. Then he remembered he had seen the turnoff one other time, at night, at the top of a long and gentle rise. Aya, thank God for brains, for a faithful memory! All he had to do was watch out for that lovely rise, make sure it was the lovely one.

When he arrived at it, Polaris was straddling the borderline, on perfect time. Bowing his head to her, he knelt to bury real tears of relief with his last tin can, then headed east. Now it seemed he could not go wrong. He had run almost no time at all, keeping to the firmer sand, when he came upon the Sun's first light—the village lay at his feet, the imitation mesquite sign was on his left. Sonorla was coming awake. From a centerly hut rose the highest smoke. Wasn't it that smoke which had led him safely home?

The people looked sleepily out their holes on him as he trotted past, at a good brisk pace, directly toward Mantilla's hut. Her own smile was a far from sleepy one as he ducked in; she had been expecting, she had been counting on him. She was wearing clean pajamas, and her eyes lit up even more radiantly than they had just twenty-four hours ago for the Señor, as John-Juan, kneeling, drew his bottles out. They were Pepsis and had not cracked, thank Polaris, the second runner's Star! Adding them to her impressive store, she selected two cleaner ones and placed them side by side on her cornmeal box. Now she drew a whiskey bottle from behind the box, set it next to them. It still had its cap, with the head of a horse on top. "Shall we have a little apéritif, then eat?" she asked.

"Thank you, señora!"

She passed him the sardine can, king-size this time, and fired them up. Cornhusk filter tip. Carefully unscrewing the horsehead cap, she filled their matching Squirt bottles with a steady hand. She passed John-Juan's first, screwed the cap back on, then raised her own. Giving his a gentle tap, she said, "To your first solo, John-Juan!"

He waited for her to drink before he sipped. Aya, it was pure essence of corn, and very strong. Tapping bottles with her same care, he said: "To Mantilla, the first lady of Sonorla!" How well he remembered all this! Watching him drink, her eyes looked searchingly into his. She did not withdraw them as she raised her own bottle to her lips. They drank deep together so.

Now she set her bottle on the cornmeal box, said, "You made excellent time."

"Thank you, señora."

"I began to worry after you left, that you might not remember where the turnoff was. Did you have any difficulty with that?"

"No no," he said, but knew he blushed, "I remembered it was at the top of that lovely rise."

"Aya, isn't that a lovely one?"

"Yes! And Polaris was perched on the borderline, so I knew I must be just about on time."

Nodding, she looked up at him from lowered eyes. Softly then, "And at the Sun's first light did you see my smoke, John-Juan?"

"Yes, Mantilla," he said.

Smiling, "I made it extra big."

"Thank you, Mantilla," he said, also lowering his head.

Now they shook themselves, waved smoke aside, and drank again.

"You passed the other man?"

"Yes, we passed," he said.

"Did he seem serious?"

"Oh yes."

"Was he fast?"

"Oh yes!"

She shook her head regretfully. "He's a bad one," she said. "That's the man you replaced, you know. He begged to be given another chance, so I dropped him to number five and put him on the southbound ten P.M. Tomorrow I'll have him erasing tracks."

"He seemed to be doing quite well, from what I—"

"No no, it's all show," she interrupted him. "By now he's probably stopped for lunch."

"Well . . ."

"That other one, Ray, there's a runner now," she said. "He's serious."

"The one on the northbound ten A.M.?"

Nodding, "He cares," she said.

He was drinking and did not say. The smoke was too dense now for her to see his face. "Well, enough of this business talk; you must be tired!" he heard her suddenly cry out, and something gave his bottle an awful blow. The fire hissed as his corn sprayed out. The same gesture had partially cleared the smoke: John-Juan could see Mantilla staring in shock at the handful of broken glass he held. She was quick to regain control of herself, and held her own bottle up to the door-hole light, closely examined all sides of it. Hers was all right. "That was an imperfect one," she said, taking the broken glass from him, tossing it in her garbage pit. "You can share with me."

"Thank you, señora," he said.

Accepting her bottle, he took a sip, held it back out to her, but she was busy with her cooking now. What, didn't she trust herself? She had nothing whatsoever to apologize for, an accident like that could happen to anyone, it was not clumsiness. He did not want to embarrass her, of course, or appear to reject a bottle that had touched her lips. He sipped some more, and waved his hand, clearing the air for her. As a matter of fact he had been a little miffed himself when his bottle broke. This was good stuff. He helped himself to another swig. "Drink up, drink up!" Mantilla said. For a second the thought flashed through his mind, was she trying to make him drunk, but he smiled at it. He trusted her, it was impossible not to trust one so beautiful. Whatever she might do would be all right with him, tonight. He drank up. "These are fritters," she said, handing him his coffee can.

So they were; not pancakes after all. Prodding them with his sticks, he covertly watched her rinse his—their bottle out. He watched her fill it at her well. They would be sharing water now. Hmm, of all people could Mantilla lack consideration for a guest, would she deprive him of his fair share, because of her own clumsiness? She knew that her bottle had been more than half empty when she handed it to him. His own had been almost full. She had heard how much noise it made when it hit the fire, seen the flames shoot up. But now she smiled as she handed their bottle to him, and he drank water first, with thanks.

They ate their fritters in comparative silence, harmony. These were pretty good. On flavor they were a cross between her pancakes and her tarts. They had a somewhat different consistency. Aya, it was too late to tell if any were in the shape of a heart—he had poked at them too much.

"John-Juan, did you enjoy your lunch?"

He blushed. "Thank you, Mantilla, yes!"

So it was true, he hadn't just imagined it. How he disliked himself for having sat sullenly poking, when he could have been lifting the corners in search of hearts! What might Mantilla think—that she had chosen as second runner a hopeless alcoholic? He wanted to reassure her that whatever of that he had had before he had left up north. But Mantilla asked no reassurance, seemed totally unconcerned. Stacking their dishes, she poked at the fire with a tire iron, discovered a large ear of corn beneath the coals. As soon as it had cooled enough, she stripped back the husks, freeing a delectable steam. Her timing had been perfect, the ear glowed like burnished gold. She added salt! Suddenly John-Juan realized how truly hungry he was, what a long way he had come since lunch. Mantilla passed the first ear to him, did not take one herself until he was on his fifth.

"You like corn, don't you, John-Juan?"

"Yes!"

Smiling, she poked among the coals, shrugged humorously at finding nothing there, offered him another king-size cigarette instead. Having lighted his and her own, she leaned back against the cornmeal box, stretched her sandaled feet before the fire, inhaled. From a certain point of view, the fingers overlapping are even prettier than the legs. From where he sat he could see her delicate ankles, and a glimpse of flesh above her pajama cord. "John-Juan," she said, looking him directly in the eye, "you're from California, you know what's happening."

Inhaling deeply, he nodded, yes.

Her look was even more intent. "How much time is left?"

Exhaling smoke, he said, "Not much?"

"Have we been working fast enough?"

"Mantilla?"

She waved her hand with the cigarette expansively, to indicate all the village and the land around. "Will we have everything ready soon enough?"

"Oh yes!"

"We try, we try," she said. "We've enlarged our shifts. Tomorrow I'm going to put two extra men on the distillery. We'll have enough for all, including some visitors. We've retouched our sign, did you notice that?"

"Oh yes."

"You sound hesitant, John-Juan. Did you find some error or fault in it?"

His lowered eyes watched his cigarette go out.

"You can speak freely to me, John-Juan."

"Well . . ." he said. "It was a little hard to read, coming in."

"Aya, it is, it is," she said. "You are perfectly right. Sonorla isn't a large city, you must realize that. We have our own to provide for first. You've seen," she said.

"Yes . . ."

"Oh, we aren't exactly *hidden* here! Last year we had three hundred and twenty-eight."

"Three hundred and twenty-eight?"

"Of visitors. We do welcome them if they can find their way. I'm sure the majority leave Sonorla with a far higher opinion than if they had found it crowded here. They spread the word. Of course, there are always scoffers in any crowd, no matter how limited it may be."

He nodded, yes.

"They will remember though. There will be room for some. Oh, I know that Sonorla isn't for everyone. Let's not delude ourselves! Not everyone could live on Corn, any more than everyone can live on reoads and airplanes. We grow our Corn not just to remind how things used to be, but to remind that Corn is good, that the Earth is good. People have forgotten that. They spend most of their time *attacking* the earth. You've heard the terrible noise they make! With all the grrrrrinding, how can they think? They can't, of course. They can't even hear what's said. Soon nothing is said. They are only waiting for the final attack, the silence it will bring. They think they won't care by then, that they will be glad instead. Here in Sonorla they are reminded that there is another way, that there is no need to wait, that there is gladness in a pancake or an ear of Corn with salt. That's what we want to say to them, John-Juan. We even send out invitations now and then."

"We do?"

"Also little gifts. In the old days they used to make mistakes. They used to send rich gifts to the conquistadors, ask them to stay away. We send poor gifts and ask them to come. If they cannot come, we ask them to pause and think —not just of us but of themselves and everyone. Few people today have any idea what's inside themselves. We of Sonorla know very well. I see you smile, John-Juan! It's not just Corn, believe me, please! We do have Love. . . ." Before her tender yet mocking smile, John-Juan blushed. "If they come," she went on presently, "we only ask that they leave their money and guns at home. If they forget, we ask them to check their guns under the mesquite bush. There's a little sign on the far side of it, you may not have noticed yet: 'Come As You Were.' On their way out they can pick them up again. In all this time we haven't lost but one. It is very safe in Sonorla."

"Yes, I can see it is."

"You haven't missed anything yourself, John-Juan? You still have your brush?"

"Yes, when I last looked," he said, "yesterday."

"John-Juan, do I see you stifling a yawn?" she chided him, but smiled. "Well, it has been a long day for you, hasn't it?"

"Yes, señora, it has."

"Oh, I know I pushed you a little hard by giving you the ten A.M. But time is wasting, and you ask for such confidence, you know that." She was no longer leaning back against the cornmeal box, but far forward to see him more clearly through the smoke. "John-Juan," she said, "I have plans for you."

"You have?"

"Oh, we've made runs to Mexico D.F., when we go after our mail, and to Acapulco once. That doesn't help. Those are only the Ministers down there, they are out of touch. They always say they haven't room for us in their communiqués. As soon as we begin to be known to one, he is called back home, a new man is sent in his place. That never helps. No, John-Juan, I've been saving you for the U.S. route. That way we'll be able to get to the Administradores direct. We won't be wasting our time so much. You're fast, and you can speak better English than the other boys, we all know that. It will be easier for you to pass. Well, John-Juan?"

"Thanks."

"John-Juan? Have you any questions, doubts before you start?"

"Well . . ."

"You can speak freely to me, John-Juan. Speak up, speak up!"

"Well, I was wondering if something more practical . . ."

"Speak! Like what?"

"Well, couldn't you start a student exchange program or something. . . ."

"We will! We will!" she cried approvingly. "We will as soon as you get back! Is there anything else?"

"Not that I can think of now. . . ."

"Well, when will you want to start?" She was on her feet, and lifting him to his. "You'll want to leave in time to cross the border before tomorrow's light?"

"I suppose I will."

"That's all right—the Señor is off duty today. He'll have time to see that you get started straight. What day is this? Ah, you'll miss your fish!"

"Aya," he said.

"I'll pack you a good lunch, John-Juan."

"Thanks."

"Meanwhile you would probably like to brush your teeth."

"Thanks again," he said, ducking out the doorhole with Mantilla's help.

"John-Juan!"

"Yes . . . ?"

"You're *red*," she called.

"That's all right."

"John-Juan, take a little time to rest your ankles first!"

He did not even answer that, but staggered hell-bent for the ladies' hole.

5

Five minutes later, squatting a little sheepishly in his own hut, he consoled himself that at least yesterday's old girl had not been opposite. This had been a younger one. He was running a little behind schedule today, it seemed. One thing, the ladies did have soft husks. What did they take him for, dumb? They might want to think again. Meanwhile what was all this talk about hospitality? His fire was out. Suppose he had wanted to warm his ankles before he left, had anyone thought of that? It somewhat disappointed him to find his brush still here, but neither had they freshened his ravioli can. Brushing his teeth without water for the second time, he looked around for other signs. There was no telling whether his bed had been made or not. On the other hand, someone did seem to have been tampering with his cornmeal box. The lid was up, revealing weevils inside. Welcome to Sonorla! You may hardly have time to put your toothbrush down, but you'll have a nice greasy pack to carry it in on your way out. He decided to leave his Glisterine behind; a tip.

"John-Juan, you have a visitor!"

It seemed to him an unnecessarily regal way to announce oneself, but he presently joined her outside the hole, after shaking the spit out of his brush. "Shall we talk out here, señora? It's a little chilly in there."

"Ah, did Coyoacyl let your fire go out? Well, it's a beautiful day to walk! Isn't it, John-Juan?"

"Yes, it reminds me of yesterday."

"Doesn't it! Did you bring your toothbrush, John-Juan? Ah, there it is, in your pack. That's all right. There will be room for your gift, and your map. We may have to squash your lunch a little bit. We'll work it out. I'll wait for you here, John-Juan."

She gave him a little bit of help toward the locker room, where the smiling Señor sat waiting on the bench for him, alone. He held John-Juan's lunch in one hand, in the other his pajama top. It seemed he was to go fully dressed this time; they knew it would be cold up north. The Señor first packed his lunch. No canteen this time; he was to be traveling light. Then the Señor put his pajama top *over* his pack, showed him how nicely it fit by patting it. A little secret of his. Nobody would know what he carried in there. John-Juan slouched over to the starting line, and the Señor found room to toe the mark in front of him. Then out the hole in low.

"That was fast, señores!" She approached John-Juan with outstretched gift and map. "Turn around, John-Juan!" Giggling, she lifted up his pajama top. "I'll put your gift on the bottom, John-Juan. Then your lunch. . . . It fits! It fits!" It might have fit better if she hadn't wrapped his gift in so many husks. "You can carry your map in your pocket, John-Juan. I've marked U.S. 22 on it." That was all she had marked, a long, wavering line on a yellow folding map probably made of cornstalk pith. "Stay well off the highway, in the woods. Don't bother with the cans," she said. "You follow U.S. 22 until you reach the river there; you'll find the Administradores on the other side of it. They will be meeting in their summer hut. We are told it is made of rock!"

"All right."

"Remember to give them their gift first, then their invitation, John-Juan."

"All right."

"Be sure to find out if they are coming or not."

"*All right.*"

"John-Juan . . ." She had turned him around, and now she took both of his hands in hers, drew his head down to hers, so close that he could feel her lips in his ear, whispering, "Come back, John-Juan."

"All right, Mantilla," he said, straightening up again, looking at her through blurring eyes. His eyes were still blurred as he turned to stagger after the Señor among the huts and the sleeping dogs. At the edge of town he could scarcely read the sign. It seemed to say: "You are now leaving Sonorla, friend—come back again *soon* sometime!"

Partly, it was the sun. The sun was burning harder than yesterday, even through his pajama top, or he was growing tired today. The Señor himself was in marvelous tone. He had been off duty all night, you could tell by the shape his ankles were in, by the cocky way that he tilted his head. He was out to give his star pupil a little test, see if he was serious. Thus they hit the road in record time, or rather one hundred yards this side of it. The Señor had got the lady's word, it seemed. Yet something still drew him irresistibly to the road; he would make little side trips to the edge of it and then dash back. John-Juan dog-trotted straight ahead, ignoring him. But it soon turned out those weren't just visits the Señor was making to the road, he was playing tin can with it. The eager beaver had a stick. After each foray he would run back holding his can in such a way that John-Juan could not help but see inside: almost half full. Ow-wow.

What did they take him for? He could run, he had found

that out long ago. He had not needed them to show him how. So he had picked up a few pointers along the way, he admitted that, but this time they were overdoing it. In short, this was his last run. He had other plans for when he got back. A figuring man would already have been the Minister of Student Exchange by now, and living in Mantilla's hut. A man could do worse. A man could have good fun with that, once he got the upper hand on it. Oh, she was not unimpregnable; he had noticed she didn't tie her cord in a double knot. There would be other things, fringe benefits. She did have a good store in there, no denying that. What had she said—two extra men on the distillery? In the morning there would be the natural spring, with plenty of clean bottles to dip it with. She was a little far from the men's hole perhaps, but—aya—he would have to be better about that. She had her own garden, and garbage pit. The husks in her bed had looked softer than his, with a finer chaff underneath. There he was, back on that again. A man gets big ideas when running a lot; it becomes a struggle to keep the feet on the ground.

As Minister, he might well be able to make use of the Señor in some suitable way, and he himself would want some help, of course. Beyond doubt, the man was serious. He would be a good one to get the kids started straight, also meet the kids from foreign lands. A rendezvous could be arranged somewhere near the border, at the office perhaps. (Was Señora Ramírez at this moment receiving hairs in the four o'clock?) The Señor would know how to make good use of the kids on the way in; *and* the way out. John-Juan made a side trip to the road, attracted by a sauerkraut can, and then dashed back. Presently he found a stick. Returning from a foray of his own, the Señor nodded and smiled approvingly. Yes, John-Juan would be able to make good use of the man. Meanwhile he seemed to be finding his second wind.

He had almost lost it again by the time the sky started turning dark; Polaris could be seen twinkling far to the north. Why was it they weren't at the border yet? Wasn't this usually about time for lunch? True, they had started late, but not so late as all this. No, it was those damned side trips that were bugging things up. The Señor didn't follow instructions very well. Perhaps he would like to make this delivery himself, John-Juan thought, dumping his can and stick. In that event, John-Juan was prepared to accommodate him; he could duck off at any time to a good roundhouse he knew; the Moon would lead him there. Let the Señor trot on to the Administradores without a gift, then report back to the boss about that. John-Juan meanwhile could catch a few winks. But the Señor seemed to have other plans: he was beginning to veer away from the road, off to the right. There were lights to the left. Maybe the man knew what he was doing after all. At least it was still dark when they hit the ditch.

The ditch was a little clearer out here, more like bean soup. The Señor knelt at its edge, stirring it with his stick. Now he backed off a few paces and ran up to it, but he didn't jump. John-Juan could handle that part. The Señor was already into his act, high upon his toes, jabbing with his forefinger down and out, far, far to the north. Flopping onto the sand, he munched an imaginary, no doubt heart-shaped tortilla tart. He looked up expectantly, smiled and nodded when John-Juan said, "Lunch." On his feet, he patted John-Juan's back. Anyone could be taught anything if only you handled him right. Shrugging him off, John-Juan jumped the damned ditch, from a standing start.

But once on the other side, he turned to see the Señor

standing there waving a little forlornly with his stick. It seemed to John-Juan that there were tears in the other man's eyes. Perhaps he too was wondering what was ahead, what U.S. 22 would be like. Were there as many bottles up there as some people said? Returning his wave, John-Juan trotted off to find out. Who knew, maybe the boss had made this whole thing up. There was no road anywhere in sight, not even a track. Way out here there were not many signs, and only one neon one. "Brother, Are You Insured? See Lord and Son," in red. Home again. John-Juan sat down in its blinking shade to study his map.

He had about decided that the lady was serious but a hopeless drunk, when he looked up to a call from the south. Had the Señor too discovered a mistake, come to hail him on back? In the distance he could make out a figure approaching slow on the run. This man was short, wore dark, rather disheveled pj's or suit. He was carrying a hat, and long hair flapped above his mustache. It wasn't the Señor, but John-Juan had thought he looked familiar, even without his example case. "Comrade!" called the amigo's friend, goose-stepping the ditch, but John-Juan was already folding his map. The man looked a bit hungry tonight, probably wanted some lunch. It wasn't time for that yet, and John-Juan made a habit of never sharing his brush. What had the lady said—stay off the highway, stay in the woods? He could find neither one. But even on open sand the man was no match, his legs were stiff. That hat was a drag. When John-Juan looked back, he was collapsed against a signpost adjusting his tie. The sign said "U.S. 22 ten miles northeast." There was no time for thanks, if he was to reach the river in time for lunch. Happily, the second runner's Star had stayed up with him; John-Juan ran with its twinkle in his left eye, thinking to himself, Aya, the old lady must have been sober for once.

In part. The highway wavered up ahead, right on course, but not a tree was in sight. Either she had mistaken a creosote bush for a woods, or her map was outdated, they had since converted all the trees into posts. Giving her the benefit of a dilemma, he kept to the billboards a hundred yards east, was soon glad that he had. There was just no working this road. The Señor's pajamas would have popped. Out here, a man had to watch for the broken glass; a bottle thrown this far never had a chance except where the Kleenex was unusually deep. There were other things too, seldom seen down south. Perhaps he would collect a few on the way back. The Señor might want to use them to get a better grip on his stick; but John-Juan thought to offer them to the lady first.

These were big thoughts, but not so big that he failed to notice warning signs announcing a frontier ahead, everyone must have their passports out. Aya. Slicing farther east, he dropped behind a billboard (SMOKE COTTON!) to unpack, bury his AMIGO brush. Let them come and dig that. Repacking, he took a quick feel of his gift, but couldn't tell much through the husks. Quickly up on his feet, he headed south, parallel to the fence, until he came to a cattle guard. They were either asleep on the job or just now changing shifts: one sniffed at his pack, lowed for him to stop, but then let him go with a shrug. He seemed to know that John-Juan was too fast for him. To the left lay a brick-windowed powerhouse, surrounded by another fence, enjoying privacy. Those woods lay ahead! Two other fugitives were aiming for them, one dark and one light, running shoulder to shoulder much as John-Juan and the Señor had run, but away from the road. John-Juan followed them in.

They seemed to know their way in these woods, and they knew how to run, were fast and serious both. They stayed close together unless a tree got in the way, then closed quickly together again. Now they made a sharp turn, probably north, and John-Juan did the same. When they stopped to peer through underbrush at a clear space ahead, he stopped too. It was the road. After a whispered consultation his guides started across. Two other men were running up the road, armed and uniformed. Light and dark, they drew their guns, waved them at John-Juan's guides. "Nigger lover!" the lighter, hairy one yelled, taking aim. "Kike lover!" the dark one yelled, but by now John-Juan's guides were across and out of sight. The two started after him. "Over here, Jocko!" John-Juan called, ducking back into the woods. Yells and shots followed him for a while, but they were no match for him. Mantilla was right about the roads. And upstairs the airplanes grrrrround on.

The woods were denser here, almost crowding out the signs, but John-Juan did not stop for any of this. He was traveling lighter now, without his AMIGO brush. His gift turned out not to be so much; the only real weight he carried was lunch. Somewhere he had lost his second slipper heel, probably at that cattle guard, which also helped. Too, he was learning the meaning of fear. He ran hard, but soon, seeing a clear space ahead, he knew when to stop, peer through the underbrush. This was not the road again, only a small bald spot men had scratched in the woods. They had uprooted the trees, tossed them in a pile to one side, and now dressed in white they were stamping the brown Earth. Each man carried a handful of twigs from the tree he had felled, a flaming victory torch. One man in black stood high on the arms of a wooden cross, crying to them. "You know the

truth but you lie, you lie!" he cried. "Amen!" they roared.
"Amen!"

"You know the truth but you lie, you lie!"

"Amen! Amen!"

The man in black tossed his torch onto the pyre, and roaring they added theirs. The burning trees roared back. John-Juan could feel their furious heat as he circled around them, not toward the road. The men in white were running that way, bearing their leader on his cross.

"You know the truth but you lie, you lie!"

"Amen! Amen!"

The fire, igniting the living trees, flew after them: Could it catch them before they reached U.S. 22?

"This way, Jockos!" John-Juan called, plunging into the woods. He could hear them roar "Amen!" but could not tell where it was coming from. Running alone, with the fire behind him and the dark ahead, he could only hope. He had somewhere to get before time for lunch, and the woods in here were little help. Had she said *woods?* It was almost a jungle now, a mass of leaf and stem gone mad at the touch of slippery skin, trying to smother him in a wet embrace. How long it had been for them! He slid this side and that, under and over, like a snake. Behind him the fire was sputtering out. He did not worry about the road, for he knew that her river had to be somewhere in the middle of all this mud; he did not need her outdated map. In here there could be no reading that anyway, but he would find good use for it when he got out. Right now he dared not stop. Even the second runner's Star had given him up—it blinked at him when he hit the river's edge. He turned left.

It might have been worse. At least she knew the difference between a river and a ditch; he would have need of her bridge. Soon, there it loomed in the car light a few hundred mud turtles north; he stopped underneath to show them the map. He wasn't the first. Quickly up again and onto the bridge, traveling lighter than he had since the southbound 10 A.M., he crossed to the other side for lunch. It was not so bad under here, for a picnic ground. Easing map turtles aside, he could sit with his back to concrete and his feet on a rock, hold his pack in his lap. Still, things seemed all wrong. Either he had stopped sooner than she had meant for him to stop, or he was running far ahead of schedule tonight. She had packed pancakes. For the first time, he had no stomach for them, heart-shaped or not.

Before returning them to his pack he drew out his gift, spread open the husks. Why hadn't he guessed? It was a pipe. Inside its bowl was a map-paper note: "Made in Sonorla by Sonorlans. Genuine Cob," he read by Polaris' reflected light. It seemed that any invitations had been left up to him. Less flattered than annoyed, he was about to repack, but there was something else underneath. A cigarette, regular size. She had meant it for him. She must have, for there was also a match! It was wrapped in green husks; she had known this would be a wet trip. Inside was a note. "Best wishes to John-Juan from the Señor," it said. Mantilla had written for him. Carefully repacking the pipe and the lunch, John-Juan settled himself, scratched the Señor's match high up on concrete. It went off first time. He fired up his cigarette and held the match until it burned his fingers, then with his other hand held it by the tip until it had burned to the end. He laid it gently on a rock, in its husks, keeping only the note.

Resting his head against the bridge, he inhaled deeply, sighed. The Señor would have gone wild underneath here had he seen all that his unbroken match had revealed. John-Juan could picture him now, packing with a length of drift-

wood, into gallon cans. He would be down on all fours trying to bury in muck. Turtles would be scurrying away from
him. There would be a great rush for the river, not just an
occasional plop. What would he think of John-Juan sitting
here quietly, smoking a cigarette, even though lit with his
match? Would he think John-Juan was too tired? Probably,
if he were here. But the Señor, with his penchant for roads,
would never have gotten this far. The Señor had no restraint.
He would probably have gotten no farther than that cattle
guard. If he had, he would have been an easy target for
Jocko's gun. He might have thought Jocko was supposed to
be there. John-Juan was glad the Señor had not tried to come.
It comforted him to think of the Señor safely at home now,
even in Mantilla's hut. Someone had to make this run, and
she had chosen the right man, he thought.

Flipping his cigarette in the river, he set off to find that
other hut. It was not a hard one to find, a three-storied hut,
made not out of rock but of brick, on a hill. John-Juan
waited for a convoy of cars to pass by before sprinting across.
There was blinding light on this side, from the hut and the
steel posts lining the yard or field they had cleared. One tree
had been spared, painted white. John-Juan did not use the
brick path that led to the main door, but staying to one side
of it, he slowed to a walk. There was no sound from inside
or out, not even a bark. Nothing could be seen through the
windows, though the shades were all up. The door was wide
open, but now a uniformed doorman filled it. He peered
down from beneath his big hat. "What do you want?"

"Good evening!" John-Juan called from the steps.

"What do you want?"

"Is this the Administradores' hut?"

The doorman looked not at his eyes but at his straps.
"What do you want?"

"I have an invitation for them."

The man smiled now, shaking his head. "I'm glad to say we're all filled up."

"I have a gift."

"Try again someday. Right now we're all filled up."

"I won't stay long!" John-Juan promised, climbing the steps. "I brought my own lunch!"

The doorman's smile had begun to fade, but he was trying to be patient with him. "I told you, we're all filled up."

"I brought my lunch!"

"The hell with your lunch." The doorman was closing the door.

"A memento!" John-Juan cried to the crack, running to the top of the steps. "A memento!"

The door swung halfway open again. The doorman leaned halfway out, half careful, half curious. "Who are you any-way?"

"I'm John-Juan."

"Try that again?"

"John-Juan! John-Juan! . . . Here, see here," he said, handing the doorman the Señor's note.

The doorman had a little difficulty making the handwriting out. "Best wi . . . ?" He quickly folded the note, jabbed it into John-Juan's pocket. "Hide that," he whispered, swinging open the door. "Step inside a minute, you bastard," he said loudly.

"Sir?" John-Juan followed him in, or through the door. It led to a narrow gallery, with four or five rows of seats, tiered, facing a glass wall in front; through that was in. The doorman gave a paper to him. "Now what was that invitation about?" he asked underbreath.

"I have to give my gift first."

"Quieter, kid! Don't you know this place is bugged!" The doorman rattled his programs: "What kind of gift?"

"It's a simple one—"

"Quieter, I said! *How* simple?"

"A pipe."

"Holy shit. . . ." The doorman waved his programs at a seat. "Sit down, you bastard," he said.

John-Juan sank thankfully on. How long had it been since lunch at Señora Ramírez' house? A few other people were seated here and there in the rows, but they were asleep. Soft music floated down from above. How long had it been since the Moon's roundhouse? The doorman had left, but John-Juan was not yet ready for sleep. His program helped to keep him awake. It was real paper, printed on one side, in bold print: "FIFTH (5th) NIGHT—SECOND (2nd) SESSION," it read. That filled the page, but John-Juan's eye was caught by other words nearby on a wall, not quite as big: "No shooting in this gallery, please." Leaning far forward, he could see down through the glass wall in front, where five men sat at a white, star-shaped table one story below, each man facing the rest from his own point. Through the thick glass he could not hear what was said, but they were all talking, and there was music up here. Suddenly they all stopped, and the music did too. A secretary was reading to them. They sat hunched in their chairs, staring moodily into their hands. When she stopped, one man raised his right hand and she made a mark in her book. That was Mr. 2's vote (they all had their numbers on their backs and their chests). Now she read again, and a hand went up when she stopped: Mr. 5. She read more and Mr. 1 voted for that. Mr. 4 liked the next part. The last man to vote was Mr. 0'3, at the end. Now they were all talking again.

They stopped short, looking up, when the doorman opened their door and spoke briefly to them from there. Mr. 0'3 asked a question of him. When the doorman answered, all of them talked. The doorman said something else. Now those who were so seated that they could glare at the gallery glared, while the two others sat shaking their heads. The doorman closed his door, it seemed quietly. At once they resumed talking, but Mr. 4 kept watch on the gallery until the doorman arrived there. The doorman spoke loudly to John-Juan.

"They-smoke-cigarettes-and-they-don't-like-this-foreign-propaganda-of-yours."

"It was only meant as a token of good wi—"

"Kid, I told you this place is bugged—say something else!"

"Did you mention the invitation?"

"I'm-glad-to-say-that-we're-all-filled-up."

"Tell them about it, *please!*"

"Say something else!"

"Excuse . . . What are they voting on down there?"

" 'Whom shall be left?' "

The doorman went quickly, before John-Juan could say more, and Mr. 4 resumed surveillance. The gallery had been awakened by their talk. The spectators, who had been scattered, were huddled closer together now. They stared curiously at the glass wall in front, without speaking. Those nearest John-Juan huddled with him, as though impartially. Now they could see the doorman open the downstairs door again, put his head inside. He withdrew quickly when Mr. 0'3 said something to him. This time all five men arranged to direct their heads so as to look up at the gallery, glare harder than ever. They continued glaring until the doorman got up there.

"Did you tell them?"

"We-are-all-filled-up."

"Take it to them! Take it to them!" John-Juan cried, on his feet and unpacking. "Take it . . . !" His hand dug under his lunch frantically, then went stiff. Where was his pipe? He looked around the gallery: the other spectators had gone. Someone had switched presents with him. The music had stopped, and in the sudden quiet he could hear his pack ticking. What he had felt under the husks was hot and metallic. "Watch out!" he cried, running.

The doorman held the door for him. It took him nine ticks to run downhill, to the river, one more to fling his pack, lunch and all, far out toward the middle. There was a small splash as it hit, then another one, much larger, then a muffled explosion. John-Juan felt cold water splashing over him as he looked back up the hill to the hut. People were coming down toward him yelling. He started for the bridge. He was still faster than any of them, but had stopped too long at the river. Something hit him hard on the backs of his legs and he flew headlong into the bank of the highway. Whatever had hit him hung on. People were yelling.

"Nice work, Jocko!"

John-Juan could not get up. He turned halfway onto his back to look up at the face panting over him. "It was a bomb!" he yelled.

"There's no bomb, man," Jocko panted. "Bragging won't help anything."

John-Juan turned on his side to yell at the others crowding around him. "I wanted to save you!"

"Hear that, chief?" Jocko slugged John-Juan hard in the stomach.

"You don't understand!"

"I understood . . . plenty . . . the first . . . time . . . I . . . laid . . . eyes . . . on you," Jocko said, grunting each time he slugged him.

"You know this man, do you?"

"Sure . . . chief," Jocko said, slugging harder. "We've had . . . our . . . eyes . . . on this . . . man . . . for a . . . long . . . time. . . . He's wanted . . . in . . . Calif . . . ornia . . . on two . . . counts of . . . indecent . . . language. . . . One each of . . . contempt . . . of . . . deceit . . . and . . . not . . . carrying . . . firearms. . . ." Jocko was aiming at the head now, the mouth.

"Where—is—the—*doorman!*"

"We've got him in custody, chief."

"Good, you can take this man too. Book him on unlawful flight, until we check with California."

"You—don't—understand! I'm—John—Juan!"

Jocko's big fists stopped pounding long enough to wrap the broken arms around the broken legs, slap handcuffs on. "O.K. . . . George," he said.

Betrayed again.

Author Biography

Douglas Woolf was a child of privilege (prep schools, Harvard, yachts) but after driving an ambulance in Northern Africa for the American Field Service during World War II, he chose the life of the underclass, and of the wild. When he worked it was as a window washer, groundskeeper, ice cream man, migrant farm worker, messenger, or—just as the hero of *Ya!*—selling drinks in sports arenas. Once there was enough money Woolf took to the woods, the desert, or ghost towns to write.

That didn't take much, for he required little in the way of cash, physical belongings, or material comfort. What Woolf did need was time, silence, and the company of the animals and plants of the forests and plains. The ability to travel (he identified with the lone and migratory wolf) and to remain as utterly independent in his daily life as he was in his writing. And books: Woolf built walls of the great English-language novels to make the room in which he died. His first question was how to make paper, and his last words were, "I have to write."

Douglas Woolf combined a great intelligence, deep knowledge of literature and history, and intimate knowledge of life across class, culture, and place. The result was the extraordinary sophistication from which he gives voice to the voiceless, reporting on worlds otherwise unknown. Woolf is considered a "writer's writer" because of his mastery of language and independence of vision and style; his 1978 collection *Future Preconditional* won the first American Book Award for fiction. He is likely to find an ever-larger audience over time because of the clear—and funny—vision he provides of post-World War II America. Just as Kafka insisted that the world he portrayed was real, not fantastic, so Woolf described *Ya!* & *John-*

Juan as "two serious novels about America today, its recent past and near future." The prescience of Woolf's work becomes ever more evident.

These two novels mark Woolf's turn from writing about others to the self as hero. The hallucinatory *John-Juan* explores the rending of American identity wrought by the assassination of JFK, a friend of Woolf's from Harvard days. Out the other side of that hallucination, *Ya!* begins a series of novels in which Woolf literally describes the world in which he lives. These two novels also played a role in that life, having been among the first to be remaindered after the 1974 change in U.S. tax law that radically changed the book publishing industry, making it far more costly to publish avant-garde writers and to keep great writers with relatively small audiences in print. Hundreds of copies of *Ya!* & *John-Juan* were bought back from Harper & Row and sold on street corners across the country. With a sign reading "Author's 1/2 Price Sale," Woolf met readers on 60 college campuses in 30 states over 3 years during the mid-1970s. It was during this trip that Woolf came to believe that the era of the book was reaching an end.

With this new edition of *Ya!* & *John-Juan*, almost all of the novels and short stories that had been published by the time of Douglas Woolf's death in 1992 are back in print. During his lifetime Woolf's work appeared in every major literary journal, was published in seven countries besides the U.S. and translated into half a dozen other languages, and served as the basis of the Oscar-winning movie *Harry and Tonto*. First editions of his books were published by the premiere avant-grade presses: Robert Creeley's Divers Press, Evergreen, Grove, Jargon, Tombouctou, and Black Sparrow. A major autobiographical novel *(Woolf's Guide to New York)* and a book of poetry *(God's Teagarden)* have not yet been published.

LANNAN SELECTIONS

The Lannan Foundation, located in Santa Fe, New Mexico, is a family foundation whose funding focuses on special cultural projects and ideas which promote and protect cultural freedom, diversity, and creativity.

The literary aspect of Lannan's cultural program supports the creation and presentation of exceptional English-language literature and develops a wider audience for poetry, fiction, and nonfiction.

Since 1990, the Lannan Foundation has supported Dalkey Archive Press projects in a variety of ways, including monetary support for authors, audience development programs, and direct funding for the publication of the Press's books.

In the year 2000, the Lannan Selections Series was established to promote both organizations' commitment to the highest expressions of literary creativity. The Foundation supports the publication of this series of books each year, and works closely with the Press to ensure that these books will reach as many readers as possible and achieve a permanent place in literature. Authors whose works have been published as Lannan Selections include: Ishmael Reed, Stanley Elkin, Ann Quin, Nicholas Mosley, William Eastlake, and David Antin, among others.

SELECTED DALKEY ARCHIVE PAPERBACKS

FOR A FULL LIST OF PUBLICATIONS, VISIT:
www.dalkeyarchive.com

SELECTED DALKEY ARCHIVE PAPERBACKS

FOR A FULL LIST OF PUBLICATIONS, VISIT:
www.dalkeyarchive.com